one
more
day

one more day

DIANE CHIDDISTER

Paperback ISBN: 978-1-63337-552-9
E-book ISBN: 978-1-63337-553-6

Manufactured and printed in the United States of America

One More Day is dedicated to all the Sallys in the world, mostly women and some men, who work long hours for little pay as certified nursing assistants (CNAs or STNAs) in nursing homes, memory care units, and assisted living facilities, providing daily care for our most vulnerable elders. To those who do the job with love, joy, and compassion, like the young woman who inspired this book, I bow to you.

1.
a new country

On his best days, Thomas thinks of getting old as living in a new country, a remote island nation perhaps, someplace only recently found. He's sending reports back to the mainland. The world waits for his findings! Well, perhaps the world isn't actually waiting. This place isn't quirky, certainly not sexy. It's just old people living together, packed in one building. It's the culture here at the Grace Woods Care Center.

But the world should perk up its ears. Strange things are happening. For instance, they're happening right now at the table where he sits having breakfast. The woman sitting opposite lifts her plate high. She tips it. Now eggs fall through the air. A streak of yellow! Potatoes tumble down too, brown and oily. Goodness, here comes the garnish, little pieces of kale drifting like wings. And the woman tipping her plate, the one with the tiniest nose Thomas has ever seen (Thomas tries not to study her nose when they're eating)—she seems to be smiling! Aides are swarming around her. Oh, yes. She's having a wonderful time.

Thomas tries not to smile. He likes the women who work here, doesn't want them to think he's in cahoots with the plate-tipping woman. He's sorry they now have to work harder, scrub the table, mop up the floor. But this place is curious. It's definitely curious.

Curious. As an anthropologist, it's his favorite word.

Thomas aims his attention at his own plate. He's new here, and this is curious too. This is worthy of his attention.

He studies the gleam of his plate's blinding whiteness. Each part of his meal seems precise and symmetrical, a perfect circle of scrambled eggs, a neat square of potatoes, three Little Pig sausages all in a row. A ruffle of green leafy vegetable adorns the side of the plate; on top, two slices of pink candied apple. Red on green, then yellow and brown, a rainbow of color adorns gleaming white. Who came up with this thoughtfulness, this attention to detail? What could be the underlying purpose of such precision?

He's only an anthropologist; he's not God. He can just speculate. But he feels certain the underlying purpose is the creation of hope. All is not lost! That's what the food is telling these people. The forces providing these perfect circles and squares are benevolent, the world is benevolent, there is more good than evil, that's what this symmetry says. Yes, you are old, his meal says, your body is failing, you may lose your mind. But here at Grace Woods there is order, there is reason; just look at the perfect circle of eggs, the tight square of hash browns. This orderliness will not let you die a meaningless death. Perhaps you won't die at all.

The symmetry of the food creates the appearance of a world rich in meaning and order.

Of course, the tiny-nosed woman is having none of it. That's for sure.

Maybe she knows this doesn't make any sense. Most cultures don't try to spark hope in their old people. No, they kill them! Thomas knows this. Indigenous peoples the world over, since time began, have been marching their old people off the edge of a cliff or abandoning them in the wild to be eaten by bears. Or drowning them. Or bashing in skulls. Thomas used to lecture his classes on these practices and his students ate it right up. They loved it.

And of course, killing old people makes sense when there's a shortage of food, and there's always a shortage of food. Take your weakest people, your sickest, your most vulnerable—and that's old people—and dump them. Get rid of them.

So the strangest part of this new land of aging is that it puts old people together in buildings and keeps them alive.

It's true that the food here sometimes doesn't taste good. While the presentation is attractive, the taste often is not. Does that undermine his theory? Thomas isn't sure. The eggs are barely warm (of course, that's his own fault for not eating more quickly) and as tasteless as pudding without butter or sugar. The hash browns are just slippery slices of potato that have no zip, no zing. Which means not enough salt, of course; that's the problem.

It's a puzzle, for sure. Thomas needs someone to talk to. He needs someone to spin theories with. He needs Hal. He and Hal just let their thoughts roll; first one speaks, then the other, then someone tweaks and embellishes, the new energy taking wing in unseen directions like the kale floating from that gleaming white plate. Then one or the other sees something deeper; the theory becomes both airborne and rooted. Ah, he loves this part. And then he or Hal gets carried away and go a step too far; they're ridiculous, they laugh, and it's the best laughter Thomas knows, the laugh of new thinking, of pushing the edges. Sometimes he and Hal pause for a moment and just stare at each other, filled with awe. Hey, look what just happened! Look what we did. We thought up something entirely new, we brought new thinking into the world.

But where is Hal? At home Thomas could count on him each Monday morning, could count on his old friend showing up for an hour and they'd spin theories, they'd laugh at old stories from the department. After that hour, for even the rest of the day, it made sense to Thomas, this business of getting old. Then Thomas could see things in perspective, a perspective that buoyed him, kept him bobbing up on the surface, just north of despair. Yes, he is old, very old; his time is short. But he had a life! He was an anthropologist of some standing. He published papers, taught classes. He had tenure, for God's sake.

But recently Hal seems not to have visited. Is he sick? Thomas feels his heart race for a moment. He can't lose Hal, not now, not anytime soon. He's lost too many friends. Thinking about Hal, Thomas feels a slip of memory floating just past his awareness. Did he die? How could Thomas forget?

He pushes his plate away. He's no longer hungry. It's the worst part about this new country. It's a country in which you don't meet old friends again. They fall off the edge of the earth. They vanish.

Sometimes Thomas imagines he's gathered all of his old friends, all of his colleagues, in a large room where they're waiting for him. In his mind there are tables overflowing with platters of salmon and cake, his friends drinking champagne while they wait, saving a glass for him. All he has to do is find this room and there they will be: his old friends.

On bad nights, nightmare nights, he can't find the room. But on good nights he finds it, opens the door. He sees himself greeting everyone. Perhaps they clap when he arrives? His colleagues from the department are mixing with old tennis buddies, grown-up kids from the neighborhood. Of course there is Marjorie. Is Sarah there? His heart beats faster imagining this. Maybe she's off by herself in a corner. Thomas clinks his glass, gets their attention. Do you know what you meant to me? I honor you, Thomas says to each one, I honor our friendship. He bows to each friend, deep and low.

But Thomas doesn't want Hal to be at the party. No! Hal needs to be here at the center, in person, still alive, laughing his hearty laugh. Thomas has to get his heart to slow down. He has to stop worrying about Hal. Focus. Focus on the food in front of him, the food of this curious culture.

No, he's not hungry. He hoists himself up from the chair to a standing position. Ouch! Pain slices his hip; he is trembling. This is the hardest part. He's not just observing the people who live in this country. He lives here as well.

"Thomas?"

It's the girl he likes, the tall, plump one. Such a smooth face, such smooth skin.

"You're not eating. Is it okay? Can I get you anything else? Would you like some French toast?"

Thomas does his best to smile and nod. Yes, everything's fine, thanks so much. It's important to be easy, not too demanding. She's kind, yes, but she's busy, too, and he doesn't want to add to that burden.

People around Thomas are leaving the table. He's the last to leave. He's observing. Observation takes time.

The room swirls a bit. Damn. He grabs the table again. Okay, that's better.

He takes a deep breath. What sort of dizzy is this? Sometimes when he traveled to a new country, Thomas felt dizzy. He got dizzy trying to take in the new things around him, the new ways of seeing the world. He was struck by a vertigo from all the options of human behavior, the options he'd never considered. A room in the Filipino village where he lived decades ago, where people grieved a dead person, the body right there before him, but only a few feet away young people chatted loudly and flirted. Wait a minute! Too loud, too raucous. That's disrespectful. But in this culture it was not disrespectful, no others seemed bothered. This was life going on; this was a part of the grieving.

When this sort of dizzy came on him, Thomas tried to stay with it. He tried to take a deep breath, allow himself to live in the vertigo, to feel the complexity of human behavior. It's what makes him a good anthropologist, he believes. He can stay with the dizziness, breathe into it.

Now Thomas takes a deep breath. Stay with the dizziness. Okay, that's better.

Some of the residents are now sitting in front of the television, where they seem to spend most of their days. Watching what? The weather channel. Good lord, can't someone change the station?

Thomas heads back to his room.

Damn. He hugs himself. This pain blasts his groin, sharp and hot. Breathe through it. He can breathe through it.

Okay. He stands upright. It's better. It's almost gone. He'll move on. Is the pain happening more? Maybe. He's not sure.

Partway down the hall, he stands still for a moment. What's

with the bears? Little stuffed teddy bears sit on the windowsill, some with red bows on their necks. Thomas closes his eyes. He needs to calm down. Sometimes he's annoyed at those in charge of this culture, how they seem to think he's a child, that all of these old people are children. Teddy bears.

He could complain. But the best thing would be to forget it, just let it go. Don't be a crabby old guy.

He walks on. Here's a table, a chance to rest for a second. On the table a puzzle is partly completed. He could see this as a child's toy too and feel insulted. But adults like puzzles, too. Still, he notices that puzzles always show rolling pastures with contented cows, or Victorian villages with happy people galore. Again, it's a systematic attempt to blot out the ugly, the bleak. Things like death, for instance. There's not a single puzzle scene of the Holocaust, nor any of war. Is he being unreasonable? No puzzles showing Vietnam with helicopters overhead, Asian men throwing rockets, American soldiers dead on the ground. Not a single puzzle that shows the storming of Normandy.

No, only puzzles of Christmas trees, Santa Claus, families with kittens and puppies. Again, the propaganda. Life is good! Life is meaningful; it makes sense.

He can't wait to talk to Hal about this. It bolsters his theory.

Sitting next to the table is the woman with the tiny nose, the one who dumped her eggs at breakfast. Now she's bending over the puzzle, studying it. She pulls her arm back. She seems to be getting ready for something. Oh shit. He wants to see this. There she goes; her arm sweeps the table, the pieces scatter, fall to the floor. Now she bends over again, pushing more pieces off. It's a farming scene, rolling hills, a happy farmer with a horse and a cart, but now the pieces tumble on top of each other, and it's destruction, just piles of cows and horses and farmers lying helter-skelter all over the place. The woman steps back from the table. She smiles. Thomas feels himself smiling as well. A small rebellion here in the hallway.

What was he doing? Ah yes, finding his room. When he looks up quickly, he's dizzy again. Where is he now?

It's a long, white-walled hallway with doors on the side, like the hotels where he stayed for professional conferences. He's been to conferences all over the country, all over the world. Where was the last one? Tokyo? Sydney?

But he's not at a professional conference. A door opens. Out comes an old woman pushing a walker. He's an old man living in an old people's home.

His heart needs to slow down.

It's been a long time, maybe five decades ago? It's been a while since he was out in the field, living in that Filipino village. He was so young then, before the college ran out of money to send him.

Here's what he told himself ten times every day: you are just like these people. Don't think of all the ways you are different, the ways you're astounded by how they get through the day. Don't see them as strange or misguided. And whatever you do, don't think you would never, ever, eat their most unsavory food, you would never put a whole baby duck in your mouth.

No, don't do that. Instead, observe your hand as it scoops up the balut. But don't see it as a whole baby duck if that thought unsettles your stomach. No, see it as something moist and soft, then aim your hand to your mouth. Observe yourself chewing, hear the approving sounds from the others. Whatever you do, don't think of the baby duck feathers tickling your throat, the tiny bones that crunch as you swallow. Think that you can do this new thing. Know you can do things you never imagined.

The woman walking ahead in the hallway is small and hunched over, and she seems to be flinging the walker before her. Her face is thin, beaky-looking. She reminds Thomas of a bird, a big bird, a bird of prey—a hawk perhaps, a bird that does what it must do to survive. She must keep moving. She looks fierce. Her arms are pale and stick-like, yet she's heaving the walker like a strongman, a teamster.

In the Filipino village Thomas ate the whole baby duck. He grew to like it. Sometimes he asked for more.

He can do this. He is doing this. He can be an old man in an old people's home. He can do things he never imagined.

2.
taking deep breaths

"Bradley Cooper in a white suit! Oh, God. I just about went crazy."

As usual, Sally has nothing to say as Deborah commands attention in the staff room. Deborah and Charlotte are giggling, leaning their heads toward each other. They're sipping coffee a few seats from Sally. Wait a minute. Nobody left on the floor? That won't work. Someone has to go back out and be on the job. Sally looks at the clock and gulps her coffee. She starts to stand.

"Hey." Deborah takes a glance at the clock. "It's okay. I just needed a quick cup. Just one. You don't have to do everything, you know. You're not the only one here." She seems annoyed.

Sally sits down again. Deborah's been working here forever, although Sally doesn't know why. She doesn't seem to like the residents much, and she's old enough to retire. But then, no one actually retires from nursing home care. People just work till they drop.

Deborah's looking over her glasses at Sally, the way she usually does. Does she mean to make people feel small? Probably.

"Anyway?" Deborah says now. "Mike didn't like it. He didn't

like it one bit. He didn't like me losing it over Bradley Cooper in a white suit. He kept saying, 'Can't you just sit back like a normal person? Do you have to sit on the edge of your seat?'"

She and Charlotte are shaking their heads, laughing. These are their two favorite topics: popular entertainment and husbands. Today they're covering both.

"God, Bradley Cooper is old!" Charlotte says. "He's not hot. Now Chris Evans. He's hot."

Watching Deborah and Charlotte laughing together, Sally wants to join in. "Chris?" she says. "Chris who?"

Now Deborah and Charlotte look at each other, eyes wide. They burst out laughing again. Sally feels herself heating up. This always happens. She doesn't end up joining the conversation; she ends up feeling alone. She has to stop and think before she says something. Because whatever Sally says, it's the wrong thing. Most often she's said something that's not only wrong but ridiculous. Ridiculous to the others, that is.

"Oh God! Oh God! I'm so sorry," Deborah says. She wipes her eyes, she's laughing so hard. "Chris who? He's Captain America! Sally, you are just not living in this century. Not that that's a bad thing! Nothing wrong with that! Oh no!"

Now Deborah and Charlotte shake their heads again and lean back in their chairs. They are trembling with laughter, holding their sides. Sally feels hot. She knows her face must be bright red. Why does she even care what they think? So what if she doesn't fit in? So what if she can't make small talk? There's a reason they call it small, she once said to her mom.

"That new guy?" Charlotte says. "He looks like Bradley Cooper. I think he does."

"Him?" Deborah says. "Not even close."

Deborah shrugs. "Anyway, Mike just about lost it. Finally he went to bed, huffing and puffing in that way he gets when he's mad and he won't say why. Because he's embarrassed he's jealous over a movie star. He knows it's ridiculous but he can't help it. Men!"

Sometimes Sally feels she has her own language that no one else speaks. There's space for pauses, for breath. When someone is speaking to her, Sally falls silent. She feels herself stilled, as if a spell has washed over her. People open their mouths and sound comes out. Isn't that something? Sally finds it amazing.

"Well," Deborah says now.

Charlotte makes a little grunt and flips her hair over her shoulder. How does her hair get so shiny? What does she put on it? Charlotte doesn't have a husband, but she has a string of men who seem to waltz in and out of her bedroom, sparking the stories she tells to the staff.

Now they lean in and talk to each other again.

So what if some people find her annoying? Her mom did. *Hey! Stop that listening!* her mom used to say when she'd had too much to drink, which was a lot of the time. *Don't look at me like that. Talk faster! Talk more!*

Okay, she waits too long between sentences. She waits for a pause after the other person stops talking, but as she waits, someone jumps in. And when Sally jumps in, it's always the wrong place, the wrong time.

Also, she doesn't have stories about men. She gave up telling those stories years ago. One day she realized how much room she used in her brain thinking about one man or another and whether they loved her or not, but the guys never stayed with her anyway. Sally doesn't know why, but they didn't. She's a bit chunky, is probably why. And once she gave up the hunt, she could think about so many new things. She has so much more room in her brain.

Now Deborah and Charlotte are whispering together. They always seem to be whispering, to be close, though Deborah is so much older. They act as if Sally's not there. She stares at her coffee.

The worst thing about loneliness is trying to push it away. Because when she lets it come, loneliness isn't so bad. It's just a space in her body, a deep space, an emptiness. A tightening. But it's not pain, not a feeling of sharpness and knives. No, it's more like a softness. A feeling of sadness, sure, but in a soft way. Not a hard feeling. Not like getting cut with sharp things.

Now there's static on their walkie-talkies. Deborah holds hers close to her ear. "It's Thomas," she says. "The call button." She wrinkles up her nose. "Probably poop. He's doing that more. It's gross."

Sally stands. "I'll go," she says. "You can stay for a while."

She goes out the door before the others can argue. It's all right, really. She wants to see Thomas.

• • •

The thing to do is breathe through your mouth. That's the trick with poop, as long as Sally can do it. Because poop makes her gag, and Sally can't gag, she can't make these old people feel worse than they already feel, pooping their beds.

This has to be the worst time for her people, the worst out of many bad times in this process of getting old, really old. People are spilling food down onto their shirts, they are slipping and falling. They're leaving pee stains in their underwear. The stains say to the world: *I am falling apart!* But nothing's as bad as pooping your pants, and almost everyone here poops their pants.

So Sally gets them talking about something else when she cleans up. Something they love.

Thomas is facing away from her. He looks out the window. He's new but already one of her favorites, though she doesn't feel good about having favorites. He's wearing one of his blue button-down shirts and a tie, like he always does. It's as if he's getting ready to stand in front of a roomful of students, teach them about anthropology. Anthropology!

"Thomas," she says now. "Tell me again."

He grunts, turns his head toward her. "Tell you what?"

"About that place you told me about. That island."

He takes a deep breath. He's shaking his head. "My dear," he says, "I just pooped in my pants."

"I know. But I want you to tell me. Tell me about the island where they had those strange dinners."

He turns back to the window. Sally believes he's thinking about it. His skin is so warm. She can't get over old people's skin, how warm it is. Like all their lives their thermostat has been low and now, toward the end of their lives, they're heating up. They're getting hotter and hotter. They're giving it all they've got. And then dying happens so suddenly! How can a body go from being so warm one day to stone cold the next? It doesn't make any sense.

She pats Thomas's shoulder, then his arm, then his middle. She's working her way down to his bottom. "Thomas," she says. "I have to clean you up. But go on. Tell me, please."

"I know," he says, his voice just a whisper. "I'm sorry."

Sally leans in close. "Tell me if the water's too warm."

He grunts in response. He smells like breakfast, like sausage. She will work quickly, efficiently, so as not to give him any more discomfort than he already feels. She's good at this. She knows what she's doing.

Her people, these old people, they're speaking her language. They aren't making small talk, no. *I need to go to the bathroom. I can't find my glasses, my hearing aid. I need help getting dressed, my shoe is stuck in my pant leg. The water's too warm.* These things are meaningful. They're not small.

"Well," he says. "The potlatch. It's the Tlingit tribe on Vancouver Island. I wasn't there, but I know about it. It's sort of famous."

Sally turns her head. What was that noise? "Thomas? Did you hear something?"

He shakes his head no. Okay, she must have imagined it.

Thomas looks out the window. He tells her again how different groups on the island prepared for months for a great feast to which they invite a neighboring tribe, where the chief brags about how rich he is, how strong. They prepare so much food that members of the invited tribe eat too much and then vomit. Then the guest tribe goes home but later returns to eat too much once again. Actually, that's the point, to make the guests vomit. The point is to prove that the host tribe has more, that it's superior. That is, the point is to prove what a great leader the chief is.

"Humans," Thomas says, shaking his head. "Humans do crazy things."

"Guess not much has changed," Sally says.

"Ha," Thomas says. "You've got that right."

The strong stench of poop envelops her, and Sally has to take another deep breath. She gulps air. This almost always works. But she has to move fast. She's beginning to lose control. "There," she says now, after rinsing the cloth one last time. "You're done, Thomas. It's over."

"Thank god," Thomas says, turning toward her. "I'll never do that again. Never!" He slaps himself on the thigh, laughing.

There's a scraping sound in the closet. Thomas and Sally both turn toward it. The closet door opens, and a tall guy steps out. Sally's heart races. Who is this? How did he get in? What can she use as a weapon?

"That was interesting," the tall guy says. "I never knew that about the Vancouver tribe."

Sally's eyes widen. She had no idea there was someone in Thomas's room. Apparently, neither did Thomas.

"Sorry," the stranger says, ducking his head as if he's used to making this gesture, constantly ducking beneath ceilings and doors. "I'm Shannon. New guy in maintenance? I was fixing the shelf in the closet. I didn't mean to hide. I was just in there, so, well, I stayed and listened. I didn't want to interrupt. I loved anthropology in college. I mean, I took a class once? Maybe two."

Sally blinks. This is the guy who looks like Bradley Cooper? "You need to tell people." Sally tries to lower her voice. "You can't be just popping up when no one knows you're around."

He ducks his head again. "You're right. I've got a lot to learn."

He flashes a big smile at Sally. It's a huge smile, really, the sort of big goofy smile that helps some men sail through life. This guy is used to being a charmer, that's for sure. He needs that smile since he has an odd face, his eyes set far apart like a fish. He's very young. A tall, lanky body. A nice body. Sally looks at the floor.

"Okay. Thomas," she says, "I'm leaving now. Anything else before I go?"

Thomas looks out the window. He sighs. "You know, in some indigenous villages, old people just go out into the cold to die. They just walk and walk and when they're tired they sit down and then they freeze to death. Alone. So simple! And then the animals eat them, bobcats and such. I think that makes sense. I really do."

Sally closes her eyes. She walks to the side of the bed, sits down. She takes his hand. "I'm glad we're not an indigenous village," she says.

Thomas turns toward her. Are those tears in his eyes?

"And anyway." It's the maintenance guy again. What's his name? Some girl's name. He's still standing there, by the doorway. Sally thought he had left. "So around here there's no bobcats. No bears. You'd just be eaten by squirrels. That's just silly. That's ridiculous," the guy says.

Sally feels herself heating up. Wait a minute! This guy needs to be more respectful to Thomas. But Thomas is laughing.

"That's right," he says. "Squirrels. Not much dignity there."

Finally, the new guy turns and walks out the door. But he turns back. "Whoops. Forgot these." He reaches into Thomas's closet, brings out a hammer and screwdriver. He flashes his big smile again. He's wearing a tool belt. Sally feels herself blushing. She loves to see a guy in a tool belt. But that's just silly. It's silly, is all.

3.
flocks of birds

Lillian doesn't intend to dump her eggs on the table. In fact, the thought never occurs to her. But still her hand scoops her plate right up and lifts it. Some mysterious force boosts her arm higher, higher, up in the air. She can't stop. When she tilts her plate just so, the eggs slide right off, falling smack dab to the table below. Plop!

Oh my. These eggs move, they go places! What's that Dr. Seuss book she reads to Annie? The places you'll go! These eggs are traveling. They are making strides. They are scooting right off the edge of the plate and then vanishing. For a moment, Lillian gazes as eggs float before her.

Eggs in the air! Potatoes too, little slices of fried vegetables falling through space.

It's something you don't see every day. Something Lillian has never seen before, ever.

Oh! It's the fizzy feeling, bubbling up in her body. Like fireworks, hot and explosive. Bursts of colors, reds and greens, blues and silvers. Golds are her favorites. The fizziness starts with heat in her feet, then shoots up her legs, into her arms and middle. Now the heat roars right up her neck. Here it comes, shooting through bone in her skull, exploding in air. It's life! It's adventure.

Isn't it exciting, to see new things? To see that eggs can take off, to see potatoes blast into space like rockets? To see kale take wing and soar? Isn't that something to see? Doesn't that make the world tip on its side just a bit, shake everything up? Doesn't it make new things possible?

Shouldn't this make everyone happy?

But it's not making them happy. That old woman across the table is frowning. Well, Lillian doesn't like the old woman anyway. She has no neck. Her name is Bull, Elsie Bull, or something like that. She looks like a cow. Sometimes Lillian tries to talk to her and the Bull woman just looks off into the distance. Like right now.

And then there's the too-skinny woman with pouches on the sides of her face who sits next to Lillian. Her eyes have widened, but not in a good way, no, not at all. She is looking at Lillian as if she's disappointed, as if this is one more in a long string of things Lillian has done to disgust her. The little pouches hanging on the sides of her face look even bigger than usual, as if marbles could perch right on top.

"You are out of control," the face-pouch woman says to Lillian, shaking her head. Yes, disgust seems to be what she's feeling.

Didn't the others see what happened? The moment before the eggs went flying, Lillian studied her plate. What she noticed was how gleaming her eggs were, how shiny, how they reflected the light in the room. Slightly moist, too. These golden eggs looked poised to shine in a magazine on good eating, on healthy living, on how eggs should appear in a perfect world. Steam rose from her eggs like energy, like desire, and Lillian thought these eggs might levitate all on their own, might possess some magical power. She lifted her plate. Lillian was proud of her eggs. She wanted to hold them high, to honor them.

In that moment, Lillian felt herself honored too. She felt herself rising up, up with her plate in the air, hovering a bit over everyone. And she wasn't only honoring her eggs and herself. No, she was holding up everyone here, honoring each and every one of these old people. Look at us! Look how we sparkle and glow, just like our eggs.

Look at me!

Shouldn't these people be grateful? Well, they are looking at her. But not in the way she had hoped.

Mischief! *What sort of mischief are you making now, my little man?* Lillian's mom used to say to her brother, as if mischief was highly desirable. Frankie was the mischievous one, the boy, the trailblazer.

And Lillian didn't make mischief. No, she was good, she toed the line. What line? Where was the line? Lillian was never quite sure where the line was, and maybe that's why she tried not to move too fast or too far; she didn't want to go over the line. She never made problems, never talked back or made out in the back seats of cars with boys or smoked cigarettes. She got married when she was supposed to get married, when someone asked and she had no good reason to say no. And it was to Dan, and he was a good man who held the line with him always, the line she needed to toe.

She was so good. And now she feels fizzy, just dumping her eggs on the table. Here is life, adventure, exploding inside her. Mischief. What a surprise, what a pleasure!

Lillian opens her mouth to speak. "I..." she begins. "Eggs do..." Lillian stops. She takes a deep breath. This time, this time. This time the thing she is thinking will glide right out of her mouth smoothly and surely, it will land squarely, just like how the eggs plopped down on the table.

People are listening, even the Bull woman. They lean toward her expectantly. Something is coming. They want to hear. At a moment like this Lillian feels real, alive in the world. She's not just a strange woman trying to figure out where she is; no, she's someone with something to say. She sees herself on a stage in front of an audience, ready to put on a show. The curtain is rising, a dark-red velvet curtain, it's lifting, farther and farther. Here she is, in person.

Look at me!

But the birds. The birds have landed again, the birds in her mind. So many birds. When Lillian forms a thought to tell someone else, the birds take off, they whirl and twist in the wind of her mind, they dive and dip in graceful arcs. And Lillian loves birds, so she watches them. She follows the birds as they lift up into the sky. But then the words in her mouth fly away, too. Lillian loses her thought. Her mouth is still open, but nothing comes out.

Now the others are frowning, shaking their heads. Lillian feels herself squirming. The velvet curtain drops down, right in front of her. No show today. It's been canceled.

Someone's face is close by, right beside Lillian. It's the nice brown woman with the long hair, and for a second Lillian is sorry she upset this nice woman. "Here, let me take that. Let me take your plate, sweetheart. Your eggs are falling right off."

Well, of course they fell. Lillian dumped them. Doesn't she get credit for anything? Still, she lets the woman take the plate. The woman begins scrubbing the eggs off the tablecloth, her mouth bunched up in a little O. Now the woman leans down and washes something off Lillian's stomach. Oh! It's cold! But Lillian can smell the citrusy smell of the woman's hair. She leans forward to sniff it. It's a good smell, a summery smell, and it makes Lillian suddenly happy. She leans into the woman's head. It smells so good that Lillian rests against it.

"Oh, sweetheart," the nice woman says. "I like you, too. But you need to give me some space."

Lillian moves back. She scoots in her chair. She's feeling the cold, dark feeling inside, the feeling that she did something wrong but she doesn't know what. That feeling makes Lillian freeze. If she freezes, if she doesn't move any more, not an inch, maybe she won't do anything wrong ever again. Maybe she won't cross the line.

But it's time to get up from the table. On the TV screen people are rushing around, trying to get out of the storm. There's always a storm on TV. People are continually hammering wood over their windows, just like today. It's a hurricane! How come there are so many hurricanes? When Lillian looks out the window it looks like a regular day, not a hurricane, but on TV it's always a hurricane. Or a tornado, and floods are popular too. The no-neck woman and the others are just sitting there, watching the storm.

Lillian stands close to the TV. What was that movie? The one with the little girl with dark braids and ruby red shoes who got swooped up by a storm? The wind whirled her around and around and then dropped her down somewhere new. At first it was scary. But then she ended up in a magical land, a land with comforting trees and singing lions and kind men wearing tin hats.

Lillian leans into the screen. What would it be like to be picked up by this wind, whirled around in the sky? Sometimes Lillian feels she knows that little girl, knows what it's like to be spun by a big wind, to be scooped up one place and dropped off in another, a place new and frightening. Sometimes it feels like her life.

"Hey," someone says. "Stand back. You're in front of the picture."

Enough of this hurricane. She wants to go back to her room. Is this the right way?

There are so many hallways, and they all look alike. Lillian starts down a hallway, but it stretches out endlessly. It goes on and on. Her room is here somewhere, but where? Big pictures hang on the walls, pictures of oceans and mountains. Here's a picture of fields of corn, like in Indiana where she's lived her whole life. Now she's walking into one of those fields, the one next to her grandmother's house. The corn sways in the wind. Any minute she'll come to the end of the row and turn left. At the house her grandmother will be frying chicken. Such a sweet crackling sound, such a wonderful smell. And her grandmother will lean down to give her a kiss, smelling like talcum. But now as Lillian reaches out to touch the silky tassels dangling from corn husks, she hits something hard. Wait a minute, this isn't a field! It's all flat, like a wall. It is a wall. There's no grandmother here. Lillian feels her heart racing.

Where is she again?

Little dark animals sit on the windowsill. Lillian picks one up. It's a bear. Her heart's slowing down. It feels good to hold this bear, so furry and soft, with big black button eyes. But the bear's dark eyes appear puzzled, as if the bear's thinking, *What am I doing here?* She sits for a minute, cradling the bear in her arms. Lillian holds the bear close, rocking. She tries singing, a soft, soothing tune. But the bear still looks puzzled.

"I don't know what you're doing here," she whispers into the bear's little ear. "It makes no sense at all."

She has a room somewhere, but where? It's a room with a chair and a bed, and when she's lost in the hall the worker ladies point, they say, *Look, Lillian, your room is right here.* As if that makes any sense. And Lillian wants to say, *Really? My room?* Because none of these rooms look like any room she's ever known—not her childhood room, not the rooms she and Dan shared.

She walks and walks. Ah, here's a puzzle on top of a table. She likes doing puzzles. Sometimes they help her calm down. And maybe she'll find her way back. Maybe if she puts the exact right piece in the right spot in the puzzle, she too will slip into place. Perhaps she will find her way home.

Lillian sits at the table. It's a farm puzzle that looks just like the place where her grandmother lived. There's the red barn, the fields of ripe corn. Here are the goats and the pigs and the garden. But where's the right piece? Lillian tries squeezing the pieces of cardboard together, tries fitting curved pieces into curved empty spaces. But none of them work. It's making her mad. It's the fizzy feeling again, rising up in her legs. Oh my. What if she pushes this puzzle right off the edge of the table, right now? What if she does? What will it look like?

Here it goes, all these tiny slices of field and garden and people cascading onto the floor. There goes the farmer!

Oh my! Lillian likes the way the pieces look now, tangled up on the carpet. Cows and pigs and fields collapse on each other, all smashed up in a pile.

Did anyone see it?

There's a man standing close. Yes, she has seen him at her table and walking around. Sometimes he smiles at her, unlike the others.

He's looking at her now. He is smiling.

"Mom? Mom!"

Now here's a woman with frizzy grey hair standing beside her, a woman who looks familiar. Calling her Mom! But she doesn't have a grown-up daughter. Not one with grey hair. Lillian's daughter is little. Eight or nine maybe? Something like that.

Where is Annie?

What's Annie eating? Lillian feels her stomach drop to her feet. Is Annie at home? It feels like a long time since Lillian was home. Has her daughter been starving? Is she roaming the house looking for food? Annie likes grilled cheese sandwiches and tomato soup, but she's too little to make them. She can barely reach the top of the stove. What if she forgets to turn off the burner and ruins the soup? What if a fire breaks out?

"Where is she?" Lillian asks.

"Where is who?" the frizzy-haired woman says. She is frowning.

"My little girl," Lillian says. Her skin is itching, she feels frantic. "Where is Annie?"

Now the frizzy-haired woman has tears in her eyes. She

looks at the floor, then back up again. "I'm here, Mama," she says. "I am Annie."

Now the frizzy-haired woman's face looks crumpled and old. Lillian's sorry to make her sad, but how can this woman say that she's Annie? How can she say something so mean?

Now a worker lady appears and grabs Lillian's hand, places it on the arm of the frizzy-haired woman. "Look!" the worker lady says. "It's your daughter!"

Lillian jerks away. She hates it when the worker women do this, when they point to a room and say, *Here's your room*. They point to a stranger and say, *Here's your daughter*. As if Lillian's a dunce, a dodo. As if she knows nothing at all.

Here it comes, the big wind. Oh! Now it's lifting her up, up, and away. This is how it feels to be picked up by a whirlwind, to be scooped right off the ground, spun into space. Lillian gulps air. Her body's spinning, her head spinning too. She's getting dizzy. So much wind. It's a little like flying but more like falling, like tumbling down a dark hole even though she feels herself rising higher. Her head spins and spins.

She looks down at her shoes. She doesn't have red shoes, no, not like in the movie; she wears the shoes the worker ladies put on her feet every morning.

Now the whirlwind pitches again, drops her off on the ground. She sees her ugly shoes hitting the carpet. Oomph! Lillian lands with a thud. Here are her feet, on the ground once again. She takes a breath. Okay, she's standing now, her feet on the carpet. But there's no tin man here, no friendly lion, no grandmother trees. And at the end of the movie, the little girl got to go back to Kansas. She got to go home.

Lillian's home is a big red-brick colonial house with white pillars in front, almost a mansion. Daniel bought it for her and they've lived in it ever since. Her little girl is inside, maybe Daniel, too. She'd know her home anywhere.

This isn't her home. No, this is a hallway, a stiff white hallway like one in a scary movie, a hallway that goes on and on. This isn't like being Dorothy, with her perky dark braids and red slippers. No, there's no magical land, no home at the end. There's only more spinning, more whirlwinds coming her way.

4.
fresh flowers

There's a man walking in the front door of the center. He doesn't sign in. Now he stands just inside, frowning, looking around.

Beth's in the dining room just inside the front door, dispensing her evening greetings. As her residents eat dinner she bends toward them, kissing cheeks, saying hellos. Seeing the stranger, she stands straight. For the zillionth time in her life, Beth wishes she were tall. Even just a tiny bit taller. She wishes she'd chosen those spiky high heels she almost put on this morning.

She's glad she has Harmony with her, although Harmony isn't exactly a watchdog. But the man doesn't know that. Still, Beth wishes the dog wasn't wagging her tail quite so feverishly.

This man is tall, very tall, with a fresh-scrubbed, pink-cheeked look. He's dressed in a dark suit and tie, more formal than most visitors. After all, this is small-town Ohio, and most show up in T-shirts and jeans. She knows pretty much everyone who comes to the center, and she's never seen this guy before.

Beth moves toward him, holds out her hand in a way that

she hopes is crisp and professional, Harmony trotting beside her. The man looks down as if from a great height. His is a big hand, a huge hand, and as his skin touches hers, something jagged moves through her, some jolt, some physical warning.

Shit! Her Mama Bear self rears up, stands on hind legs. Watch out! These are her people, and she's damn well going to protect them. She'll take him on. She looks up into the face looming above her. Of course this is ridiculous. Standing tall, she doesn't even come up to his shoulders.

"Can I help you? I'm Beth Hughes, the executive director." Did she just say executive? Beth hates that term, its pretension, and never uses it, though it's her official title. But perhaps the word gives her more height. A few inches, anyway.

"I'm Charlie. Charlie Earnhart," the man says. His voice is low, a bit nasal. "From New Horizons? I'm just here to, oh, take a look around," he says, flashing one of those smiles that come a second too late and seem pasted on, an afterthought when a person wants something from you.

Residents are looking up from the tables. Edward eyes Beth first, then the tall man, his eyes widening. Beth has to smile. Edward keeps trying to find her a boyfriend, and only he would think this young man a candidate. She shakes her head no, no way, this isn't the guy. There is no guy. Edward makes a face, goes back to his dinner.

The man nods toward a chair in the living room area, right next to the tables. "I'll just sit here a few minutes. Just getting a look around. Don't let me disturb you."

Right. New Horizons. What could possibly be disturbing? It's the company that might be buying Grace Woods Care Center.

Beth can't imagine what board members are thinking, selling out to a for-profit company. The center's been non-profit since the beginning, sponsored by the Brethren Church, not too much religious connection but just enough to ensure a center with ethical standards. Beth's proud to be part of it, and she knows that, in the nursing home world, pride is a hard thing to come by these days.

Charlie is not sitting down after all. He's picking up a vase from an end table and examining it as if at a yard sale. Now he's running his hand over the top of the table. Checking for dust? Good lord. He doesn't own this place, at least not yet. Does he?

Beth takes a deep breath. Okay, calm down. She heads back to the residents, leans over Lorraine. She kisses the old woman's cheek. The cool softness of skin feels like a surprise. This is Beth's favorite part of the day, mingling with residents. She tries to stop in each evening as they eat dinner. She's a director who knows each person by name, knows their loved ones. And she knows the loved ones love her; they appreciate a leader who's out and about, accessible, not hidden behind her desk.

"Lorraine," she says now. It's important to call each person by name, by the name each chooses to go by. It says this: *I see you. I know you.* It matters so much, especially because her people are old, and too often the world passes them by. More than anything, Beth wants her people to understand that they are seen. Lorraine turns toward her, flashing her smile.

"You're so beautiful," Lorraine says to Beth, looking up from her meatloaf, gazing as if she's in love. It's what Lorraine says every evening. You're so beautiful. Beth pats Lorraine's hand, moves to the next seat.

She kneels beside Monica. "Monica," she says as the old

woman looks off into the distance. But the name doesn't get a response. "Monica," Beth says again.

It's here again, the darkness that sometimes pulls Monica away from the others, down, down as if she's drowning in sadness. Sometimes Beth calls her name over and over, and the old woman's name feels like a lifeline pulling Monica back to them.

"Monica," Beth says again, louder.

Now Monica turns toward her. It's a deep look, a piercing look, and Beth holds the gaze. It's a gaze filled with sadness, and Beth wants to look away. She feels Monica pulling her down. But she doesn't look away. Here's the thing: a gaze thick in sadness, in despair, even that gaze, if two people feel it together, even that gaze has buoyancy. Beth feels it. It's the end of the day, Beth is tired, she'll go home soon to a house that's too quiet and empty. Yes, she's pulling Monica up, up, out of the pit she is in, yet Monica is pulling her too, she's also throwing a lifeline. The force of this gaze, this shared humanity, is pulling them both up, bringing them back to the world.

"Monica," Beth says again, holding the old woman's hand. "I'm happy to see you."

Monica's eyes are still locked on hers. That's the thing about old people. They're not in a hurry. They're not checking their phones or needing to be somewhere else.

Always people ask: Isn't your job depressing? No, Beth replies, no, it's not. Or rather, yes, it is, but that's not all. Sure, there's sadness, lots of it. But mainly there's this: the warmth, the buoyancy, of connecting, deeply connecting, with people whose time in this world is short. They teach Beth how to live every day.

Now Monica goes back to her food. Beth stands, surveys the

dining room. There's a tug on her consciousness from the edge of the room. That man, the New Horizons man, Charlie. What is he doing now? He's still sitting there, frowning, just looking around. He's making her nervous. She'll try to ignore him. There are fresh flowers on each table, as she requested. But wait a minute. Her first choice is daisies, for their optimism, their sunny brightness. Where are the daisies? These are carnations—better than no flowers, but not much.

Beth studies the plates. Lorraine's having meatloaf, while beside her Monica takes a bite from a hamburger. It wasn't easy making this happen, getting the board to approve meals restaurant-style, allowing people to order rather than be served the same meal as everyone else. But it's so important. At a time when her residents have lost so much control over their lives, she wants to give them this—choice over what they are eating.

She touches Monica's plate. Not warm enough. Okay, she needs to make a note of this, too, keep on top of the kitchen. Still, it's an experiment that seems to be working. Is she making this up, or are her residents happier now? Beth thinks they are. It's too soon to know if they're eating more, but Edward's in his suit coat and Lorraine wears lipstick. Her people seem to be dressing up more, seeing meals as an occasion.

Does Charlie notice this, that her residents dress up for dinner? That they have choices in meals? She sneaks a peek. Okay, she's definitely distracted by him. And he's looking off in the opposite direction. Fine.

Here's the new guy, Thomas. He was some sort of professor, and he has that professorial air about him, sort of observant, bemused. He's wearing a shirt and tie, as if about to teach one more class. She hasn't yet met any family; the arrangements took place over the phone and through lawyers, sort of unusual.

"Professor?" she says, bending toward him. He has lovely dark eyes.

"Thomas." He smiles. "Call me Thomas."

Is it too much to put her hand on his shoulder? He doesn't flinch, so Beth keeps it there. Here he is, a college professor eating at a table with three strange women, all of them old, very old. He looks lost, in a good-sport sort of way, but lost just the same.

It's the hardest part, seeing people soon after they move here. It's a good facility, and good care happens here, but it's a facility nonetheless, a place full of old people, of strangers, and no one, not one single person, has ever wanted their final days lived like this. All the fresh flowers in the world can't take this away.

There's so much more she wants to try. Last month at the symposium, the Dutch woman spoke of that country's efforts to revamp elder care, building cottages to house people rather than bigger buildings, so residents can live in family sized groups based on shared interests. And according to the Dutch woman, it seems to be working.

Okay, Beth can't tear down this building. She can't start over again. But couldn't she find new ways to bring her residents together in small, like-minded groups? Help them bond with each other? Thomas and Edward, for instance, both highly educated, could be a good fit. Maybe add Lucy, the retired librarian.

"I'll stop by your room this evening," she says now to Thomas. "Just to talk. Get to know you." She squeezes his hand.

Thomas nods as Beth moves to Lillian beside him. Thank goodness Lillian still has food on her plate; she hasn't yet dumped it. "Lillian," Beth says. "How are you?"

Lillian can't answer, not really. She looks at Beth blankly. Beth always means to say something pleasant to Lillian, not ask questions that make her feel put on the spot, but here she did it again. And now Thomas is watching too, looking quizzical.

"You look lovely tonight," Beth says, and Lillian gazes up at her, smiling.

Now she feels the eyes of the New Horizons man following her. What is he thinking? Beth is sorry she hopes he's impressed that she's mingling with residents, but of course that's what she's thinking. She wants to keep her job. Still, if he weren't here, she'd be doing this anyway. She's good at this work. She wants him to know it.

Now he's standing behind her. She feels a chill.

"I'll just look around more," he says, his eyes narrowing. He seems to be gazing above her, right over the top of her head.

What's that sound? Beth can't believe that Harmony seems to be growling.

"So sorry!" she says, although of course she's not sorry at all. "Harmony never growls. Never."

"Of course," Charlie says, frowning as he walks away.

• • •

After finishing paperwork, Beth's ready for home. But she told Thomas she'd stop by. At the door to his room, she hears voices. She hesitates. If he has visitors, she won't interrupt.

But it's a familiar voice. Beth sighs. Apparently Sally and Thomas are hitting it off. But you can't just sit around chatting, not if you're an aide with others to care for. She and Sally have discussed this repeatedly. Sally is both Beth's best aide and her worst.

Now, as Beth walks in the room, Sally stands, her face reddening. "I was just leaving," Sally says.

Thomas is frowning, looking from Sally to Beth.

"Lillian needs some help getting ready for bed," Beth says.

"Of course." Sally gives Thomas a wave, heads out of the room.

Thomas widens his eyes. "The boss lady," he says, when Sally is gone.

"Hmm. Sorry. Did I come on too strong?"

Thomas shrugs as Beth looks around. The room no longer smells like disinfectant. He's only been here a week, maybe two, but the room has already taken on Thomas's smell, a little bit of peppermint.

Thomas lies on his back, dressed in his clothes, a blanket spread on top of him. Is he still wearing a tie? Yes, he is.

The room still looks bare, not quite lived in. What Thomas has mainly is books, spilling out of his bookshelf, still in boxes next to the bed. She takes one from the shelf. It's an anthropology text from the looks of it. She leafs through the pages, stops at photos of Maasai tribesmen wearing in their ears what appear to be saucers.

When Beth turns back to the bed, Thomas's eyes are closed. He's snoring softly. She won't bother him now. She'll come back tomorrow.

• • •

As Beth heads out to the parking lot, she's surprised to see Charlie walking in front of her, his tall silhouette framed by shadows. What's he been doing all this time? Where has he been?

In her mind, another tall man emerges from darkness. Was her father as tall as Charlie? Even taller? She blinks, blinks again. Of course it can't be her father. He's dead. It's just Charlie, bending into his car.

As a child, Beth thought her father was the tallest man in the world. Was it her first memory? An early one, anyway. As she and her father took their evening walk in the neighborhood, she would be looking at him, looking up, and his head seemed to reach clear up to the sky. Always, Beth was looking up at her father. His hand was huge and warm holding hers, and she felt safe, safe and happy walking with the tallest man in the world.

Too often, though, people came up to them, neighbors who wanted to talk. Her father had an important job in the world; she knew this. He was a judge in a room with big windows and he wore a black robe. She'd seen it once. And even without the robe, in just his regular clothes, people wanted her father's attention. They would start talking and he'd listen. And there she was, surrounded by legs, so tiny, so close to the ground, just waiting for the people to stop. Sometimes she tugged on his hand.

Then he looked down at her, and even though his head was way up in the sky, she felt the warmth of his smile. "Beth," he would say, squeezing her hand. "Bethie."

That was all he said, and she knew what that meant. It meant you need to be patient with people. You need to give them their due. They each have a story, a struggle, and the least we can do is listen. That's what he told her, over and over.

"I'm trying," she says now to the parking lot. "I'm doing my best."

• • •

Backing her car up in the parking lot, she looks at the place where she spends her days. It's an average brick building, not that big, a rectangular block structure one story high. There's the concrete slab of a porch on which sit rocking chairs and a swing, a sliding glass door that leads to the dining room. From the outside, there's nothing remarkable.

Yet some nights, like tonight, with the lights blazing, the building seems to be trembling. There's a quiver and throb, the brick structure wiggling like Jell-O. Beth squints. Is that so?

It makes sense to her. Of course the building is trembling. Yes, people are living their last days here, but those days are still filled with the sorrow and pain and sweetness of life being lived. This building should be shaking and throbbing, the ground rumbling beneath.

Beth rolls down her window. Sometimes, like tonight, when she looks at the building she hears something too. It's a low hum, a buzz, and while perhaps it's the HVAC system, Beth could also believe it's the sound of her people, their coughs and harrumphs, their many hearts beating away.

Is the building really trembling and humming? Maybe not, but it should be.

5.
too much fuss

What's with these people in this strange land? Why get so excited? It's another custom that doesn't make sense.

Why are they doing this?

It's always like this, as far as Thomas can tell. So much commotion over nothing. Now residents are lined up in the dining room with their walkers, their canes, so you'd think the queen of England is about to arrive. Some have dressed up, women wearing lipstick (although most often smeared), the one man in a coat and tie. For what? For a dish of ice cream. Thomas leans in closer. It's only vanilla!

That activities lady keeps these old people whipped up, that's for sure; she makes a big deal out of everything. She must be the one who puts little bears in the windows, who puts out the ceramic pumpkins that leap out at Thomas from tabletops, from the corners of hallways.

Of course, not everyone in this old-person culture is having fun. About half are sleeping in chairs. They showed up for ice cream, but now they sit slumped, heads dangling on chests, snoring softly. Some are drooling. But others seem remarkably blind to how depressing this is.

The tall psychiatrist, retired for years, is leaning in to a group of old women, smiling down on them. Of course he's talking to women—he and Thomas are the only men here. And the woman who always says "yeah, yeah"—well, she's saying "yeah, yeah" now, gazing down at her bowl full of ice cream as if she's never seen anything like it before.

Humans! He still hasn't figured them out. His students always wanted the weird stuff, and there's plenty of weird stuff. Cultures that eat live snakes and bugs, men who put sticks in their ears, in their testicles. There's weird stuff galore. And what he's seeing now is pretty weird too. It's curious, that's for sure.

Now he imagines himself at a lectern, talking to a huge room of students. Sometimes he had four hundred! His classes were popular year after year.

Delusion! he says now in his mind, his voice full of wonder. You have to show students the wonder, and he's doing that now, his eyes widening, his hands gesturing.

These people are old, more than old, they are ancient! And they're excited about ice cream. They put on a dress to meet up in the dining room with other old people! Pay attention to this. Delusion! It's rampant in this culture of aging.

"Hey, everybody! Hangman!"

What's this? Now the perky activities lady stands next to a whiteboard on which she's just drawn a head in a noose. She's Vanna White of the gallows, waving the others over to join her. Thomas rubs his neck. Hangman! It's an odd choice of game for a nursing home. Does anyone see the irony here?

The perky woman puts up a bunch of blank spaces—how many? seven?—and the old people start calling out letters. They seem excited to hear their own voices—*P*! *G*!—and thrilled even when the letters are wrong, when the lady draws a neck on the man in the noose, then one arm hanging down.

Thomas closes his eyes but still he hears people calling out the most ridiculous letters, the ones with no chance of winning—*X*! *Q*! He hears the scratch scratching of the perky woman drawing another arm, the torso of a man on the board.

Call out a vowel! Someone, anyone!

"*A*!" Thomas hears someone call out. It's the old guy, the shrink. Thomas opens his eyes to see the perky woman smiling, writing a big *A* on the board. The doctor is leaning forward, smiling.

"*R*!"

Now people are clapping wildly as the perky woman writes an *R* up in the first blank space on the board. "Any other letters? We have an *R* and an *A*. Thomas? Anyone?"

The woman who pushed her eggs off the table keeps clapping, and the "yeah, yeah" woman says "yeah, yeah" again.

"Rainbow!" the shrink calls out, and the perky lady grins, fills the remaining letters in the blank spaces. Damn. Even the Hangman word is a happy word, a word that has now sent all of these old people into fits of clapping, of pleasure. The old shrink is smiling, taking a bow.

In Thomas's mind he's at the lectern again, addressing a full auditorium. *The level of delusion is remarkable*, he's saying. *These people are ready to die. They've lost their mobility, much of their functioning. Some have lost most of their minds. Yet they seem to be having fun.*

Thomas sees himself shaking his head in front of his students, holding his arms out wide, conveying his sense of astonishment. They're nodding back. Some are laughing, making fun of these people. He's sorry to have sparked this old-person ridicule, but it's hard to stop when he's making his students laugh. He loves making them laugh.

But of course, what he's doing is cheating. He's labeling. He's reducing the endless complexity of human behavior to a single word, a concept easily grasped. It's what good anthropologists try to avoid, and he's good at his work, or he once was. So he shouldn't be thinking this way. He shouldn't be diminishing the remarkable scene in front of him to this single word, this simplification. No, he should instead be opening to it, exploring it, feeling himself step into this new culture without judgment, without preconceived notions.

And there's something else, too, the worst part of his chosen profession. All of this observing, this judging—all of it keeps him off to the side, at a distance from others. He's on the outside, looking in. It feels safe, a natural inclination, maybe the way that he's made. But it's a cold place, too, this distancing. And it's lonely.

What is this? This phrase is his mantra. Or it was. It's what he said to himself to help himself open, to leave judgment aside. *What is this?* It's what he repeated a hundred times a day in the field in the Philippines, when he felt himself slipping toward labels that were simple but wrong, way too easy. Now Thomas remembers. At best, *What is this?* came with a feeling. It felt like a loosening, his skin slipping away, a letting go of all that kept him apart from the others.

Yes, he's feeling it now.

"Thomas?" The perky lady is calling to him, smiling her blazing smile. "Will you join us?"

"*E*!" Thomas hears his own voice calling out. The old shrink is smiling, leaning toward him. The lipsticked old ladies are clapping in his direction. The perky lady puts an *E* on the board with a flourish in the first of nine spaces. Okay, he's here now with the others. He joined in.

Here's what it feels like. A sharp intake of breath, a humbling, a stark moment of truth. These people aren't different from me. I am here now; I am old and alone and living among other lonely old humans. This institution, this strange land of teddy bears and shuffling old women, of tasteless food and delusional games—this is my home now.

And yet. It's a softening too, an easing into the moment. A relaxing. Yes, this is me. This is who I am now. This is where I belong. These are my people.

"*X*!" someone else calls. The perky lady writes *X* in the second space.

"Excellent," the shrink calls out as hooting and clapping explode in the room.

But whoa. Thomas sucks breath. He closes his eyes to the pain; maybe not seeing will take it away. Okay, the pain's going. It's gone. But now a wave washes over him, a wave of fatigue. He is suddenly tired, so tired, deflated, a tire that's gone suddenly, inexplicably flat. He wants his bed. But the hallway he has to walk down appears to be endless. He just has to begin.

"Thomas?" He hears the perky lady call after him, but even waving goodbye seems exhausting.

He keeps walking.

He's barely started the long trip down the hall when the retired shrink stands in his way.

"Can I walk with you?" the man says. "I have something for you. Let's just stop in my room."

The room they turn in to has a big bookcase. Old books—they smell musty. Medical books? Thomas reaches out, runs his hand over the bindings. They feel soft, almost alive.

There's a computer next to the bookshelf. On the table, so many photos. Maybe the psychiatrist brought him here to show off his family? There's an elegant woman who must be his wife, surrounded by people who must be his children. Four of them from the looks of it, standing with equally elegant young adults, healthy and happy grandchildren. And the psychiatrist in the center of things, surrounded by all that love.

"Beautiful family," Thomas says. But the man just grunts, digging into a pile of papers. Thomas doesn't think he can stand any longer. He holds on to the back of the chair.

"Sorry," the man says. "I can't seem to find it. I'll keep looking. I'll bring it down to your room."

He heads into the bathroom. Okay, Thomas can leave.

Once he's back in his own room he lies on his bed, catches his breath. He tries not to compare the photos on his own bedside table with the other man's family. He has several photos, but only one person in each, and it's the same person. He hasn't seen her in years. She's somewhere in California. Lexie always wanted to leave Ohio and she did, straight out of high school.

Thomas studies the photos. In each of them Lexie is alone, first as a little girl holding a stuffed bear, then as a high school graduate, then a young woman. In the photos she seems to be drifting in space, engulfed in a background of blue, on her face a hesitant smile. His stomach tightens seeing her like this, alone, floating in air.

He'd like to hear more from Lexie, but the ball's in her court. And when he thinks of her, he also thinks of what he did wrong as a father, so many things. His stomach balls into a fist. Mostly, Lexie's been angry since he left her mother for Sarah. Of course Lexie has a right to be angry. But that was thirty years ago! Or maybe forty. Even more?

"Thomas?"

It's hard to tell who this is. Is she a nurse? Nurses don't wear those hats anymore. This one has a very round face. He doesn't recognize her. He wants to tell Hal about how nurses wear barn-yard scenes on their clothes. Where is Hal? His stomach tightens.

"Thomas, we need to do testing," the woman says. "You've been falling, you know, and there's the diarrhea. So we made you an appointment for next week at the hospital. Someone will go with you, of course."

"Fine," he says, although it's not fine at all. But what can he do?

"Should I turn on the TV?"

Thomas shakes his head no.

"A book?" the round-faced woman says.

"Sure." A book would be wonderful. One of his favorites, by Mary Catherine Bateson, sits on the edge of the bookshelf. He points to it. The nurse hands it to him before leaving.

It's a lovely book about Bateson's life as an anthropologist. She's a wonderful thinker, a lovely writer. Reading it, Thomas always feels proud of his chosen profession. He'll start from the beginning.

But the words swim. They dip and skitter in front of his eyes. Thomas blinks, tries again. He just needs to focus. He wants the words to stand still, he wants to savor the start of a sentence, then the movement through to its end: subject, verb, predicate. He wants the thrill, the pleasure of her graceful writing. But these words are tangled, like the puzzle pieces that fell to the floor, cows and chickens all smushed up together. It makes his head spin.

It takes him by surprise every time. He always forgets. He can't read anymore. Or at least, he can't read easily. When he opens the book, tries again, the words once more tremble and lurch.

Thomas closes the book, looks out the window. The feeling is hollowness deep inside, as if something has carved out his core, leaving only a shell. He watches a blue jay dive-bombing a robin until both fly away. Is this what the Buddhists call emptiness? But it doesn't feel spiritual, no. It just feels empty.

He can still hold the book in his hands. He can raise the book to his face and smell the foresty smell of print, of words on a page. It's a wonderful smell. He licks the cover. Okay, this is crazy. He licks it again.

• • •

When Thomas wakes, the old psychiatrist is sitting by the side of the bed. Outside it's getting dark. Was he napping?

The psychiatrist leans toward him. "I don't know what your interests are, but I've been protesting the death penalty. I write letters to men on death row. They're all men, of course."

Thomas sits up, rubs his eyes. The death penalty?

"Here's one I wrote yesterday. That's what I was looking for earlier." He holds out a piece of paper. "I use a computer to keep up with the cases," the man says. "But not to write letters. Oh no. These guys want something handwritten. I mean, how many people are writing to them? Not many, I'd guess."

This old guy has his own death sentence in the not-too-distant future, and who's writing letters to him? Nobody, that's who. Yet he's taking the time to do this for others, for those whom society says should be killed. He's writing these letters by hand. Thomas looks at the man's hands, which appear gnarled by arthritis or simply aging. He must find it uncomfortable, even painful, to write. This is curious, more than curious. Thomas doesn't know what to say.

"Anyway," the man says, handing over the piece of paper. "I just wanted to show you. You seem like someone who might be interested. You could join me writing letters, if you want."

Thomas nods, maybe too vigorously. He'd like to be the person the man thinks he is. But now his eyelids feel heavy. He just wants to sleep.

• • •

Was he napping again? Apparently. Now it's dark outside, almost night.

Ow! He sucks breath. These flashes of pain come out of nowhere. He holds on to the side of the bed. It helps if he doesn't think pain, if he just thinks of this feeling as, well, a feeling, a blast of heat, getting squeezed very hard. Thinking pain makes it worse. There, it's passing. It's almost gone.

What is this?

It's a warmth on his forehead. Something soft and wet, soothing him. The warmth, the softness, takes his mind away from the pain. Someone's hand is guiding the cloth, a gentle touch on his face.

He opens his eyes. It's the tall, smooth-skinned aide, now at the side of his bed. She's stroking his forehead with a warm cloth.

"Thank you," he says.

"That was bad," she says, looking into his eyes. "The pain. I could tell."

Thomas sighs. "Pretty bad. But the washcloth helps. It's still helping. Sally. Have I got that right?"

She smiles. "Yup."

She stands, disappears into the bathroom. He hears water in the sink. When she comes back, the cloth is newly warm and wet.

"It's so soft," he says, as she lays the cloth on his face.

"I have special washcloths," she says, shaking her head. "I send away for them. They're bamboo. The ones here at the center, they're not soft enough. So I carry my own stash for times like this. Then I wash them at home. Some folks here think I'm crazy."

"That's not crazy. It's not crazy at all."

He closes his eyes, lets the cloth soothe him. He hears the chattering of squirrels outside the window.

When the cloth is cool again, Sally takes it away.

"More?" she asks.

"It's gone now. The pain. I love the sound of the word. Bamboo. Lots of bamboo in the Philippines, where I did some research. Way back then people saw it as sort of a pest. But now. They're building houses with it, eating it. Apparently, they're making washcloths, too. Anyway, bamboo! I just like to say it."

There's a wistfulness, a hint of sadness in this lovely woman, and he's pleased to be making her smile. She picks up the book on his table, the one by Bateson. "Looks good," she says, turning it over. "Is it good?"

"Yes, it is." He looks down at his hands. "The thing is, I can't seem to read it. I can't read anymore."

He's surprised to hear himself say this; he didn't mean to say it out loud. Now Sally studies the cover. She opens the book. "I'll read it to you."

Thomas shakes his head. "Oh, no. You have things to do, I know that. You might get in trouble."

Sally tilts her head, speaks slowly. "Not for long. Maybe I'll just read part of a chapter."

Thomas closes his eyes. It is soothing, the words of his favorite author wrapped in Sally's soft voice. Sally's taking a risk now, taking the time to tend to him. He's worried for her, yet grateful. He feels like a small boy at night in his bed, his mother reading before she turns out the light. It's a wonderful feeling. He thinks of the retired psychiatrist writing letters to strangers who live on death row. The old man is writing letters by hand, by a hand that perhaps finds it painful to write.

Thomas feels himself drifting, drifting into the night. Now he sees himself again in front of the lectern. It's the last day of class. He's zeroing in on the one thing his students most need to know, the thing more important than this quirky stuff he's been discussing all year. The students lean forward, ready to write. Yes, they need to take notes. It's not good to label, no, not good to simplify things. But it helps to find patterns. Patterns help us see repetitions, find order in chaos, grasp the whole picture. Patterns help us to understand. There's a pattern here, and he wants his students to see it. He wants to leave them, at the end of each term, with something important.

Kindness! he's saying at the top of his voice, waving his arms, almost yelling. *Pay attention to kindness! It's kindness that matters the most.*

Did he actually say this, or is he just now making it up? He hopes he did say it. Perhaps it doesn't matter. He closes his eyes, lets Sally's soft voice envelop him as evening light leaves his room.

6.
a dead cat

Sally wants to paint the walls of the break room. She asked maintenance if she could paint, but no one got back to her. She wouldn't charge for her labor if the center takes care of the paint. She'd make the room a soothing shade of Southwest terra-cotta.

A lovely terra-cotta on the walls here would help. And some good coffee in the vending machine. This coffee tastes greasy, as usual, greasy and strangely sweet even though it's supposed to be black. Still, she drinks it all day. It's coffee.

She sits alone at the table. There's only one table.

Now Deborah bursts in the room. No matter what room it is, Deborah always bursts in. While she's petite and Sally is tall, being around Deborah always makes Sally feel small. She feels herself shrinking. Deborah is followed by Megan, the new girl. Are all young women named Megan these days?

"Damn!" Deborah says, grabbing a chair. "That woman! First she wants one thing, then another. Then she doesn't want the first thing anymore, not the second thing either. So she's mad at me. That new woman in twenty? She's a handful."

Sally looks at the table. She doesn't like talking about residents like this.

Megan sits down, begins peeling the wrapper from a candy bar. "You're telling me. Yesterday she drove me insane. Insane! Today she's all yours."

Sally feels her face heating up. She should say something, but what? She looks down at her cup.

"Have you had her yet, Sally?" Deborah is staring at her. She peers over the little glasses that she keeps on the edge of her nose.

"Once. A few days ago," Sally says.

"Was it okay? Did she make you crazy?"

"No. Yes," Sally says. "She's old. She's unhappy. I don't know."

Silence now from Deborah and Megan. Megan turns toward Deborah. "I went in about five times last night after she called me. She wanted water, then she wanted the water taken away, then she wanted some crackers, then I had to go take the wrappers away. They were making too much noise. That's what she said! The wrappers were crackling when she was trying to sleep."

"She was frightened is all," Sally says, before she remembers she should say nothing.

Deborah stares at her, frowning. She shakes her head. "Mother Teresa over there."

"I'm not Mother Teresa," she says, although she's sorry to hear the whininess in her voice. "It's just that I think she's frightened is all. She just moved in. It's a lot to take in."

Deborah looks at Sally. "Honey, we're not hurting anyone. We care for them too, just like you do. We're just blowing off steam. You have to blow off steam once in a while. We all do. Even you."

"I know," Sally says.

Now Deborah and Megan get up, throw their cups in the trash. As they leave the room they lean into each other, laughing at something. Sally feels her gut tighten. Why doesn't she know how to be with people? She just doesn't is all. She's amazed at these women whose words just flow out of their mouths, how strong they are, how articulate.

She should have been quiet, just stayed out of it. Or not been so high and mighty, so goody-two-shoes. She'll replay the conversation over and over in her head, insert the words she wishes she'd said. For a second she'll feel good about herself when she hears the new words in her head, but then she'll remember the words that actually came out of her mouth. She'll burn with shame. Why doesn't she know better?

When she was a kid she loved coming home from school, opening the door to the kitchen even though no one was home. The kitchen so warm, smelling of bacon from breakfast. Her mother and father were working, and she was an only child. But she didn't mind being alone. She liked it. After school Sally felt exhausted from all those children, how rough and tumble school was, kids talking and laughing and rushing around all day long. Sally trying to figure out what to say, when to say it. But at home she could make tea and be quiet. She felt at ease, finally. Well, until her mother or father appeared.

Sally looks around the room. The only other place she felt at ease was here at the center. Was she in high school? It was a hard time, so much drama, not enough friends. Some guy always breaking her heart. Then she took a job here after school and everything changed. She never left. These old people saved her.

The door to the break room opens again. It's the new maintenance guy, the tall guy who popped out of Thomas's closet. He smiles his huge smile at Sally, then grabs a coffee. When he sits beside her, his legs are so long they stick out the other side of the table, next to her. She scoots away, gives him more room.

"I've been wanting to tell you something," he says, looking at her. His eyes are light blue.

Sally nods. He makes her nervous. He's so young, and young men usually ignore middle-aged women. What could he want to tell a forty-two-year-old woman like her?

"That day, the other day, when you were helping that guy who pooped in his bed? What's his name, Thomas? Anyway, the way you were talking to him? It was, you know, sweet. I was moved by it. I was standing in the closet about ready to cry. That's the real reason I didn't come out sooner."

Sally feels her face getting hot. "Oh. Okay. Well, I like him a lot. He's a good guy, Thomas." He looks at her, smiling that devilish smile. He smells amazing. He smells like Tide detergent, a clean, fresh smell that wafts off him like steam from a hot sidewalk. Sally catches herself leaning closer, just to smell him. She pulls back.

Is he flirting with her? Of course not. Still, Sally is suddenly aware of her hands holding her cup. How dry her skin looks, how old. She wishes she'd put on lotion today. Now he stares into his coffee, then looks up at her. He is sort of handsome, but in a strange sort of way.

"There's something else, too," he says, leaning over his cup. "There's something in my car I want to show you."

In the car?

"Well, I should tell you about it first. I should prepare you. It's a cat. But she's dead. My dead cat."

Sally's eyes widen. Okay, this guy is crazy. She begins pushing her chair back from the table. He reaches his hand out, puts his hand over hers. Now she's staring at her old dried-up hands again.

"I'm sorry," the guy says. "That sounds weird, I know. She died a few days ago. I just can't seem to take her down to the vet. I want her cremated, put in a little box so I can have her in my house. So I can take her with me wherever I go. But I don't want to leave her there at the vet without me. She'll be alone." He looks down at the table, shakes his head. "I mean, she's dead. I get that. But I just can't seem to take her away."

Sally nods. She understands now. He's looking for comfort. People come to Sally for comfort. She knows how to act now, what's required. "I'm so sorry," she says.

Now he looks up, his eyes wet. His strong features look sort of crumpled. "She was my best friend. Silly, I know. Just a cat. But I'd just moved to a new town, and I didn't know anyone. And, well, she loved me. She followed me around. She'd sit in the bathroom and wait for me when I was taking a shower! She helped me feel not so—I don't know—not so alone."

"Of course," Sally says.

"You don't have to see her if you don't want. She's wrapped up in a blanket and all, and she's in the back seat. It's not grotesque, not just a dead body. But I keep meaning to take her down to the vet and then I drive there, it's about ten miles away, and then I just turn around and drive back with my dead cat still in the back seat. That's crazy, I know."

Sally smiles. "It's not crazy."

"Well, it's a little crazy. But I can't help it. I can't let her go." Now he stares into his coffee. "Would you come along? When I take her? I know it's a weird thing to ask, but after I heard you with the old guy I thought, she's so kind. Maybe she'll help me. Maybe I just need someone to go with me, and then I can drop her off."

He looks up at the ceiling, then at her. "I don't have friends here, not yet. I just moved. I just have my cat. Well, I had her."

Okay, it is weird. But there's a sweetness about him she didn't expect. "I can go. I'm off tomorrow, or some other time. I'm glad to do it. Well, not glad that your cat died. You know what I mean."

When he looks up at her, Shannon's eyes seem more deeply blue than before. He wipes them. "Wow. That's great. Thank you so much." He looks at the table. "Do you want to see her? See what you're getting into?"

He seems to want this, so Sally nods yes. Walking out to the parking lot, she's aware that other staffers are turning their heads, watching. Sally's ashamed that she's proud being seen with this young man, even if only to look at a dead cat. Shannon seems oblivious to people looking.

He has an old car, some kind of Chevy. When Sally looks in the back window she sees a lump under a blanket, little grey ears sticking out. Now he opens the door, leans in. He's petting the blanket.

"Poor baby," he says. "She doesn't smell or anything. It's cold enough in the car. I wouldn't let her smell. I would never do that." He closes the car door again. "Thanks. Thanks for not thinking I'm crazy. Or for thinking I'm crazy and doing it anyway."

"Sure," Sally says. They're heading back into the building. Of course that's what he wanted. He wanted her help. He's not interested in her as a woman. Doesn't she know this by now? Why is her heart such a sucker, so quick to waltz off in a fantasy of being loved by a man, and especially this man, this young man who sees her only as kind? She's aware of his body now walking beside her, his arms swinging, almost brushing against her. But she can do this. She can be kind. She knows just what to do.

7.
where is home?

Some blonde lady comes on TV and begins talking about weather patterns in southwest Ohio. But Lillian doesn't live in Ohio! She lives in Indiana. What is she doing listening to the wrong weather report in the wrong state?

Who are these old people anyway? Why did she just eat dinner with them? She doesn't know who they are. They don't even like her and she's not fond of them, either.

When she begins thinking like this—*Where am I, anyway? Why am I here?*—a giant claw twists its way into her stomach. A claw with long nails. Ouch! She hugs herself, but it doesn't make her feel better. But it does help to walk. When she walks, the claw feels more like a tickle, and if Lillian tries hard, the tickle turns into an engine, a tiny engine propelling her forward.

Lillian starts walking. There's the big pictures of mountains and oceans and fields of corn, but she's not going to fall for them, not today. No, she's not walking in fields of corn, she's walking in circles. She knows this.

Here comes the woman with pouches on the sides of her face. The woman's dark glares make Lillian feel dirty, so she darts into the room she's passing. After all, the door's open.

Someone is lying in bed. It's a man, the tall man who sits on the other side of the dining room. Sometimes he talks to her. He's nice. Now he makes little puffy sounds as he sleeps.

She sits on the edge of his bed. Out his window, birds peck at seeds on the boxy feeders that stick up from the ground. Lillian loves birds. How fat they are, on such tiny legs. How do they keep standing up? Why don't they fall right over? Birds give her hope. Now the man grunts. He opens his eyes.

"Hello, Lillian," he says. "Here you are. Again."

"Hello," Lillian says. "Yes!"

It feels good to just sit for a while in silence, watching the birds. She also likes all the people standing around on the man's table next to his bed. They look so happy together, such a tall, handsome family.

"Lillian," the man says. "Please don't take your clothes off." He's sitting up in bed now, fully dressed. He has a blanket pulled up to his chest. "It's fine if you sit here a while," he says, though he's frowning. "If you don't take off your clothes like last time. That makes me uncomfortable."

Did she do that? Lillian doesn't remember. She reaches out, takes his hand.

"Okay," he says. "I guess it's okay to hold hands. For a little bit." But now he drops her hand. He's reaching for one of the photos next to the bed. "I have a wife, you know. Well, I had one. But I still have her, of course, in my heart. She's with me all the time. She was, what do you call it? The love of my life."

The man hands her a photo of himself standing with the woman who must be his wife. Lillian is supposed to do something with the photo, though she isn't sure what. She hands it back to him.

"What…?" Lillian says, and the birds in her mind take off.

She doesn't like the birds in her mind as much as the ones at the feeder. Would it help to know what sort of birds they are, the ones in her mind? Today they're little black birds soaring up into the sky. Too small for crows. Maybe grackles? The same sort of birds that nested in the big tree in the backyard when she was little, and when so many birds took off at once Lillian sometimes thought the tree itself was flying away.

Whatever they are, these birds are flying. Her words are sprouting feathers and wings. Her mouth full of feathers!

"What…?" she begins again, but more birds begin flying. They're not like the birds at the feeders outside; those birds have little black caps and white tummies.

The man tilts his head, looking at her. "I'm sorry, Lillian," he says.

Sorry? What is he sorry about?

"It must be hard," he says, looking right at her.

Now someone walks in. A thin woman, young. A perfume smell is following her. "Lillian," she says, "you have to leave now. This isn't your room."

The man looks up. "It's okay. I don't mind, for a little bit."

But the young woman sounds brisk and sharp, like Lillian did something wrong. Like wherever the line is, she didn't toe it. "Go back to your room," the woman says, her voice deeper this time.

Lillian stands. Go back to your room! She feels like a child, a dog. Her room? She wants to tell the young woman she doesn't have a room, not here in this place. She opens her mouth, but the birds begin flying.

"Go now," the young woman says, with a snap in her voice.

Ouch! The claw is twisting again, telling Lillian she's been bad, so bad that she lost her place in the world, and maybe she'll never find it again.

Lillian starts walking. She needs to calm down. And here she is in the big room again, the one with the TV. On the screen people are still hammering boards onto their windows. The bull-necked woman looks over at her, then looks away. The others keep staring at the storm on the screen.

Where is Dan? Where is Annie? Why isn't she at her own home?

Her home. It's a red-brick colonial with white pillars in front. It's almost a mansion. She fell in love with this house long ago when she and Dan had just married and lived in an apartment, after Dan returned from the war. They took evening walks in this neighborhood, dreaming, and always stopped in front of this house. It was her favorite. And he began fixing root canals and pretty soon they had enough money to move. One day Dan came home with a key and said, *Come with me.* Then he led her to the beautiful brick house she loved and said, *It's all yours. This is our house now.*

It was her house! And she never got tired of it, not even after living there years and years and years. Sometimes she felt bad that Dan made so much money off of people's bad teeth, but she tried not to think about it.

In her mind Lillian walks in the front door of her house.

She turns off the front hall to the kitchen. She likes to keep the table set. She keeps four place settings on the table, one for Dan, and Annie, and herself, and the other for who knows who else might show up? She loves having a place for whoever shows up, although it rarely happens that someone shows up. A stranger at the door! An old friend who needs a place to stay for a while. A relative lost for decades who suddenly appears on the step. Even though these people never show up, she is ready for them.

Lillian likes to think of herself as that sort of person. Always food for guests. Always a place at the table. She knows people who have houseguests over and over, so-and-so staying a few days, or a week at a time. But no one ever stays over at Lillian's house. Why not? She was ready.

Dan and Annie used to kid her about the place at the table, the extra place setting that no one used. Truthfully, she also set the extra plate because only three plates look sad. Only three plates at her table! Only two people, plus her, in her family. Just looking at the paucity of plates on the table seems to say something dark about her love for Dan, his love for her, that there just isn't enough of it. That she and Dan aren't fecund, aren't robust with love, that in their decades of marriage they could only squeeze out one tiny human, not two or three like their other friends, or seven or eight like the Catholics. Maybe people thought she and Dan never have sex. Maybe Dan doesn't like her body, her tiny breasts and thick ankles. Maybe he's not really in love with her. That's what this small family, these three measly plates, say to the world.

Lillian closes her eyes, looks back to the TV screen where

boards are still being nailed to windows. She's sorry to be thinking this way about Dan. He loves her. He does.

Her kitchen cupboards! Lillian never gets tired of opening them. Sometimes, when she's alone—and for some reason she's alone a lot—she goes to the kitchen and opens her cupboards. She gazes at her plates. There are the silvery and sleek plates for special occasions and the Italian ones for every day, hand-painted with tiny flowers and leaves. She loves those plates, how they seem to promise not only good meals but Italian villages perched on a cliff, vistas of the blue sea. The plates say, *We're waiting, just waiting for you to come and put us out on the table.*

Something grey ripples in Lillian's mind, like a soft scarf in a breeze. Something about her daughter, about Annie all grown up. But that can't be. She's a little girl, waiting for her mom to come home.

Where is her home? Why isn't she there?

Lillian turns her head. Someone just walked in the front door of the building, the man with the ponytail who comes to visit the tall man.

Wait a minute. The door that's too heavy to push open herself hasn't quite closed yet. It's still swinging shut. She can slip through the door before it closes.

She can walk outside. Just like that! She can take a step forward, into the parking lot.

"Miss Lillian!"

Now someone is tugging her arm. It's the nice brown lady, the one with the good-smelling hair. Now the woman has grabbed Lillian's arm.

"Come with me," the brown woman says. "Come back inside. It's too cold."

Cold? Lillian isn't cold. But this woman is strong. Lillian feels herself being pulled back inside.

The lady leads Lillian toward one of the dining room tables. "Sit here, sweetheart. I'll get you some cocoa. You like cocoa, no?"

Lillian does like cocoa. In the living room area, people are still watching the storm on TV. Okay, she'll sit for a while.

But she watches the door. Her house is out there somewhere. She will find it.

8.
red plates

When Charlie, the New Horizons guy, leans forward, Beth believes he's looking at the photo of Jack. Of course, keeping her ex-husband's photo out on her desk likely reveals all sorts of embarrassing things, but she keeps it around just the same. For times like this. Sometimes it helps to show off a good-looking man, a man who lends credibility, a professional man in a suit. It's stupid, of course, but also the way the world works.

And they don't know Jack's an ex. Most days she has the photo turned toward the wall, but today she's turned it around, facing her visitors.

Now her office seems overstuffed. Charlie brought along his young female assistant, the three of them sitting in chairs so close they could touch knees. But they needed privacy, and so here they all are in her office. Still, Beth didn't expect to feel quite so exposed as Charlie swivels his head, seeming to take in every last thing. What else might they find out about her? That she likes Matisse, or at least the poster up on the wall. That she has a photo of a dog on her desk, but she's sure they don't care about her dead dog. Still, she looks at Daisy first thing each morning and the last thing at night. She misses her all the time.

And there's the fedora hanging on a hook over her desk. Charlie is eyeing it. It's her dad's hat, the one he wore each morning when he went out into the world, when she was a child and he the person she most wanted to be. After he died, she claimed his hat, had Norm put a hook in the wall.

Now Charlie's frowning at the door to her office.

"I always keep the door open," Beth says now. "It's important, showing the staff I'm accessible. But we can still be private."

He tilts his head as if trying to figure her out.

"We're at full capacity," Beth says now.

Charlie and the woman are nodding happily as they look at each other. "Well," Charlie says. "That's good news." The woman is wearing a scent, something citrusy, which dominates the small room. Beth tries not to breathe in too deeply.

It's the first time she's met with them. A week ago the sale went through, and nobody knows what it means to the center. She'll let everyone know what she finds out, she told her staff a few days ago.

A wet, sputtering sound floats up from the corner, followed by two tiny yelps. Ah yes, Harmony sleeping, chasing her doggy dreams.

Now Charlie looks toward Harmony, then back at Beth. "The dog," he says, with a frown.

"Harmony? Yes, she's our center dog. We've had her, oh, maybe five years? The residents love her." Beth is sorry to hear an edge of desperation in her voice.

"We like visiting therapy dogs," Charlie says now, frowning at Harmony. "But they don't live at the centers. They visit."

"Oh, it's no problem," Beth says, trying to slow down her words. "Our staff takes her out three times a day. They love her. She's well behaved." Beth hopes Charlie doesn't remember that Harmony growled at him. "We have aides who have been here for twenty-five years," Beth finds herself saying. "That's unheard of, as you know, in this industry. We have a waiting list for residents. Last time I checked there were, oh, about six on the list. Maybe seven. We're at full capacity."

Is she repeating herself? It's what Beth does when she gets nervous. She also talks too fast and too much. And she's nervous much of the time. She needs to slow down. She stops talking, takes a breath. She looks at her hands. Such little hands, Jack used to say, tracing her fingers. Like a child's. He loved saying that as he held her hands in his. His hands so much bigger. Beth squirms. She stuffs her hands under her legs, sits on them. She doesn't want these people to see how little her hands are. She's not a child. She's a woman who knows way more than they do about the work they're all doing.

Now Charlie leans toward her. "Have you read about us? On our website?" He has a wide smile, very white teeth. "We're not corporate! We're a family business," he continues. "My father started it. He wanted a place for my grandfather in his last years. But he couldn't find a place good enough. So he started one, and we've been doing this work ever since. We have, oh, maybe thirty facilities now? I've lost track. But we hope to expand throughout the state. Maybe the region!" Charlie flashes his white teeth at Beth.

She feels sick to her stomach. Right, they're not corporate, yet they have thirty facilities. Grace Woods's small size, its independence, is what makes the place work, makes it special.

"Our intent is to keep things here that are working," Charlie says. "That is, keep them working. In fact, we'll make them work better. You'll have more resources. We want to help."

Now Harmony sits up, having awakened from her nap.

"Why don't you make a wish list?" Charlie says now. The young woman eyes Harmony. "We'll be back soon to talk about it. See what we can do."

Beth feels herself exhale. More resources? A wish list? Okay, perhaps this is promising. With the non-profit center board, it was like pulling teeth to fund anything new. It's been a while since Beth made a wish list. "Yes," she says. "We need some red plates."

"Red plates?"

In the hallway, someone is moaning. Loudly. Damn. Who's on duty? "Red plates," Beth says, hoping the New Horizons people don't hear the moan. "It's this new thing. Studies show that red plates help people eat better. People with dementia, especially. It's a small thing and no one knows why, but it seems to work. I'd love to try it."

Charlie frowns at her. At least the moaning has stopped. "Well, this isn't a memory care unit."

"Yes, but almost everyone here has dementia. A little bit. They're old people."

"If we have dementia residents, we need to lock doors. Insurance and all," Charlie says. "There shouldn't be people here with too much dementia. That's what I'm saying."

Beth smiles at him. She should stop herself but can't quite.

"Not too much dementia," she says. "Just the right amount."

The New Horizons people look at each other. Damn. Sometimes Beth's humor falls flat. When people don't know whether to take you seriously, you make them feel awkward, Jack used to say. People don't like to feel awkward.

Sally sticks her head in the door. "Oh, sorry," Sally says, taking in the stranger's presence. "It's just, one of Edward's bookshelves looks like it might fall. Could you send one of the maintenance guys around?"

"Yes," Beth says. "But we're busy here."

Sally shoots her a frown, then leaves. Charlie's eyeing Beth. Was she too abrupt? She was nervous. Probably she was abrupt. People tell her she's abrupt with the staff, although she's always surprised to hear it. She doesn't mean to be.

"Speaking of plates," she says to the woman and Charlie. She's just getting going. She shifts into her deeper voice, the one she hopes makes up for her lack of height. "We started offering residents a choice for their meals, like in a restaurant. They seem to love it. I think it makes a difference, helps them feel more in control of their lives. There's all sorts of things I'd like to try, things like that."

Charlie leans forward. "This is a small facility, have I got that right? About twenty residents?" When Beth nods, he clears his throat. "Ordering meals and such—that doesn't sound cost effective," he says.

Beth blinks. What about all those resources?

The New Horizons people squirm in their chairs. They're getting ready to go. Okay, she'll put off the rest of her wish list. As they stand, Charlie looks down at Beth. She stands too, although it doesn't help much. He still towers above her like a tree. Now he's eyeing the photo of Jack again.

"So," he says. "What are your plans?"

"My plans?"

"Yes."

Beth takes a deep breath. "I'd love to add more pathways out back, so our residents do more walking," she says. "More outside furniture too, picnic tables and such, to encourage them to get out of the building. And I'd love to do things the Dutch are trying, placing residents into family-size groups."

Charlie frowns at her. "I mean," he says, "what are your personal plans?"

"Personal?" Beth's stomach has flipped. "I don't know. I intend to stay here at my job."

"For how long?" he says, leaning in.

"As long as I can," she says. "I love working here."

As Harmony gnaws on her kibble, the room seems to throb with the sound of crunching.

"How old are you?" Charlie asks.

Beth feels her heart racing. Isn't there some sort of law against asking this? She could lie. But they have the paperwork, or they will soon. "Fifty-nine," she says.

"Hmmm," he says, glancing around as they leave. "We'll be in touch."

When she hears them go out the front door, Beth sits down again. She looks at the photo of Daisy. Did she screw everything up? She wants Harmony to come sit beside her. But the dog just looks at her, then walks out the door. Daisy wouldn't do that. She'd see that Beth feels bad and come sit beside her, put her head on Beth's knees. She'd look up with her big brown eyes and nuzzle Beth's hands. Beth would feel the dog's cold nose, her warm skin, and she would smile. Daisy would make everything better.

• • •

As she walks toward her car, Beth feels there's someone behind her. She turns to see Lillian walking near the back of her car, carrying a stuffed bear with a red ribbon.

"Lillian!" Beth is sorry to sound alarmed. She doesn't want to upset the old woman.

"Yes!" Lillian says. "Hello!"

For an old woman, Lillian moves quickly. Beth takes her arm. Who is working tonight? How did this happen? "We need to go back inside," Beth says. "I'll go with you. It will be dark soon, too dark to be out."

"Yes. Hello!" The old woman stands still for a moment looking perplexed, as if trying to figure out how she ended up in a parking lot. Beth is relieved that Lillian doesn't resist, turns toward the building. Beth didn't want to use physical force.

Now one of the aides, the new Filipino woman, bursts out the door. Beth is sorry that she doesn't like this woman. Is she being racist? The woman seems well-meaning but gets worked up over everything, escalates unnecessarily. In this case, though, she should have been paying closer attention.

"I'm so sorry!" the aide says. "She just slipped out."

Beth feels her voice deepen. "It's your job to keep that from happening."

"I know." The woman looks at the ground, shaking her head. "I know it is."

The two of them flank Lillian as they go back inside. Beth ducks into her office as the aide leads Lillian to a table.

As Beth leaves for the second time, Lillian is sitting down, the aide bringing her a hot chocolate, the stuffed bear sitting upright on the table.

As she walks toward her car, Beth checks behind, making sure Lillian's not following. No one there. No, the center doesn't lock doors, not until late in the evening. It's policy, and Beth wants to keep it that way. Still, it shouldn't be the Filipino woman's job to keep Lillian from walking right out the front door. The New Horizons people were right. Lillian doesn't belong here.

Beth still doesn't know why she gave the okay, except that Lillian's daughter, when they met, seemed so frazzled and yet so well meaning, yet another middle-aged woman overwhelmed by trying to care for her mother.

It was how many years ago, maybe ten? It was after her brother and his wife gave up, said they could no longer care for their mother as her Alzheimer's worsened. Could Beth quit her job, stay home and care for her? No, she could not. She never felt close to her mother, felt always the disappointment in her mother's look: Beth worked too hard, she never had children, she caused a good man to leave her. Beth and her brother looked all over for a top-notch facility and thought they found one.

Each time Beth visited her mother at the facility and got ready to leave, her mother insisted on walking with her to the door. It was a metal door, heavy and locked. No one got in or out without knowing the code, and Beth tried to punch out the code quickly, while her mother was looking away. Then she slipped out, alone, shut the door as fast as she could.

As Beth walked away, she couldn't help looking back. There was her mother, her face pressed to the small glass opening in the door. Each time Beth turned and looked behind, her mother was standing there, face pressed to the glass. Her face didn't hold disappointment, no, it held something worse: it held fear, the bewilderment of a child. Where are you going? Why are you leaving me here?

Take care of your mother, her father had said when he died.

There had to be a better way. Her mother died a few years later. When Lillian's daughter asked if her mother could live at the center, Beth had said yes. And no locked doors.

9.
sky land

Is this what death feels like?

Thomas feels like he's orbiting, circling the earth. He blasted off in a spaceship and now he's moving through air. If he were an astronaut, he'd be looking through a window out into a sweet blue horizon. Would it be blue? More likely grey, dark, and scary. But as long as he's fantasizing, he'll think of blue, he'll think of this strange place as a carnival ride, his little ship traveling through space but still tethered to a creaky machine operated by a grizzled man who looks deranged but knows what he's doing, knows how to keep this ship from hurling itself into an endless expanse and never, ever returning to earth.

What is this thing called? An MCI? MRI? Whatever it is he's inside it, a metallic tube-like contraption. The doctor thinks this test will get a handle on what's wrong with him. The nurse who positioned Thomas inside had a tight smile as she said, Relax! Right. She seemed nervous, which of course made Thomas nervous as well.

He has an alarm button he can press if he wants to stop. He's trying hard not to press it. Instead of a window, Thomas looks at his own blurry self, reflected back from the metal just inches away. In his reflection, Thomas looks both larger than life and cartoon-like. He looks frightened.

He is frightened.

It helps to imagine himself doing research, heroically circling the earth. The world waits for his findings!

Some indigenous people think you rise up and live in the sky after death. You travel to Sky Land. The Navajos? The Hopi? Thomas likes the name Sky Land, the beauty of it, the simplicity, the irony. What would Sky Land be like? Well, you wouldn't be in a spaceship, that's for sure. No, you would float; you'd be a human soul simply floating on air. Do the Navajos believe in a soul? Thomas doesn't remember. And what's a soul anyway? Can a soul float? Thomas has never believed in a soul. Still, it feels good to think of himself drifting on air, listening to the soft swish of wind whooshing by. It would be sort of like flying without flapping his arms.

Thomas would like to believe in Sky Land. But this is not what death feels like. Death feels like nothing. And he won't be aware that he's feeling nothing. He simply won't be. All that Thomas is now, all that he's has been for eighty-seven years, will be over. Done. He'll be finished. Extinguished.

A chill swoops through Thomas. It starts in his chest, then blasts through his arms and legs, fingers and toes. He feels frozen, except that his heart's beating wildly.

Damn!

Can we even begin to think about death? Because when

we're thinking, we're conscious, and yet we're trying to think of not being conscious. Thomas doesn't know how to do this.

Weird Ways to Die. It was the class he taught about death, and the students flocked in. He talked about the Tibetan Buddhists who smear corpses in bull urine, then leave the bodies out for the vultures. There's the tribe in which people cut off their fingers when loved ones die. The people who spread the guts of the dead on their relatives to keep the dead person's strength in the tribe.

Weird ways to die. Is there any way to die that's not weird? No, there is not. One moment you're breathing, and the next you are not. That's just weird.

All these decades on Earth and he's still as frightened of death as when he was a child. Then Thomas would lie in his bed and try not to sleep. If he slept he might die! So he watched the lights of cars on the street flash by his bedroom window over and over. He sang to himself when he felt himself getting sleepy. When he felt his eyelids drooping he'd sit up, horrified that he'd almost fallen asleep. Sometimes his mother stopped in his room, and once he told her how frightened he was of dying. He's surprised now that she didn't talk about heaven, give him some comforting vision. He suspects she didn't believe in it. Rather, she was honest and practical. Oh, that's such a long time away, she said in her soft voice, bending down to give him a hug. So many years. He remembers the woodsy smell of her perfume.

Not so long after all.

He takes a deep breath. This contraption is loud, very loud. This is clanging and thumping. Lots of metal banging into more metal. This sounds like he's in a spaceship that's falling apart, a spaceship that needs maintenance soon. Or like he's stuck in a clothes dryer with tennis balls. Metal tennis balls.

But the sounds aren't the worst part. Being enclosed in this tube is the worst part. He's supposed to lie still, no moving allowed. The metal so close to his face he can smell it, sharp and chemical. Arms by his side. No room to move. Now Thomas knows he's not in a spaceship, no. He's in a coffin. His stomach squeezes into a lemon. His heart races.

Damn.

Is this what death feels like?

Some people find it comforting that death feels like nothing. Who are those people? Thomas tries to remember. People who seem fine with some day becoming extinct. People who say, well, of course we die, that's just the way of the world. No big deal. People like this tend to be academics. Or men. Male academics. It's all bullshit.

He is terrified.

He wishes he believed in an afterlife. Marjorie held these New Age-y beliefs, but Thomas just couldn't abide them. He couldn't abide heaven or any sort of woo-woo meeting up again with your loved ones. Oh, he tried not to let on. The one time he tried to talk about it, it was a mistake. Isn't that sad, Marjorie said to Thomas, isn't that just too depressing? Of course his beliefs are depressing. But Thomas can't help what he believes. And she made it hard. He felt her recoil from him as if he were dirty, stained somehow. After this talk he felt that in some basic way he and Marjorie didn't belong with each other, didn't understand each other's essential foundation. Sometimes he thought she wasn't smart enough for him.

An image lodges in his mind, one he hasn't remembered for years. He and Sarah, lying in bed, talking about death. Not long, probably, after they began sleeping together, after the first and last time he fell in love with a student. He smiles thinking of Sarah as just a student. She was so much more than that, an intelligent, wounded, complex human being. A human being who loved him. Whom he loved, deeply.

Sarah. Thomas feels himself smiling, even though he's in this contraption. His reflection shows his smile as outsized and goofy, just as he feels.

It was a cold afternoon, snowing outside, and they had just made love in her room. Something about the warmth of their bodies, their nakedness, led to one of those talks about deep-down beliefs, deep-down feelings. He said he believed death to be simple and bleak, a human being simply was over, done, extinct for eternity. He told her how frightened he was. He felt his body chill as he said this, and he wondered how many times he had said this before. More than that one awful time, with Marjorie? He wasn't sure. He worried that Sarah would recoil from him as Marjorie had.

And then Sarah took his hand and they lay for a while in silence. Then Sarah spoke too, she looked straight up at the ceiling and said she felt the same. She said this bleak vision sometimes felt like the deepest part of herself, a part that seemed to alienate her family and friends. So she didn't speak about it, not to anyone. How lonely it was.

Thomas held her hand tightly. He felt so close to her then, as close as he'd felt to anyone. Ever.

What Thomas remembers so clearly is the two of them

staring straight up at the ceiling, staring into the truth of life's bleakness, holding on to each other, the snow falling outside. He remembers how the ceiling light overhead looked like a grapefruit. Then they turned toward each other and made love again, and it felt as if for the first time in his life Thomas actually shed his skin, shed everything that kept him apart from this woman he loved. He clung to her, feeling stunned and humbled and no longer alone.

Afterward they lay silently, watching the sky darken outside. Neither moved to get up or turn on the light.

Where is Sarah?

Thomas wants to see her. He closes his eyes against the glaring metal of the machine, the *thonk-thonk* of it.

Of course he won't see her. She left him years ago. She was too young for him, in years, in life stages, though in no other way. She wanted children, she was just at the beginning of grown-up life, while he was way past the middle. He just couldn't see having more children. He hopes she found what she wanted.

He tried once, maybe a decade, two decades ago, to find her. He was in New York for a conference and he looked up her address. He took a bus to her home. She lived on the Upper East Side, and he found her brownstone along with a sign that said, Sarah Miller, Psychologist. Well, of course. Of course she's a psychologist. He heard voices inside the building, and it sounded like someone was coming outside. He stood at the gate just a moment. Then he left.

What will Sarah feel when she hears of his death?

Ah. He won't know, will he? No, he will not ever know.

He will be gone.

Thomas closes his eyes. His stomach has balled up again. He's learned nothing, absolutely nothing in the last eighty-odd years. Thomas thought studying anthropology might help, studying the many ways that humans face their inevitable end. But it didn't help. It didn't help in the slightest.

What if he imagines the world going on, other beings that benefit from his death? There's that new kind of burial, where you get wrapped in a sheet and just put in the ground. That seems a good idea, environmentally sustainable and all. Thomas imagines being the earthworm that finds his body, inviting all his worm friends to come to the feast.

Getting eaten by worms. Thomas squirms. No, this is not comforting.

He feels himself taking small, fast breaths. This metal contraption looms closer, squeezing him. He closes his eyes.

He tries again to imagine himself in Sky Land, the gentle whoosh of the wind, the soft touch of a breeze. No. His stomach keeps churning. He can't breathe.

"Help," he hears himself say. But it's a soft voice, a tiny voice. Is that his voice? It sounds like the voice of a child, a small helpless being, and for a moment he feels like his little-boy self, trying to stay awake through an endless night.

"Help," Thomas says again, louder this time. And again. His heart slams into his chest. Now he's punching the metal. His hand hurts, but he can't stop.

"What? Are you okay?" A voice from outside, the nurse's voice.

"Claustrophobic," Thomas calls out, although he can barely push out all the syllables.

A pause.

"Okay, just about done here. Can you go for a few seconds longer? That would help."

Thomas breathes deeply. He says that he'll try. He needs to keep his eyes closed.

But when he takes a deep breath, Thomas smells the sharp metal smell. What will his bones smell like, when they burn? Now his stomach is squeezing into a golf ball. His whole body feels cold.

"Help," he calls out again, as loud as he can. "Get me out!"

"Sorry," the woman calls back. "We're done now. Thanks for hanging on."

And just like that, Thomas feels himself shuttled out of the cylinder, into the room. Oh! The lights above, the scent of the nurse's perfume, the worried look on the face of the doctor hovering above him. All of these seem magnificent, larger than life. He's back in the world. He takes a deep breath. A swoosh of relief sweeps through his body.

"Sorry," the doctor says, bending close to Thomas. "That can be hard on people. But you did great."

Thomas feels himself shaking. He did great. Well, not exactly.

• • •

As the nurse wheels him out into the lobby, a tall pretty woman stands up. She walks toward him. He knows her.

"The center wasn't busy, so Beth said I could come with the ambulance guy to meet you," Sally says.

"I'm glad it's you," he says.

She holds out a book. "I brought the one you like, on your table? The one we read from before. It's good! I could read more."

"Thanks," he says. "I can hold it." It does feel better having a book on his lap. He clutches it as Sally wheels him out of the building. A young man in sunglasses lowers a ramp at the back of the van.

"What's your name?" Thomas asks.

"Charlie. I'm Charlie," he says, as he buckles Thomas into the seatbelt.

"Thank you," Thomas says.

Charlie seems nice, but he drives like a maniac. Thomas hangs onto the seat next to his chair.

Sally is smiling at him. "You always ask who someone is. Like with Charlie. Like he's a real person to you."

Thomas shrugs. "He is a real person. He's helping me. Like you are, too."

"Sure, I just mean. Well, lots of people don't do that."

The van careens around a corner, and Thomas holds tight to the seat. Now the van's slowing down.

"I hated that. The MRI," he looks down. "It was like being dead."

She looks steadily at him. "I'm sorry," she says. "Would you like me to read?"

"Maybe later."

Now the van jerks to a stop before revving up, blasting forward. When the book falls onto the floor, Sally picks it up, puts it back in his lap. As the van swerves once more, Sally reaches out to him. Thomas takes her hand. It's warm. He holds on.

10.
at the vet

In the rearview mirror, Sally watches as Shannon strokes his dead cat. He's asked Sally to drive. In the back he holds the cat—is it Princess? Queenie?—on his lap. He's pulled the blanket back so the cat's head is visible.

"Good kitty," he says. "Such a good kitty."

Every so often a sob erupts, a jagged little sob that takes Sally by surprise. At first, Sally sees Shannon look up at her eyes in the rearview mirror, to see if she heard. She tries to look away. He's a grown man, of course, and even more, a tall man, a big man, a man who wears a tool belt. And here he is, using a soft, little-boy voice as he speaks to his dead cat. He must be embarrassed.

So she tries to look ahead at the road. It's a warm autumn day, a beautiful day. The car ahead is moving slowly, and that's fine with Sally. They're not in a hurry. Clearly, Shannon needs this moment of grieving, and she's happy to let him have it. Still, it feels awkward being enclosed together in this metal machine, with Shannon's grief so raw and so close. She barely knows him.

Sally is good at comforting people, but this isn't that. This is trying to pretend she's not there.

Sally takes a deep breath. Shannon's car smells just like him, that clean-clothes Tide smell. It doesn't smell like the car of a maintenance guy. It looks like that sort of car, though, tools and candy bar wrappers strewn here and there, but it smells like a load of fresh wash. How does he do it?

Every so often Shannon starts speaking again, and she looks into the mirror, thinking he's speaking to her. "You've been with me so long," he says now in a low voice, almost a whisper. "You took care of me, didn't you? You did."

Ah yes. He's talking to the cat. My, he has long eyelashes. He has beautiful eyes. Sally looks away as a burst of small sobs edges into full-throated crying. Shannon gulps air between sounds. When Sally last got dumped by a guy, she drove around town wailing. Wailing at the top of her lungs in a car. It felt good in an excruciating sort of way. She wants to tell Shannon he can wail if he wants, but she barely knows him.

Now he seems to be speaking to her. "Princess! Such a silly name for a cat. But I was a little boy when I got her. I was about twelve. She's maybe twenty years old? She's a very old cat."

Sally nods. She's sorry that what interests her most is finding out that he's not as young as she thought. So he's about thirty, thirty-two? About ten years younger than she is. But still, not that old. Still just a kid. Too young for her.

"Next time I get a cat I'll give it a grown-up name, a manly name. I'll call it Spike. Or maybe Miles. I've been wanting to name a cat after Miles Davis. Do you like jazz? Turn left here. It's just a half block." He looks back at his cat. Now he's bending over it. “Oh sweetie,” he says to the cat. “I’m so sorry. No kitty will ever replace you.”

He’s chatting away now, to the cat? To her? She sees now he’s a talker, a person who loves hearing words coming out of his mouth. She usually tries to avoid talkers, but his words are a comfort now, filling up the quiet between them.

The car in front slows down even more, so Sally does too. “It’s okay,” Sally says out loud. “We have all the time we need.”

Now Shannon’s eyes meet hers in the mirror. It’s a deep gaze, a meaningful gaze, and Sally feels herself shiver. She’s tingling a bit, just looking at him. She blinks, pulls her eyes away. The clinic appears on the right. Sally pulls into the lot. After parking, she just sits for a moment.

“I can do this,” Shannon says in a soft voice to himself, and Sally watches as he leans over his cat. “Can you go inside? Tell them we’re here? I think someone will come out. They’ll come get her.” Now his body shakes, and he’s holding back tears.

Inside the clinic Sally signs a list, waits for her name to be called. She hasn’t been here since her dog died, but she used to love bringing Elliott to the vet. Well, not that she loved her dog being sick, not that. But she loved watching the people. There they sit, holding their sick kitty or dog, and each person seems so exposed, as if what they’re holding in front of them is not a cat or a dog but their own beating heart, as if they’re showing the world their deepest, most secret devotion, their spectacular love for their animal.

Across the room sits the old woman with spiky hair and a big black lab whom Sally has seen on the bike path. The dog looks old too, specks of white around its eyes, its muzzle. Sally has seen them pulling each other along. The woman talks to the dog constantly as they walk, and the dog seems to be listening; it stays by the woman's side with its head tilted toward her. Now the woman leans down, puts her arm around the dog's neck. The dog puts its muzzle on the woman's knee. Sally has to look away.

Beside the woman sits a young mom and a little girl sitting on the floor next to a cat in a carrier. The girl sticks her finger inside the carrier, leans her head on it.

Now Shannon's name is called. Sally tells the receptionist about the dead cat, and the woman looks up. Someone will come out to the car. They'll be there pretty soon. It's busy now and while the receptionist doesn't say this, Sally understands. They don't have to rush. Princess is already dead.

In the parking lot, Shannon is still bending over his cat. Sally waits outside the car. He might need more time alone with his cat. She knocks on the window, nods toward the door of the clinic. When he motions her to get in, Sally slides in the front seat.

They sit for a while in silence, Sally watching people with their pets get in and out of the cars. A man on crutches walks in with a white poodle. A white-haired lady leads a sheltie, or it leads her. Shannon seems to be calmer.

"I like working there. The center," he says now from the back seat. "I like the old people. And the people who work there. They're not all like you, but some are. Kind. Mostly they're kind. But there's no one like you. You're the kindest."

Sally is glad she's sitting in the front seat, not beside him. She knows her face is heating up. "Yes," she says. "Well."

"That Deborah, though. She's a piece of work."

Sally turns around. "I'm happy to talk. But you can just sit with Princess if you want."

Shannon nods. He's looking down. Now he leans over his cat again, rubs his face in her fur. "I'll miss you so much."

When the back door of the clinic opens, Sally looks up. Her stomach flips. This is sooner than she expected. A red-haired young woman is walking out to their car. She knocks on the window.

"Oh god," Shannon says. "Oh, god."

Sally gets out, opens the door to the back seat. Shannon's shoulders are quaking. He leans over his cat again, holds her close. Now Shannon extends his arms, places Princess in the young woman's hands. Tears stream down his face, and Sally feels tears on her own face as well. The young woman walks back into the building, carrying Princess. Shannon is doubled over in the back seat making great heaving sobs. Sally slides in beside him.

"I'm sorry," she says. "I'm so sorry."

She's silent again as he sobs. She gingerly puts her hand on his arm. Now he bends toward her, his head on her shoulder. His hair smells like lavender. His arm rests on her lap.

"I'm sorry," he says. "Forgive me."

"It's okay," she says. "It's fine." She wraps her arm around his shoulders. She feels him heaving. He has big shoulders, a thick chest. But he's making high, heaving sobs, like a small child. The sobs slowly turn into whimpers, little bursts of throaty calls escaping from him. It makes Sally's chest hurt.

Outside the car, doors slam; dogs bark at other dogs. Inside the car it feels like time isn't moving. The back seat smells like Shannon too, that clean Tide smell, like he's been driving stacks of clean clothes around town. Shannon's skin is so warm, almost hot. She didn't intend to, but realizes she's been stroking his hair. "Oh, I'm sorry," she says, pulling her hand away.

"Please," he says, his voice soft. "Please don't stop."

It's like Shannon is her cat and here she is, petting him. It feels strange at first, stroking this strange man's hair, but then it stops feeling strange. His hair is very clean, just like the rest of him. It is so soft. She strokes his hair and then his shoulders.

Pretty soon his arm reaches up. He is pulling her toward him. What is he doing? Sally allows herself to be pulled, his head turns toward her and now his lips cover hers. She stops breathing. What is this? But his lips feel so warm. They taste of coffee and toast. He nibbles a bit at her mouth. It feels good, light, playful. And now she feels something else, heat in her body. She presses her lips against his.

Shannon touches her cheek with his hand. "Oh my," he says. "Your skin is so soft. It's just as soft as it looks."

Sally hears herself make a murmuring noise. Really, she's not thinking too well. He's a good kisser. Not like some guys, grabby or hard or fast. Shannon is taking his time. His lips feel soft and sure, like he knows what he's doing. He seems to be feeling each nuance of sensation, just as she is.

It's been a long time since she kissed someone. How long? She can't even remember. She's not thinking too well. She's not thinking at all.

11.
freedom

Lillian doesn't plan to be sitting at the front door after dinner. It's just where she ends up, close enough to the TV that she can see it but far enough away that the sound of this hurricane doesn't bother her. But here she is, right by the door.

Dinner was upsetting. Dinner is often upsetting, what with the strange people who live in this place. Sometimes the woman with a bun in her hair at the next table starts moaning, and Lillian's appetite just goes away. Why is this moaning woman eating dinner with Lillian? Why are they even in the same room? And if Lillian is eating dinner with the strange moaning woman, does that mean she's the strange moaning woman herself, in some way she doesn't quite understand but that others see clearly?

Her throat tightens up, thinking like this.

At this dinner it wasn't only the moaning woman. It was also the food, little clumps of something grey and disgusting, maybe tuna and noodles. Whatever it was it looked sinister. Are these people, whoever they are, trying to kill her? She wants to make her own food! Or just to sit down with a box of Triscuits like she used to do at her home but can't do anymore.

What happened to her home? Why is Lillian here and not there?

Here comes the man with the Bible who visits each night after dinner. Lillian watches through the glass doors as this man pulls up into the parking lot and gets out of the car. He walks toward the building, opens the door. Lillian never tells her legs to buck up, stand straight, and dash forward, but that's what they do just as the Bible man bends to sign the visitor book. Before the door swings back to close all the way, Lillian waltzes right out of the building and into the world.

Well! That wasn't hard.

Here she is, in the parking lot. She's only wearing a sweater over her dress, her favorite soft salmon cardigan, but it's enough; the air's warm. It's a beautiful evening. What season? She's surprised she doesn't know if it's spring, summer, or fall, and not knowing makes her angrier still, makes her chest feel like someone stuffed it with a thick pillow. How can you live without knowing the season? What have these people done to her?

That anger shoots up her legs, through her middle and blasts her right out into the street. She hesitates. Left or right? She turns right. Her house is out here somewhere; she just has to start walking.

A woman down the street kneels in her yard, holding a handful of plants.

"Hello!" Lillian calls out.

The woman looks up, smiles. "Lovely evening!"

"Yes," Lillian says, nodding, as she walks by.

Lillian feels pleased with herself. "Hello" almost always works well; it slides right out of her mouth before the birds take off. Then people say "hello" back. They smile at her, and Lillian feels pleased and proud that she can make people smile with just that word. "Yes" is also a good word. It makes people nod at Lillian, and she nods back, so they are all nodding together. It feels like a party sometimes.

"Hello" and "Yes" work well; it's those other words that go off the rails. It's when Lillian tries to say other words that she sees people screw up their faces and tilt their heads as if saying, What's wrong with you anyway?

So she just has to stick with "Hello" and "Yes" and everything will be fine.

At the corner Lillian turns left. She's pretty sure her house is down this street somewhere, although truthfully she doesn't remember the street. But people move so often these days, there must be new people, even new houses, all over the place. New streets even!

Now there's a dark-haired man in front of a ranch house riding a mower. He wears something over his ears and he's bobbing up and down with some invisible beat. My goodness! Lillian has never seen anyone have such a good time mowing the yard. Outside that building she left it's a wonderful world! When he turns the mower her way she smiles and waves.

"Hello! Yes!"

"Hello!" he calls back, with a smile so big she thinks maybe she knows him and hasn't seen him for years. Maybe he's a friend of Dan's? She begins walking toward him, but then he turns the mower back toward the house and moves away from her.

But this "hello" business is working. People are waving and talking to her like she's someone they know or would like to know. Yes, like she's someone who, when they meet her, will have something important to say, something that makes their eyes shine. Yes, they are looking at her like she's that sort of person.

Lillian feels herself straighten, walk taller.

Why hasn't she done this before? And where is Dan? Lillian would like it better if he were with her, if people could see that she has a husband, and not just a husband but a tall, handsome husband, a husband who stands straight and takes long, purposeful steps.

But Dan isn't here. Where is he?

Lillian walks on. A bunch of kids are playing in a backyard when their mother calls out for them to come in to bed. Oh, so sweet! But where is Annie? Is she still playing outside? Has she had dinner? Lillian walks faster. She has to find her house soon. The sky seems darker. She pulls her sweater close. It's getting chilly.

People are walking their dogs. So many people have dogs! Lillian passes a couple walking a dachshund, then a little girl being dragged by a big dark mutt. A heavy-set woman is walking a greyhound, putting to rest the notion that people grow to look like their dogs.

The dogs leap forward and strain their leashes, try to sniff Lillian when she walks by. She steps back, out of their way. It's a little bit scary.

It's colder now. Lillian buttons her sweater. She needs to find her house soon.

It's getting so dark that cars are turning their lights on. There's no sidewalk here, so Lillian begins walking in grass to get out of the road. You're supposed to either walk facing the cars or away from them; she can never remember which one. She'll try both. The lawns of these houses look so smooth, so soft, that Lillian thinks if she has to, she could just curl up and sleep on the grass. But she'll find her house by then.

Inside this house someone turns on a lamp. Lillian sees the back of a head in a chair, a woman reading a newspaper. Beside her sits a man watching TV. He looks a little like Dan. Wait a minute. Is that Dan in some other house? Is he with some other woman?

Lillian creeps up to the window. Her chest throbs with the rushing beat of her heart. She leans forward. But her foot slips and now her head bumps the wood. Ouch! She steps back. But there are footsteps inside, coming closer.

A tiny house sits in the backyard, one of those places where people store things, the kind with a window box full of flowers. Lillian tries the door. It's open. She'll just sit here for a while until the commotion dies down. Her head throbs and her feet hurt. She hasn't walked like this in so long! Inside rakes and shovels hang on one wall, and the opposite wall holds garden tools. Goodness, such organization. She always wondered what these little backyard houses look like inside. Still, she's a bit disappointed. Shouldn't there be a tiny kitchen inside, a dining room set with tiny plates? Tiny people? She'd like to share this joke with someone. It is funny. Oh well. She sits down on a big bag of something soft.

Could she live here in this tiny house?

Maybe. There's a bag of bird seed in the corner. She could pick berries. She reads books to Annie about the Boxcar Children, orphans who live by their wits, making homes in a boxcar or sheds. She could live on berries and seeds, and when she finally gets to go home she'll have such stories for Annie! It would be better than eating dinner each night with the moaning woman.

Still, she has to find Annie. Annie could live with her here in this tiny house. Wouldn't that be fun, the two of them making a secret, tiny life in this backyard? Living on nuts and berries?

But it's getting colder. There's a jacket hanging by the door. As Lillian leans over to grab it, something rumbles outside. Now a fat man with a rake opens the door to the shed.

"What the..." he says, looking startled. He drops the rake.

Lillian stands. "My house..." she begins, but then the birds take off and there she is, staring at the face of a man she's never seen before and not able to talk. Goodness! She's in a tiny house with a strange man and you can't be too careful. Her heart beats so quickly she can't get a breath. "Hello! Yes!" she says as she pushes by him, out the door, down the step and across the backyard. When she looks back the fat man is standing in the doorway of the shed, shaking his head. She heads back out to the street.

That was a close call. Her heart zigzags in her chest.

Now it's almost completely dark. Where is her house? Annie must be hungry by now, waiting for her mom to make dinner. Even though her legs ache, Lillian walks faster.

In the street she follows two girls. "Young women" is what you call them now. Her feet burn. She could ask them for help. She feels wobbly. Could they help find her house? Both girls stare at their phones. Now they're putting their heads together, laughing. Are they laughing at her? Are they laughing at the old woman walking behind them? What about her exactly do they find funny? Lillian decides not to ask for help, not just yet.

Now the girls turn off the street, head down a sidewalk.

There's a big building that sits away from the street, with lots of lights on. More big buildings are close by. Lillian squints into the darkness. Other young people are walking around. "Six papers and a term paper too! It's insane," one of the girls says now, shaking her head, and the other one grabs her arm.

Is this a school? A college? Maybe Lillian could go back to college. She always meant to get her degree. She got married instead. She doesn't remember that her town has a college but maybe they built one? Whoever *they* is. How long has she been away from her house anyway? And would these young women know her house? Pretty much everyone in her town knows Lillian's house, the red-brick colonial with white pillars, the most beautiful house in town.

Lillian turns off the road, follows the young women. She will ask them about her house, to just point her toward it.

Now a car pulls up. Suddenly a man steps in front of her. When the girls turn around toward him, their eyes widen, then they walk fast in the other direction. He's wearing a uniform. He's a policeman. A handsome policeman, Lillian can see, even in the growing darkness. Goodness! She reaches into her bag, takes out her lipstick. She loves a bright red. She can put on the lipstick without even looking and that's what she does now, before talking to this handsome officer. She wants to look her best. "Ma'am?" he says. "What's your name?"

This sounds like a test. But she can pass it. She knows her name.

"I think I can help you," the man says, with a big smile. "Can you come with me?"

Help? Lillian needs help. She needs to find her house. How

lucky! Of course a policeman will know where her house is. She can get back soon to feed Annie.

"I'll take you back home," he says now.

She reaches out, puts her hand on his arm. "Hello! Yes!" she says.

The handsome policeman takes her arm, leads her to a car. Such a gentleman. She feels proud, so proud, walking beside this handsome young man, almost as proud as walking with Dan. And he's taking her home. He wants her to sit in the back while he drives. She opens the window, as the faint smell of smoke in the car makes her nose itch. Still, Lillian feels as if she has a chauffeur, and it's not a bad feeling. She imagines being helped out of the car when it stops in her driveway, imagines how all the neighbors will look out their windows to see her. Oh, they'll think, Lillian finally came home! And she has such a handsome chauffeur, in a uniform. Lillian feels all warm and sparkly inside thinking about her arrival back in the old neighborhood.

It's completely dark when they pull up to a building. Lillian blinks, sits back in her seat. But there's been a mistake. This is not her home. This is not her beautiful red-brick colonial with the white pillars. No, this is the ugly squat building she just left.

"No!" she says. "My house..." and then the birds take off in her mind; off they go, high, higher up into the sky.

The policeman has opened the car door, is standing outside. He's waiting for her. "Ma'am?" he says. "This is it. I brought you home."

Lillian doesn't budge. She's at the place where the woman moans all through dinner. "Not..." she says. She will not get out of the car. She scoots farther away from the door.

"Ma'am?" the handsome officer says, although he's not as good-looking now; no, his face is all squished up. He looks angry. Is he angry at her? He's the one who made a mistake, who couldn't even find the right house.

"No. Not," Lillian says again, staring straight ahead.

"You have to come with me. Now. Right now," he says with an ugly edge to his voice, and Lillian is amazed at how quickly some men change from handsome to not handsome at all. She's lucky that Dan isn't like that. He's always handsome. If only he were here right now, helping her! Protecting her from this evil officer.

Now one of the nice ladies who works in the building comes out the front door. She sticks her head in the car. "Lillian? Sweetheart? Will you come with me now? I'll make you some cocoa."

Lillian keeps staring ahead. She needs to get to her house. But she does like cocoa. And she's cold. She lets herself be pulled out of the car and before she knows how it happens, she's inside the building again.

12.
cinderella

What do people do when they're home all day?

It's Beth's third day at home since taking the week off on vacation. Charlie said staff need to use up their time, and Beth had more days than anyone so he asked her to go first. It's weird, though, that he wanted her first. Is he making changes he doesn't want her to see? Or trying to get rid of her? Beth tries to not think about it, which, of course, rarely works.

At home she's cleaned the house, taken walks, and gone to the library to pick up some books. She's even turned on the TV, although she turned it right off again. She hasn't sunk quite that low. Not yet.

Now she's sweeping the living room. It's not a bad feeling. What's that Disney film, *Cinderella*? The one with the lovely young woman in a white dress and blue sash dancing around with her broom, little birds swooping low as they pick up the clutter, happy mice pitching in on the floor. Beth takes a twirl with her broom. But there are no little birds helping out, no happy mice, although probably some hungry ones inside the walls.

If Daisy were here, she'd be dancing too. Whenever Beth danced in the living room Daisy would join her, leaping up on her back legs, barking, smiling ecstatically in her doggy way, not quite sure what was going on but sure she wanted to be part of it. Beth would grab Daisy's front paws, the two of them spinning until Daisy dropped to the floor or Beth laughed so hard she had to sit down.

Daisy. Beth closes her eyes. Someday her stomach won't clench at the thought that Daisy is gone. Someday soon.

What did Jack do when he lived here? On weekends he spent a whole day happily puttering around, telling her when she asked that he was working on the house. But what sort of work was he doing? She looks around. There are no cobwebs dangling from corners, no dust on the tables. Things look shiny and clean. What exactly do people do when they work on their house?

She could call Jack and ask him. He's retired now, probably home. Still, she tries not to call him too much. He has his own life now, a wife who might find Beth a pest. But he's still her closest friend. Sometimes she thinks things turned out for the best after all, their having separate lives, Jack with a woman with time for him.

She has other friends. She can call one of them, Judy or Nance.

If only she could find their numbers. Beth rustles through the kitchen drawer for a phone book. Rubber bands, masking tape, a grooming brush for Daisy. Are there even phone books anymore? Most of her old friends stopped using their landlines, and she can't remember their numbers. Really, it's been too long.

She remembers one number, will always know it.

"Hey, stranger," Pammie's voice says at the other end of the line. Beth's still amazed that she always sounds close, though she's across the country, in Seattle. "Glad you found time to call."

"I'm on vacation," Beth says.

There's a pause. "Who is this, really?" Pammie says.

Beth laughs. Pammie has been her closest friend since they lived next door to each other as children. She fills Pammie in on the recent changes at the center, why she's spending a week at home.

"Vacation, what a bummer," Pammie says. "You know, even as a kid, you never did like to play."

"I didn't?"

"When we played you always had to be an adult. Like when we played school, you were the teacher," Pammie says.

Sometimes when she's talking to Pammie, like now, Beth thinks she hears seagulls in the background. But it's likely her imagination.

"It made my mom mad," Pammie says.

"It did?"

"Well, she just told me that a few years ago, how she'd overhear us and worry that you were doing damage to me by always being the teacher, stunting my ambition or something. Sometimes she wanted to wring your neck. That's what she said. She used those exact words."

"Oh shit," Beth says. "I'm so sorry. I like your mom. I liked her."

"I like yours too," Pammie says.

There's a pause, and Beth feels the sweetness of having a friend who has known her since childhood, who knew her mom, too.

"Anyway, I don't think I did damage to your ambition," Beth says. Pammie's some kind of expert on salmon, and she teaches at the University of Washington.

Pammie laughs. "Guess not." She fills Beth in on the family, how Bob is terrified at getting close to retirement, and the kids have settled into their jobs.

"Come visit!" Pammie says. "You know how many times you've made that trip to Seattle you're always talking about?"

"Hmmm. Possibly zero?"

"That's it. That's the number. Come soon, before we have to use walkers."

Beth is still laughing as she hangs up. Yet her house still seems empty, too quiet. She knows another number by heart. She dials.

"Hey," she says, when Jack answers.

He hesitates a moment. "Hello, Beth."

She wishes she didn't love the sound of his voice quite so much, so gentle and deep. But she does. When she says she doesn't know what people do all day when they're home, he laughs. She always could make Jack laugh, one of the things she likes best about him.

"You could fix things," he says. "Get some glue, look around for drawers that don't open and shut right, stuff like that. Then you fix them. That happens to be what I'm doing right now."

"You're so handy," she says. "I'm full of admiration."

"Shucks," he says.

The silence between them feels sweet. Beth wants to hold onto it. Still, she needs to keep talking, keep Jack on the line. "That sounds like a lot of work," she says. "Rather than fixing drawers, I could just stop opening them."

Another laugh. "Okay, then, don't do it. I thought you wanted ideas."

"I did. I do. Thanks."

Why did Jack leave? Sometimes Beth forgets, especially since they seem to like each other so much. He left her for another woman. She should be furious. For some reason she's not, just surprised. He said Beth was too hard on him, that she expects too much. And she never had time for him. The thing is, Beth knows that he's right. So how could she hate him?

"I'm sorry," she says now, though she doesn't know why. There's a long pause, then she hears Jack take a deep breath.

"It's okay," he says.

Another pause. But now something moves in the background. She can tell Jack is anxious to get off the phone. But he's a softie, Jack is, and he'll stay on if he thinks she needs to keep talking.

"I miss Daisy," she says, although she's surprised to hear herself say this out loud.

Now the furnace thumps on. She didn't know it was so loud. When she pays attention it drives her crazy, but most of the time she doesn't hear it at all.

"Poor baby," Jack says. "I know you do."

"She was the best dog," Beth says.

"Yes. The very best dog."

Beth knows she should say goodbye, let him get off the phone. But for a moment she doesn't say anything. She listens to the furnace thump off and on. It feels good just to know he's on the other end of the line, to hear the steady sound of his breathing. Then she hears movement behind him, someone else at his house. She says goodbye.

• • •

Whenever Beth stops for coffee at the Burial Grounds, she's amazed by how many people are just sitting around at the coffee shop, staring into their laptops. With the soft glow of table lamps and the peach-colored walls, the place always looks cozy. She wonders what it would it be like to be part of this laptop community. But who has the time to hang out at a coffee shop during the day?

Today Beth has the time.

Most of the people at the Burial Grounds are young. There's the dark-haired guy in the hoodie at one table and a long-haired guy at another. A girl wearing a straw hat in a vintage dress is talking loudly into a cell phone, telling the whole room that her friend just had a breakdown. Does she really want to impose this intimate conversation on everyone in the room? Isn't it rude?

Still, no one seems bothered. Even though they're each at a table alone, these people seem connected by invisible wires, all part of a family, young humans with laptops. As each sips their tall cup of coffee or energy drink, staring into their screens, it's clear they know just what to do, how to behave.

Beth opens her laptop. She presses the on button, hears the big whoosh that makes her feel she's being dragged down a drain. Now the screen lights up in green. What's her password? Oh right, *Daisy*.

She used to write, years ago, stories and poems, once kept a journal. Jack always said she should write more, said that she has a charming and natural writing voice. Charming? She opens up a new document. But the template is so very white. It's so blank.

Gazing at the blank page she feels her throat tighten. Maybe it's harder to write on a screen than a yellow legal pad, where she's always written before. Maybe she needs to get one of those pads.

Where could she find a legal pad?

And a new pen. One of those ball pens.

And maybe she needs an energy drink.

What if she has nothing to say?

Beth looks around. She thought she'd fit in with these laptop people once she sat here among them, but she sees now it's not easy. Maybe she's just too old.

She clicks on Google, enters New Horizons. Now a website comes up. The photos show new facilities, memory care lobbies that look like high-end hotels, buildings with movie theaters, gyms, meditation rooms. Meditation? It's all brick and mortar, not much on actual relationships. She's not impressed. The old people in the photos look like actors, their smiles too perfect, their teeth too white.

Damn! Is her résumé still on the desktop? There it is. Beth clicks on it. Still, just thinking about updating her résumé makes her queasy.

She's here in the world of laptop people, and she won't give up yet. It's a welcoming room here at the Burial Grounds, funky sofas at one end and a piano at the other, big windows letting in lots of light. Of course, she needs coffee. At the counter Beth asks about the assortment of cups hanging on the wall behind him, and the young guy says they're for regulars. The regulars have their own cups. He doesn't ask if Beth wants a cup.

Okay.

She sits down at a different table. The chairs look and feel different from those at the table she sat in before; this one has a sturdier back but it's a little too firm. The chair at the next table feels wobbly. She checks out the sofa. Ah yes, this is better. She leans back, closes her eyes. She feels like Goldilocks, one chair too soft, one too hard, the sofa just right.

A hint of cloves wafts in the air, maybe from the girl in the hat? And now Beth hears music. A young woman and man are huddled together at a corner table, softly singing as the woman picks out a tune on the piano and the man plays guitar. Beth doesn't know the song, but she hears gentle harmonies.

She could just stay here on the sofa, take a nap. She never takes naps and now she needs one, she deserves one after so many years of working so hard. And it feels sweet to take a nap while surrounded by these young laptop people.

The sofa is soft. For a few moments Beth feels herself drifting off. She could get used to this, coming to the Burial Grounds, taking a nap. But a loud voice cracks the silence. Opening her eyes, Beth sees that a tall, heavy-set woman with uncombed hair has taken a seat in the center of the room. She's talking into a phone. I love you, sweetie, the woman is saying. Her voice booms. I'll see you tomorrow. Where should we meet, honey bun?

Beth closes her eyes again. Laughter now, loud and raucous. How can Beth take a nap? The woman's shoulders shake with laughter as her voice thunders through the room.

Tomorrow, honey bun, I'll see you tomorrow.

Damn. Beth sits up. It's too loud.

Also, how does this sloppy, heavy-set woman have a sweetheart, a honey bun, and Beth does not? She's sorry she's being sexist, or body shame-ist or whatever it is when you discriminate against someone because of appearance, but too bad. Now the young woman and man have stopped singing and are watching Beth as if they can see into her head, can see her old-person, politically incorrect thoughts. She moves back to the table, packs up her laptop and stuff. She doesn't belong here after all.

• • •

Norm the maintenance guy waylays Beth as soon as she walks in the door at the center.

"Hey, boss," he says, using his inside bellow, which is a lot like his outside bellow. "What are you doing here? You're on vacation. Go home."

Beth tries to laugh. "I know, I know. I just had to pick something up."

He shakes his head. "I'm glad to see you. It's not the same here when you're gone."

"How's the new guy?"

Norm pauses a minute, rubs his nose in the way he does when he's thinking. "Shannon? I think he'll work out. He's smart. He likes people."

"Great," Beth says. "Good to hear."

When she ducks into her office, she's briefly offended that Joan, who's filling in for her, is sitting right at her desk. Is she being groomed by New Horizons to take over Beth's job? But that's silly. Joan has no other place to sit.

"Hey, lady," Joan says. "I thought we wouldn't see you this week. You're supposed to be home."

"Yup," Beth says. "I thought I left my sweater here, the grey one? Just checking." It's the only excuse she could come up with. Really, her grey sweater is hanging in the closet at home.

Joan squirms around in her chair, and Beth feels briefly guilty that Joan is trying so hard to find the sweater. She's even ducking her head under the desk. "Sorry," Joan says, sitting up straight again. "I don't see it."

"How's everything going?" Beth tries not to sound needy.

Joan looks around the room, then at the floor. "I thought about calling and decided not to, but here you are. So. We had a scare last night. Lillian walked out."

"Oh shit," Beth says. "Shit shit shit."

"She's back," Joan says. "She's fine. She was gone only an hour; the police picked her up. A nice officer. But still."

Beth stands next to the chair. "Do you mind if I just sit at the desk for a few minutes? I'll make some calls."

"I already did that," Joan says, frowning. "I called her daughter, didn't know what else to do."

"I should call too," Beth says. "Probably good to check in with the police again. Could you get up for a minute?"

Joan shakes her head, stepping away from the desk.

"I'll just be a minute," Beth says. But when she looks up at the clock, an hour has passed. Joan has disappeared. Still. It's a good thing she showed up. She knows just what to do.

13.
out of control

Thomas opens his eyes. The furniture in his room takes shape, his blue sweater draped over the chair, his oak dresser as solid and staunch as a guardian. Outside, leaves on the maple tree lift in a breeze.

Is this his room? Well, it's sort of his room. It's his dresser and chair, his blue sweater marking his territory. It's his stuff, squeezed into a tiny space in assisted living. His home has been shrunk, all of his worldly goods stuffed into this room, his clothes smushed into the closet, only two pairs of shoes askew on the floor. Remnants of his vast collection of books spill out from one tiny bookshelf. He's living with assistance, and so his space is diminished in the same way his life is. Still, what's left of his possessions are taking a stand, trying to make him feel at home.

Home. Huh. It takes more than a dresser and chair.

Still, it's a new day calling out to him. Damn, he loves waking. Thomas blinks, blinks again. Even in this tiny space, this old person's home, Thomas feels a shiver of thrill. The world is extending its hand. It is beckoning. Come to the party!

He smiles. Of course, he's joining in.

The birds! Oh god. Thomas closes his eyes again, listening. Even though the windows are closed, won't even open, the sounds bleed into the room. There's trilling off to the left, a staccato nearby, a *pete-pete* in the distance. He hears robins, a cardinal. It's an orchestra out there every morning. With his eyes closed, Thomas feels a part of the orchestra, an instrument, an oboe perhaps, a clarinet. Ah, Mozart's Clarinet Concerto. He's vibrating to the soft, haunting melody.

His favorite scene from his favorite movie, the Mozart concerto playing on an old phonograph as Robert Redford walks out of the wilderness, ready to fall in love with Meryl Streep.

Yes, Thomas is waking up. He's walking out of the wilderness.

Years ago Sarah said she'd never known anyone who woke up so happy. And before Sarah, Marjorie? Well, not everyone appreciated his early-morning good spirits. Marjorie seemed mostly annoyed.

But how can you be anything but amazed when you wake in the morning? New beginnings! Each morning we have one, a chance to start over again.

Thomas always meant to look at this moment closely, the moment when we awaken. He meant to look at how cultures differ. How humans sleep got all the attention. Years ago, the anthropologist from Minnesota. What was his name? When he traveled to some island for research, he found that all the villagers wanted to sleep with him. All of them, at the same time. Because that's how they slept, like puppies, in a big pile outside their homes. People in the village couldn't trust the anthropologist until they had slept with him. So he did join the pile, and of course he wrote about it as well.

God, Thomas was jealous. That lucky guy, stumbling on human behavior so quirky and sweet. Of course the Minnesota guy got lots of press, while Thomas slaved away on his own obscure studies.

Is how we awake universal, the very same across cultures, across centuries? The moment we open our eyes and suddenly our minds comprehend: here I am again! In person! Thomas always intended to research this moment. He still wants to know.

His throat tightens. Oh god. He closes his eyes. A thick fist is punching him. He sucks at the air, tries to breathe. He won't be doing that research. Damn. He's about to lose control of his bowels.

Soon he will no longer wake up in the morning.

That's what the doctor said. A few months perhaps, maybe less. It's cancer, already spread, softly and silently killing him. No chance for surgery, the cancer too far gone, deep in his pancreas. Chemo, too, isn't an option. Maybe, the doc said, maybe some experimental treatment, yet it's unlikely. He'll check this out soon.

Very soon.

How can this be? How can Thomas stop waking up?

His nose twitches. He smells sausage. Damn. It's hard to think about death when you smell sausage.

How many mornings in his life has Thomas awakened? Let's see, 87 years times 365 mornings, plus some extra. This is the sort of thing he used to do in his head. But when he tries now, the 5 in the first column slips from its spot and then he can't remember how much to carry over. He tries again and again, and that pesky 5 keeps slipping away. Well. He doesn't know for sure how many mornings. But it's been a whole hell of a lot. Shouldn't the weight of all those mornings somehow tip him toward more mornings, toward more waking up, instead of diminishing that possibility?

"Thomas?"

It's the round-faced nurse, the one with frizzy brown hair. Oh God. "How are you?" She sits on the side of his bed, looking down at him.

Thomas closes his eyes. Please, no, don't shit in your pants while the nice nurse is sitting on the side of the bed. He grunts. Okay, he can do this. He can control his bowels. "Okay," he says. "I'm okay." Really, he just wants her to leave. He wants to go to the bathroom.

"Your daughter?" she says now, putting her hand on his. "I'm thinking we should call her, fill her in. What do you think?"

Ah yes, his daughter should know he is dying. But why? And he must go to the bathroom right now. "My daughter," he says. "She doesn't like me that much."

Now the nurse closes her eyes, as if this sort of difficult information must be taken in privately. She turns, looks out the window. He wishes she'd hurry up.

"I'm pretty sure she'd want to know," she says slowly. Very slowly.

Thomas shrugs. Please hurry! "Do what you want," he says. "It's okay."

"And others? Are there others you'd like us to call?"

Damn! Thomas squeezes, trying to keep from shitting his pants. Others? Who would they be? When he was living at home, Thomas finally understood the phrase "rattling around the house." Yes, his house seemed gigantic, he felt the floor tip this way and that since nothing and no one was holding it down. He felt himself bounce off the walls, zinging from one room to another, all the rooms empty of life but for him. Yes, he was rattling around the house. Where were the people? He was long divorced, and his daughter lived on the other end of the continent. Most of his friends were dead except Hal, and now Hal is missing.

The MSNBC talking heads became his best friends. He saw them each day at regular times. He could count on them at any hour of the day to rant about Trump. That was fine by him. And there were advantages, having your best friends be on TV. He could make them as loud or soft as he wanted. He could turn them off.

"Ari," he says now. "Ari Melber."

"Okay," the nurse is squinting at him. "Do you have his number?"

"Sorry," Thomas says. "Bad joke. There's no one else."

He would like to see Sarah, that's who. But she has her own life and he won't disturb it.

The nurse is nodding. Slowly, very slowly. Thomas flinches as a hot flash of pain thrusts into his groin. "Thomas?" The nurse is frowning at him.

The pain comes and goes quickly. Thomas does his best to smile. No big deal. Ha!

She leans closer. "Shall we call hospice? They're good at pain. That's what they do."

Thomas closes his eyes. Hospice? His bowels are swirling again. He holds on to the side of the bed. "No," he says, surprised at how emphatic he sounds, how loud his voice is.

She closes her eyes again for a moment. He just wants her to leave. He has to shit. NOW.

"Okay," she says. "Maybe it's not quite time to call them, but soon."

Soon. Soon she will call hospice. As Thomas turns away from her, his bowels explode. "Oh shit," he says. "Shit. Shit. Shit."

The nurse stands up quickly. She looks alarmed. "I'll call someone to come in and clean up. It's okay. Don't feel bad."

Oh god. His shit feels hot and sticky and he knows it's all over him, all over his bed. Damn. The smell washes over him. He tries not to move. Soon a different nice woman will show up with a washcloth and wipe him off. She'll try not to gag as he stares at the tree out his window, tries to focus on anything other than the fact that he just made a huge, stinky mess in his bed.

Wouldn't death be better than this? Better than shitting his pants?

No. It would not.

He groans. Here it comes again. He feels his bowels contracting, emptying out. Oh, god. He is out of control.

"Okay. Okay," the nurse says, but Thomas can see she's shaken. She speaks into her phone. "Sally? Sally? We need you in Thomas's room. Now!" The nurse turns, stops at the door. "It's okay, Thomas. No problem. Someone will be here soon. In a minute."

No problem? Easy for her to say. She's not the one shitting her pants. Thomas stares out the window, waiting for someone to come clean him up, his pajama pants sloshing around him, about to gag from the stench. He wishes, for the hundredth time, that he could open the window. Maybe a breeze would help move this away, the smell of his body's decay. But the smell lingers, settles over the room.

• • •

When Thomas wakes up, another woman is sitting on the edge of his bed. All these women! He supposes they should make him feel better somehow. But it feels strange that he's gone from a young man trying to get women to sleep with him to an old man trying to keep them from sitting on the side of his bed.

Did he fall asleep? He vaguely remembers shitting, a young woman swooping in, changing the sheets. Sally? Now he's dry and warm. Really, these women are angels. They should wear wings.

Is this new woman a nurse? An aide?

"Hello!" she says now, turning toward him.

This isn't what he expected, not what he expected at all. She's too old for a nurse. She's the one who sits across from him in the dining room, the one who dumped her eggs off her plate. She doesn't have all her marbles. She's not bad looking in an old-woman way, slender and fit, although her hair is sort of tangled. A slash of red sits in the general direction of her mouth, most likely lipstick. He's sorry that the mis-applied lipstick gives her the look of a clown—a very, very old clown.

"Hello," he says.

The woman smiles, looking down at him. "Hello!" she says again.

Well, this could go on forever. He could use the call button, get someone to come and shoo this old woman out of his room. But it's okay, for a while. She's not hurting anything. And it's interesting to observe her up close. He wonders what it would be like to lose your memory, to be aware that it's happening. Does she know? Most people say they'd rather die than get Alzheimer's, but not Thomas. Would it be so bad, roaming around with no memories but still having the pleasure of eating a bowl full of ice cream, watching cardinals out the window? Wouldn't you still have the capacity for joy?

Thomas looks at the woman who sits on his bed. "I'm so frightened," he says.

She just stares at him now, tilting her head. Maybe he's crazy, but Thomas believes that she understands. The woman nods at him. Now she looks out the window, where a squirrel is hopping from branch to branch in the maple tree. Thomas looks too. They are both watching the squirrel.

She looks back at Thomas. She places her hand on his. "Yes," she says, looking into his eyes. She does have nice eyes, large and blue.

What is this? He repeats the phrase in his mind. Now he says it out loud. Thomas feels himself opening. He feels warmth, his skin slipping away. Here he is, in this situation he's dreaded forever, hurtling toward his last breath. He's stuck with a demented woman sitting beside him. But this moment, this particular one, is different than he expected.

Now he hears something. Is she singing? He tilts his head toward her. It sounds like an old hymn. He doesn't know the words, but she seems to know, and she's singing them, one word after another. He's read that Alzheimer's patients who can't even speak remember the words to old songs. How is this possible? He wants to learn more.

Is she singing louder? It seems like she is.

He walks with me and he talks with me.

She has a nice voice, low and melodic. Now she's looking

straight at him, and as she sings her face seems to get younger.

"I'm terrified," he says, and the woman nods again. He closes his eyes.

So dark here, under his eyelids! Thomas tries to snap his eyes open, but his eyelids are heavy, so heavy. Yet it feels good to drift off to sleep as a strange woman sings the melody of a low, soft song.

14.
enough love

Sometimes Sally sticks a book in her bag before she leaves home in the morning. It's convenient, an excuse not to join in when the others are chattering in the staff room about the latest show on Netflix or the most recent ridiculous thing that Mike said to Deborah. Sitting there now, she's glad she brought something to read while the conversation is swirling around her.

"How can you read when we're talking?" Deborah says now, although it takes Sally a moment to realize that Deborah is talking to her. "How can you concentrate?"

Sally shrugs. "I just can. I get pulled in right away. I love this writer, Michael Cunningham." She holds up the book. Wait a minute, this isn't working. Her book isn't keeping her from joining the conversation; now she *is* the conversation. Drat. She has to refine her strategy. But wait again. The others seem to be shrinking away from the book she's holding up, turning the other direction, so that Sally feels like one of those horror-film teenagers holding a cross to ward off the vampires. Please! Anything but a book! So the strategy works after all.

"Any news about the new owners?" Deborah says, narrowing her eyes at Sally. "So now Grace is for-profit? What does that even mean?"

"I don't know," Sally says, sorry to feel a sense of relief at being, for even a moment, on the same team as Deborah.

"Things will get worse, that's what it means," Deborah says. "They'll be cutting staff soon, just you wait." Deborah turns toward Megan. "It's just what happens," she says, shrugging. "Just wait. Anyway. What about Shannon? Did you do it?"

Shannon? Sally feels her attention lurch toward the others.

Megan is looking at her nails, which are pink with tiny perfect white strips on the tip of each finger. How does she make her nails look like that? "Not yet. But I will. I will today."

"Do what?" Sally is sorry that the voice she hears is her own. She's especially sorry that her voice sounds whiny and lame.

Megan seems to look at a place above Sally's shoulder rather than directly at Sally. Does Sally have something green in her teeth? Why won't this young woman look at her?

"I just, well, I want to get to know him better, you know?" she says, tilting her head and smiling. "Also, he gives me the look."

"What look?" Sally says, trying not to sound desperate.

"You know, the look. The 'I think you're hot' look," Megan says.

Sally doesn't actually know this look. Trying to imagine Shannon throwing the look to Megan, she feels nauseous. Sure, Megan's someone who thinks all men give her this look. But no doubt Shannon actually did.

"She wants to fuck him," Deborah says.

Megan giggles. She and Deborah lean toward each other. "Well, maybe. If it happens. I mean, he looks good in a pair of jeans," Megan says.

Deborah puts an arm around Megan's shoulder. "Baby, he looks great in jeans. Tight jeans. Especially from the rear end."

Now the two are guffawing again.

For a second Sally can't breathe. She needs to act normal. She stares back at her book. Of course, Megan. Why didn't Sally realize it would only be a matter of weeks, maybe days, before Shannon is hooked up with one of the pretty young women who work here? Why did she think he might like her instead?

Sally closes her eyes. It's been decades since then, since she was a little girl being chased around the playground by those boys. Those stupid boys, led by Sammy Snooks. Fat Sally! That's what they called as they chased her, as she saw the other kids turn and watch, laughing. Where was she running to? She didn't know. She just ran as fast as she could and of course that wasn't too fast. She remembers thinking her heart would explode, it was beating so wildly. Finally she couldn't run any more, she just stopped. The boys stopped too. They just laughed and threw a ball at her, then walked away.

Sammy Snooks turned back to her. "You stink," he said, and the boys leaned into each other, laughing.

That was so long ago. Still, Sally feels warm, remembering. Did she stink? Shame washes over her. But she was a child. Why was she dirty? Because her mom and dad were drunk most of the time. They weren't paying attention.

She shakes her head, trying to get the image out of her mind. And Shannon. God, what was she thinking?

She was thinking about the kiss. How many days ago? Four, maybe five. Has it left her mind at all in the days since it happened? Not much. Not very often. Not at all.

The kiss looms there in the background. The fresh clean smell of the car, the salty and sweet taste of Shannon's lips on her own. How warm his lips were, how lush. He kissed her so sweetly. Did the kiss last all afternoon? It seems like it did. It was one long kiss during which she felt things she hasn't felt in years, maybe ever. Sally feels herself heating up now just thinking about it.

Can you kiss someone like that and have no feelings for them? Could Shannon have kissed Sally like that and still latch on to Megan within a few days?

Yes, of course he could do that. He's a man. He's a man whose dead cat had just been taken away, and he was out of his mind with grief. Sally was there, so he kissed her. It was instinctive, something to soothe himself, like salve on a sunburn. It meant nothing.

Really, she's just stupid.

Sally stands, grabs her book. She'll go check on some residents. It's something she can do to get her mind off her ridiculous fantasies.

• • •

In Thomas's room, Sally tries to be quiet. He's sleeping. She's making sure he has what he needs when he wakes. His glasses are lying on the edge of the bed, ready to tumble off. There's also an open book, as always. She places his glasses on the table beside the bed, where Thomas can reach them. She puts the book next to the glasses.

It feels good to putter around in her residents' rooms. It feels good to know that when Thomas wakes, his glasses will be right by his bed where he needs them. Knowing this, that she is making their difficult lives a bit easier, she feels flooded with lightness, with purpose. She feels herself moving quickly, efficiently, in a rhythm that soothes her.

In her residents' rooms, Sally enters the places where these old bodies sleep, where they are naked. It's an intimate place. She helps people dress. She washes their bodies when they've peed or pooped in their beds. She keeps them clean. She touches their bare skin with her own. At night she pulls the sheets up, tucks them in. Sometimes she leans down, gives them a kiss on the forehead. She's not actually sure she should do this, but she does. After she tucks them in, sometimes her people reach up to touch her arm or her face. Thank you, they say. Thank you so much.

This is love, isn't it? And sometimes that love feels so strong that it lifts her right up, it carries her from one room to another. Sometimes, in the Grace Woods Care Center, she feels herself floating. She worries sometimes that working here makes her so happy, that the diminishment of these old people's lives provides work that she loves. Still. She does love it.

She doesn't need a man. Not at all.

But she meant to tell Shannon about this, about the floating. It was on her list of important things to tell him. A list! How pitiful.

In his sleep Thomas grunts, turns toward the window. Sally stands very still. Now he's snoring again. He's still sleeping. So what if the kiss from Shannon didn't mean anything? These are her people. She has all the love that she needs.

"Huh." Thomas is waking up. He reaches over, picks up his glasses from the table.

"Hello," he says, looking up at her.

Sally smiles, sits on the edge of his bed. "Hey. There you are."

Thomas starts laughing. She tilts her head. "Sorry," he says. "It's just, I have to get used to this. All these women sitting on my bed."

Sally stands. "I'm sorry. I wasn't thinking."

"No, not that." He leans forward, pats the bed. "Come, sit down again. I like it. It's just different. All these years living alone, rattling around my house by myself, and then suddenly strange women are traipsing in and out of my room at all hours. I woke up and there was that woman who lives down the hall, the one with dementia? She was just sitting on my bed, humming a song."

"Lillian?" Sally frowns. "I'm so sorry. We can keep her out. She shouldn't be here."

Thomas shakes his head. "You know, it turned out fine. We had a nice conversation. I mean, the sort of conversation you can have with her, which is, well, not much. But I enjoyed her company, in an odd sort of way." He slaps the bed. "Isn't that something. It's something I didn't expect, but it happened."

Sally smiles. He's looking out the window as a squirrel sits on a limb, holding a nut.

"We all have these notions, of course, we think we know what people will do, what they're like, really like. And of course we don't actually know, but we think we do." He's looking at Sally. "In my job, I had to learn to let people surprise me. Like that lady today."

Thomas looks out the window. He closes his eyes, tilts his

head. "Hear that? It's just a robin, I think, but they have the most beautiful songs." His eyes are so sad. "I'm dying," he says. "That's what they tell me."

Sally sucks in breath. She sits very still. "I know," she says, quietly. She takes his hand. Sally looks at her hands, holding his. "Maybe it won't happen soon," she says. "You might have some time."

Thomas shrugs, pulls his hand away. Was it the wrong thing to say? "The doc said there might be an experiment I could join. He's looking. I'll try. I'll try anything."

She should go soon, of course, check on the others. But she doesn't move. Thomas is squinting, gazing out the window at the squirrel racing up the branch of a tree. Sally watches too. Squirrel therapy, she sometimes thinks. These squirrels should be getting paid, the way they entertain residents, the way they make everyone smile and laugh in the midst of so much loss, such sadness. The ducks out back, too, with their goofy walk, their quacking. They should be clocking in every day.

Squirrel therapy was also on the list of things to tell Shannon. She actually wrote it down, in her journal. Things she wanted him to know about her. Her deepest thoughts. She wanted to make him laugh, also make him think she's, well, interesting. And profound. A list of things to say, in case she runs out of topics.

So goddamn pitiful.

"Hey." Thomas is frowning at her. "What's up? You seem sad."

Here Thomas is, dying, and he's worried about her. "It's okay. It's nothing."

As they sit in silence, the squirrel suddenly turns, seems to look directly at Sally and Thomas. But he doesn't run off. He just stands there, watching them. She and Thomas look at each other, then laugh.

Sally shifts her weight. This is what she does. She doesn't tell people hard things. She keeps them to herself. This moment, the moment in which she can tell Thomas what's going on with her, what's really happening, will soon pass and it won't come again. With Thomas it really might not come again. She hears the wind in the trees outside. She feels a little explosion inside, pushing her mouth to open. "There is something," she hears herself say.

Her stomach tightens a little more. Still she keeps talking.

"There's a guy," she says. "I like him. I thought he liked me. You know, not just like but *like like*. But now I know it's stupid. It was all in my mind."

Thomas's eyes widen. He shakes his head. "I'm sorry."

Sally takes a deep breath. She feels herself blushing. Thomas is dying! And here she is, telling him her romantic fantasies. What was she thinking?

Now Thomas is watching her, his look soft and sad. He looks out the window, then back at Sally.

"It will happen," Thomas says. "I know it. Someone like you? So beautiful and so kind. Of course. I just know it."

He reaches out, squeezes her hand. They sit in silence again.

What would it be like, to have a father like this? A father who listens, who just sits with her, holding her hand when she tells him her deepest thoughts? A father who thinks she is beautiful?

Sally closes her eyes. She doesn't know what it would be like to have a father like this. Her father always was drunk. But she has Thomas right now, in this moment. She wants the moment to go on and on.

Now Thomas turns toward her. "But this guy? I'd like to punch him," Thomas says. "But first I'd tell him how stupid he is. Then I'd punch him. If he's not too big. Is he big?"

Sally laughs. "Well, he is big. Sort of big."

But now Thomas is flinching. He squeezes his eyes shut, tilts to the side.

"Thomas? What can I do?"

Thomas is holding his side, gasping for breath. Sally bends toward him. "It's okay," he says. "It's almost gone. There." He sits up again, color coming back to his face. "Damn," he says. "But it goes away fast."

"What about stronger meds?" Sally says. "Pain meds. We can get them, you know."

Thomas shakes his head. "Not yet," he says, looking squarely at Sally. "Not till I have to."

Sally nods. She realizes she is squeezing the comforter between her fingers. She lets go. There's a knock on the door. When Sally turns toward it, Shannon is walking in.

Oh God. Oh no. Sally feels herself blushing. She stands. He looks so tall from this angle. She hasn't seen him since they went to the vet a few days ago. He looks even better than she remembered. Thomas is squinting at Shannon, then looking at Sally. His eyes are wide. Please, let him not say anything.

Shannon flashes his goofy smile. He tilts his head at Sally. "Hey," he says. "I've been looking for you. All over."

"Well," Sally says. But her throat has frozen and no words will come out.

"And Thomas." Shannon walks to the bed. "I need to check in on the shelving I put up in your closet. Is that okay? Just want to make sure it's sturdy."

"Sure," Thomas says. "Go ahead."

Shannon ducks his head as he enters the closet. Yes, he looks very good from the rear. Sally's face feels even hotter. That's why he's here. To fix something for Thomas. It has nothing to do with her. He's giving Megan the look, not Sally. Here she is, visiting Thomas, and Shannon has to say something nice to her. That's all it is.

• • •

At the end of Sally's shift, something from the corner of her eye catches her attention. Two people, one tall and one short, are standing in the dining area. They are laughing. Now Sally sees that the short one is Megan, gazing up at Shannon. Oh God, that gaze. Sally can't see Shannon's face, but she knows what it looks like; he's flashing his smile, the same one he flashed at Sally, but now he's aiming it toward this sexy woman his age, this slender young woman.

Of course he is! Sally feels balled up inside. How silly she has been. How hopeless!

She scurries by Shannon and Megan, head down. She hears Megan laugh as she walks out the front door. Did they even notice her? Probably not. The door slams behind Sally as she walks to the parking lot. She turns. She didn't mean it to close so hard, to make noise. But so what? It doesn't matter. It doesn't matter at all.

15.
an odd duck

"We don't want you to have to leave," the boss woman says now, leaning toward Lillian. "We want to make things better for you. Is there something we could do for you? What would you like?"

They are sitting at the big table in a room at the center. There are others too, the man who dresses up like Elvis at parties and the round-faced woman who looks so intently at Lillian that she has to look away. The woman who says she's Lillian's daughter is there as well, looking frazzled, like she hasn't combed her hair in a while.

What would she like? What Lillian would like is her own refrigerator from her own house, being able to open the door and gaze inside at the vegetables, at the eggs sitting in their little tray, the butter so shiny, the sturdy cartons of milk and cream. And rocky road ice cream inside the freezer. She would like this. She would like to be able to walk into her kitchen again, to smell the scent of geraniums on the windowsill, their tiny sweet petals of red and pink. She keeps them going inside all winter long. Lillian wants to walk in the front door of her house and know that she's home. She wants to hear Dan call out, *Yoo hoo*! when he walks in the door every single night after work, even though sometimes hearing this for the umpteenth time drives her crazy. She would like to be in her own kitchen, making grilled cheese for Annie.

Lillian looks around at the faces surrounding her. There's a word that she needs to say so they'll understand. She can see the word in her mind, feel its smooth shapes, its comforting sound. "Hmm," Lillian says. But that's not the word. The others look puzzled, leaning toward her.

They are waiting, waiting for her to finish her sentence. They want her to speak. Lillian sees the word again in her mind. It blazes there, as if lit up by neon, as if covered in gold. She wants to finish her sentence. She has their attention. In her mind a stage emerges, the majestic stage with a velvety curtain. The curtain is rising. She's here on the stage, under spotlights. Now she looks out, sees the audience. Yes! It's her time to shine.

But now the birds in her head take off, and there are so many today, they're flying every which way. They're flying like goldfinches, looping and swooping and swaying in the wind, moving all higgledy-piggledy. Lillian watches them go.

"Hmmm," she says out loud.

Outside, someone slams a car door in the parking lot. These people are moving away, looking annoyed. Someone begins shuffling papers. Now the boss woman leans forward again. "The next time you walk out the front door, Lillian, you'll have to leave us. We'll be sorry, but you can't stay at Grace Woods if you walk out by yourself."

The woman who says she's her daughter speaks slowly, as if

Lillian has something wrong inside her head. "Yes," she says. "My mom wants to stay here. She won't leave again."

But wait. That's not true. Lillian wants to leave. She wants to go home. Everyone stands, pushes their chair away from the table. Lillian watches a lone goldfinch swooping alone in her mind. Now the goldfinch veers off, flies away.

• • •

Lillian's sitting out by the pond with the woman who says she's her daughter. People walk by, a young woman pushing a man in a wheelchair. The man waves.

"It's so nice here, with a real pond," the Annie woman says. "And a woods! A woods you can walk in and still be safe." She smiles widely.

Sometimes Lillian thinks this might be her daughter. She does have Annie's eyes, dark and beautiful. And her fingers are like Annie's, slender and long, although of course much bigger than Annie's, because Annie's a little girl.

"Mama, this place is nice. But if you keep walking out the front door by yourself, you have to leave. To a place where the doors are all locked. Do you understand?"

All the doors locked? Lillian imagines trying to get out of her bedroom, and not being able to open the door. What would she do all day? Could she even use the bathroom? Would she have to poop in her bed? Lillian pulls her sweater tighter around her.

Now a flock of ducks swoops down from the sky, with great honking and squawking. Oh my. Lillian loves the sound of ducks, how they blast like trumpets announcing royalty. How they have to tell everyone, loudly, all the time, what they are up to. She would do the same, if only she could get the words to come out of her mouth.

Now the ducks skid to a stop on the water, sinking down until they are floating, bobbing along on the surface. But they still throw out random squawks and honks. Most of the ducks swim together, paddling along in a tight little group. But one duck is off by himself, moving in random circles. What's wrong with him? Lillian leans forward, watching.

Now the woman who might be her daughter turns toward Lillian. "Are you cold, Mama? Can I bring you a jacket?" Her voice is soft. Lillian looks into the woman's dark eyes. Yes, they are Annie's eyes. She misses her daughter so much! Don't some animals know their children by smell? Lillian has read about this. Animals like wolves. And penguins. Annie has a fruity smell, a smell like ripe peaches. She would know that smell anywhere. Now the woman is turning the other way, watching the man in the wheelchair whose helper is walking him into the woods.

Lillian dips her head down to take a sniff of the woman's neck. Yes, there's a smell sort of like Annie, beneath all the other smells that get in the way. But Lillian loses her balance, smashes her nose into the woman's shoulder.

The woman's head jerks. "Mama, what are you doing?" She looks annoyed. "Do I smell bad? Is that why you're sniffing me?" The woman reaches down, picks up her bag from the ground. "Mama, I have to go. There's so much to do at the library. It's busy, and, well, I had to come to this meeting. So I have things to make up. Work to do. A lot." The Annie woman sits up straight, puts on a coat.

Lillian scoots to the edge of the bench. She did something

wrong. This woman needs to work harder because of the meeting, because Lillian was bad, because she walked out the front door.

And just like that, the woman who might be Annie marches away. Lillian stares at the water. The ducks are still swimming. On the pond the odd duck is still off by himself. He's still swimming in circles. It looks like a mom duck and a dad duck, along with their squad of little kid ducks. And that one off by himself. Who is he, the crazy uncle duck? Some stray homeless guy duck just tagging along? Poor duck! What's wrong with him? Lillian leans forward.

"Hello!" she calls out. "Yes!"

The duck swims by himself, off to the side. Lillian knows that duck, she knows what it's like to be off by herself, away from the others. Here she is, swimming in circles as the others move in straight lines around her, as the woman who might be her daughter walks off and leaves her alone.

Lillian stands. She walks to the pond. Maybe she'll bring the odd duck some crackers. She sits down at the edge of the water, even though the grass will mess up her dress. But now there's great honking and flapping, and in a flash the duck squad lifts off, flies up into the sky. Oh my. Lillian watches them turn into tiny dark specks. She tilts her head. Now they have vanished. The pond's empty now, no ducks at all. The people who were walking have all vanished. It's getting colder. Lillian pulls her sweater tight. Dark clouds skitter by overhead, like winter is coming soon. She's cold but doesn't want to go back inside. How did she end up here in this place? What on earth is she doing here?

Her bottom feels damp, but she doesn't move. What's that sound? Music. Lillian raises her head. It's not from the pond, nor from the building. It seems to be coming from inside her head. It's the song she sang to the man sick in bed. What a surprise it was to hear the words streaming out of her mouth! It felt wonderful.

I walk in the garden alone
While the dew is still on the roses

The grass does feel wet, sort of like dew.

She hears herself singing. Just like this morning, the words are flowing out of her mouth. She's singing in sentences, whole sentences, the right words in the right order: one, two, three, just like that. She's not even thinking about singing, she's just doing it, the words tumbling out sweetly and effortlessly, like small children scampering around in a playground.

And he walks with me
And he talks with me
And he tells me I'm not alone

It feels good to sing. But shouldn't the person in the song who's walking and talking, shouldn't that person be here somewhere? Shouldn't she be able to see him?

Lillian looks around. It's getting dark. There's no one here, no one at all. Everyone must be inside eating dinner. The moaning woman is inside the building, and the bull-necked one too. Lillian doesn't want to sit at their table; she doesn't want to be one of them. She doesn't belong there. The ducks, even the odd duck, have flown away. The person in the song turns out to be wrong. She is alone after all.

16.
born for it

The New Horizons guy, Charlie, showed up at the center unannounced, wanting to talk. Beth knows what this is about. Her stomach tightens as she leads him into the conference room.

What is he thinking? He seems to be frowning as he takes in the boxes of Halloween decorations on a table pushed into a corner. Maybe he's thinking that this room is a dump. But it's not a dump, just small and messy since every meeting room here at the center performs multiple functions. Sometimes it's a conference room, sometimes storage. Like now, ceramic pumpkins are lined up on the table behind them, rows of them flashing crazed grins at Charlie and Beth.

When Beth recently toured a New Horizons facility, she was shown the building's theater. Really? A whole room just for watching a movie? But whatever happened to just dropping a screen from the ceiling, bringing in chairs, and showing a film in the conference room, which, of course, happens here all the time. When the room isn't being used for games of Scrabble and bridge, or perhaps birthday parties.

The New Horizons people were so proud of their theater! And beside it, a whole area had been tarted up to look like an old-fashioned soda shop, complete with jukebox and fountain so residents think they're young again. But do they really think that? Did soda shops really exist decades ago, other than on TV? Did anyone go to them, other than Fonzie?

Beth isn't convinced. She'll take her small, well-worn facility any day, a facility of messy rooms with multiple uses. She'll put all her money into training and staff. A good facility doesn't need to be shiny and new, that's for sure. Of course, no one is asking Beth for her opinion.

Except now.

"How did this happen?" Charlie is saying, bending toward Beth. His move seems aggressive, and Beth feels herself sitting up straighter. "How did the woman just walk right out, get loose in the neighborhood?"

Beth frowns. "She didn't get loose. She's not a dog."

Damn. That sounded hostile. Jack always said not to let her feelings spill out at work, especially when she doesn't like someone. You're supposed to hide it, he'd say. That's the way the world functions. Still, she doesn't like this guy. He's too young to be telling her what to do. Besides that, his teeth are too white.

Charlie shrugs. He has with him the young woman with dark hair he brought before. She's looking anxiously from Charlie to Beth and back again.

"Of course it won't happen again," Beth hears herself saying. "We won't let it happen again."

"It's taking such risk," Charlie says, as if he didn't hear what she just said. "She could have been hurt. Killed! Can you imagine that? The lawsuits?"

Beth sighs, closes her eyes. Yes, of course. Lawsuits. "Yes," she says. "It won't happen again. Like I said."

Now Charlie seems to be talking to the young woman rather than Beth. "That woman doesn't belong here," he says slowly, as if explaining a basic truth to someone dimwitted. Wait a minute; what woman is he talking about, Lillian or Beth? Now he's turning toward Beth. "Tell her family. She needs to be in memory care, a place with locked doors. There are so many good facilities within, oh, twenty miles from here. Close by. In fact, we have one!" Charlie brightens.

Beth takes a deep breath. She knew this was coming. "Look, I think we can make this work," she says. "There's something new, something I want to try that might help her feel settled. She's here already; we need to try this."

But Charlie is shaking his head, and not in a good way. "No," he says. "No and no." Does he think she's hard of hearing? Does he think she's that old? She's surprised how much she doesn't like this guy. But she needs to remember: he's her boss. "No," he says again, deeper this time. What could he possibly mean by that?

Now he leans forward again, squinting in the direction of the Halloween decorations. "We could take out this wall," he says to the dark-haired woman.

Beth leans toward them. "What did you say?"

"This wall needs to go," Charlie says, tapping his cheek with two fingers. His voice rises with enthusiasm.

"Why would you do that?" she says.

"Look, we have to expand. You know that." He seems to eye

her with something like disdain. "You can't be cost effective with a facility of twenty people. We need to double that, at a minimum."

Beth takes a deep breath, tries to speak slowly. "Our small size is our strength," she says. "That many people, you'll ruin what we do well. And what we do well is knowing our residents, caring for each as a unique individual. In fact, my goal is to make Grace feel smaller, organize our residents into small family groups. It works well in the Netherlands."

Charlie shrugs. When he speaks it's to the young woman, not Beth. "Well, we're not in the Netherlands. You can still give good care with forty residents. There's no reason you can't."

The young woman nods vigorously. It's clear she knows nothing.

"It would be a mistake," Beth says, but Charlie and the young woman are already standing, preparing to leave. Beth stays seated, surveying the funky conference room with its mismatched chairs, its pumpkins grinning from tables. She didn't know how different things here would feel after the sale. Now she knows.

• • •

She's still feeling shaky when she knocks on the door of Thomas's room. She hasn't yet connected with Thomas.

"Come in," he calls out. He's sitting in bed, though still fully dressed. Again, he's wearing a dress shirt and tie.

Beth smiles, sits on the chair by the bed.

"I stopped before, but you were sleeping," she says.

"Yes," he says. "I've been sleeping a lot." He clears his throat. "I'm sorry to say I won't be here long."

"Oh," Beth says. "Are you leaving?"

"Sort of," he says, closing his eyes. "I seem to be dying."

Beth feels a punch in her stomach. She should have checked his file before stopping into his room. She should have known. "I'm sorry," she says. "I'm so sorry."

He looks out the window. A branch is scraping the glass. "Sort of pitiful, you know? Dying in autumn? Me and the leaves. Couldn't I be more original?"

Beth nods. She doesn't know what to say.

"I hate it that you can't open the windows here," he says, with a sad shake of his head.

"Yes," Beth says. "I'm so sorry."

"I just wish I could hear the birds more," he says. "I wish they were louder." Outside, a bird pecks at the feeder. The two of them watch. Beth can't hear anything. He shakes his head again. "Sometimes I can make myself feel better about it. Dying. But most of the time I'm just frightened."

Beth leans in toward him. "This is hard," she says.

Thomas shrugs. "It's hard for other people, too, I get that. They need to think something upbeat, put an upbeat spin on it. Pretty much every culture does this, believe me. People can't say, oh, I'm sorry you're becoming extinct, you'll be eaten by fire and turn into ashes and never again know the sweet scent of the air or the singing of birds or…"

He looks so sad.

"Well, how can they say that? They can't. Even if they could say it, they don't believe it. But I do. I don't believe anything else. And when people try to make me feel upbeat, tell me I'll be going to some better place, it just feels, oh, I don't know." He watches the bird at the feeder. "It makes me feel lonely."

"Yes," Beth says. "Yes, of course." Sometimes, occasionally, she gets it right. Now, she's getting it right. She's sitting in stillness, taking in Thomas's words. She's making a space for his suffering. It's why she got into this work in the first place. A moment like this, a moment when someone says something hard and true, that moment pulls Beth up short. It hauls her deeper into this moment and won't let her go. She can't be bossy or fast-talking or any of the other ways she acts to get through the day. She just has to stop. She has to listen.

She doesn't try to rush through anything like she usually does. Rather, she feels very still as Thomas gazes out the window. The moment feels soft and sort of like falling, except she's not going down; she's staying right here. Right here with Thomas.

"I wish I could open the window," he says again.

"Yes," Beth says. "I'm sorry."

Thomas stares at his hands. Now his hands seem to be shaking. His shoulders are shaking. Beth sees he is crying. He's holding his head in his hands and making sobbing sounds. The sound grows louder, like snuffling, like a farm animal sound, like he can't help himself. Now he waves a hand at her, as if to shoo her away. Should she go? Should she leave him alone?

No, she will not. She sits at the side of the bed, extends her hand out on the cover. Now he takes it. She feels the warmth of his skin, hears the sound of his sobbing. They sit here together like this. It feels like this moment could go on forever. The two of them here, Thomas sobbing, Beth holding his hand, the golden leaves falling outside. The moment feels like it has no beginning and no end, and Beth feels comfortable in it; she wants it to last, to give Thomas the space to do what he needs. She can do that. She can sit with him here in silence. She doesn't know why some people can do this and some can't, but she knows that she can. Perhaps it's a gift, one she learned from her father. She doesn't have to try to make Thomas feel better, which, of course, would only make him feel worse. She can just sit here. She can witness.

This feels like what she was born for. She's not leaving this work, not anytime soon.

17.
old wounds

When Thomas awakes in the morning, another strange woman sits in his room. Damn. There's a never-ending supply of them.

But this one is different. This one is new. Wait a minute. This one is his daughter. She seems to be dozing in her chair, her eyes closed, her chin resting on her chest. She makes little snorting sounds.

His daughter looks like an old woman. Almost old. She still has blond hair, but it looks dyed, oddly metallic over her pale face. She wears too much makeup, her eyes raccoon-like, circled in darkness. She has deep furrows on her forehead, like someone constantly worried. He smiles. Lexie always was an old soul, always pondering the hard things even when little. Daddy, why do some children go hungry? Can I give them my sandwich? How old are we when we die? Are you going to die, Daddy? I don't want you to die.

Not for a long time, he had said to the question on death. What's a long time? she had asked. So many years! More years than you can imagine. I can count up to a hundred, she said. More than that?

Well, as it turns out, less than a hundred.

How long has it been since he's seen her? Thomas can't remember. Some family event years ago, maybe a funeral? She seldom calls. For years when he called he'd hear the phone ringing and ringing as no one answered. His stomach churned as he imagined her sitting in a room somewhere listening, gratified at one more opportunity to spurn him. Perhaps that wasn't fair. Perhaps she just wasn't there. Ever. Still, she never returned his calls. He finally stopped calling.

She's breathing deeply now, almost snoring.

It feels strange to be watching her. Is there some law against watching your grown daughter sleeping? He used to watch her sleep all the time when she was little, of course, poke his head in her bedroom and feel his heart swell as she clutched her stuffed bear to her chest, snuggled into her pillow, making her baby animal sounds. She seemed like a little animal herself then, a puppy perhaps, a lamb. Something soft and adorable. But watching her now feels different. If she knew he were watching her, it would just make her angry. And she's already angry.

Still, before he turns away, Thomas takes a glance at her clothes. Does she have enough money? Is she warm enough? Yes, she's wearing an expensive-looking dark sweater and what looks like wool pants. Good shoes. Thomas feels a tug of relief. She's okay, at least money-wise. He turns his head away. Pretty soon he drifts off again. The next thing he knows, someone says, "Daddy?"

His eyes blink open in spite of himself. He's surprised at the sound of her voice, how she still sounds like a little girl even though she is grown. He turns toward her. She's smiling, sort of, even though her brow remains furrowed. How does she do this?

"So," she says. "I'm here. I flew in last night."

He nods. He doesn't even know where she flew in from, where she lives now. He should know this, of course. Not knowing reminds him what a bad father he's been. Not even knowing where his own daughter lives! But asking her would get things off on the wrong foot.

"Thanks," he says. "Thanks for coming." He reaches out his hand. Her hand looks dry and wrinkled. An old woman's hand. So many years have gone by! How did he let that happen? "How's work?" he says. "How's the firm?"

Lexie always loved working, even as a little girl. She was the kid on the block who set up a lemonade stand on the sidewalk, collected quarters from those walking by. Then she embellished the idea, launched a hot tea stand when the weather turned cool, dashing in and out of the house to heat up the water. Such a little entrepreneur! He was proud of her when he pulled into the drive at the end of the day and she showed him her stash of bills, told him her plans for it. She was saving up for a horse. Did she ever get the horse? He should remember.

"Well," she says now. "I'm retired. I've been retired a while now."

His daughter retired? "Oh," Thomas says. "I didn't know that."

Thomas isn't sure how far to go, how many questions to ask. He loves to ask questions, to find out about others' lives, but some people find it intrusive. Now no one talks as a pipe rattles and he hears the furnace kick on. There's a knock on his door.

"Thomas? Is everything okay?" The round-faced nurse sticks her head in.

"It's fine. My daughter is here."

"How nice! I'll be back soon with your pills then."

Nice? Well, sort of. The silence feels heavy. What would be nice would be hearing her voice. He remembers that Lexie used to chatter away. She'd tell him the plots of the books she was reading, the movies she saw, even when she was a teenager. She was a little chattering magpie walking beside him. Now she just looks out the window and sighs.

"How is..." Oh god. He can't remember the name of her husband. "How is Hugh?"

"Oh." Lexie frowns quickly, then looks away. "We separated. We're divorced now. I thought you knew that. A few years ago."

Thomas closes his eyes. Okay, he's striking out here. "I'm sorry," he says. "I'm so sorry."

Lexie lifts her chin. Something warm washes over him and he remembers that Lexie did this a lot when she felt wronged, lifted her chin. He wasn't surprised she became a lawyer, a prosecutor, because she felt wronged a lot. Still, it's odd to be visited by so many memories of her as a child and know so little of her life as an adult.

"You always did like Hugh," she says now. "Sometimes I thought you liked him better than me."

Ouch! Thomas feels his heart pinch in his chest. "That's not true," Thomas says. "I mean, I liked him because he was your husband. But if you want me to say bad things about Hugh, I can do that."

"Well, you don't need to say bad things about him," Lexie says, looking down at her hands. "I can say bad things for the both of us. For instance, that he took off with a young woman.

Such a cliché! I hated being part of that tired old chestnut. But it didn't make it hurt any less to see how ridiculous he was being. Is still being."

"Oh god," Thomas says. "I'm so sorry."

Now Lexie zooms in on him with her fierce laser look. He remembers that look. He used to feel sorry for defense attorneys facing Lexie in court.

An older man taking off with a young woman. Thomas knows he is guilty as charged.

"Yes," Lexie says, narrowing her eyes, then turning away from him. "Well."

Now both are looking out the window, as if expecting some entertainment to materialize there. Dancers, perhaps? A magic show? The room feels deeply silent, their awkwardness a bass note thumping beneath everything else. Now the pipes rattle again. Thomas has never been so aware of the pipes.

"Did you know?" he asks. "That some native tribe, I can't remember which one, anyway, the children call their father the same name as God. It's what they do. Or used to do. And then in other tribes there's no name for father at all because mostly no one knows who the father is, so why have a special name? Anyway, as far as fathers go, names run the gamut."

Lexie tilts her head, frowns at him. "Why are you telling me this? Do you want me to call you God?"

Thomas pulls himself up, sits. "No. Of course not. It's just been a long time since you called me Daddy. It felt good."

Lexie looks at the floor. "I guess so. I guess it has been a long time."

Another knock at the door. Now it opens; in walks Sally.

"Thomas. How are you? Oh, you have company."

"It's my daughter," Thomas says. "She flew in last night. It must mean I'm dying."

Sally and Lexie look at each other and frown, saying nothing. His words hang in the heavy air. He didn't mean it to come out like that. He meant to be funny. Lexie looks at the floor, then jerks her head as if trying to shake something out of her hair.

"Anyway," Sally, says. She's straightening the blanket at the end of the bed. She nods toward Thomas. "This guy, he's my favorite."

"I am?" Thomas says. "I'm your favorite?"

"Sure you are. You tell the best stories."

Lexie sits back in her chair. "He always did like younger women," she says as she stares at her hands.

Thomas closes his eyes. He feels slightly nauseous.

The room stays silent. Sally is bustling around, ignoring what Lexie just said. "Do you want to get up, Thomas?"

"Sure," he says. He nods to the walker next to the bed. "But I hate that thing."

Sally stares at the walker, frowning. "Whoops. I forgot. I have to get a wheelchair, Thomas. It's the new rule. You've been falling, the dizziness, you know. You have to be in a chair."

A wheelchair? Thomas tries to see himself sitting in a wheelchair in front of his daughter. He can't even imagine it. "I don't want a wheelchair," he says.

"Sorry," Sally says. "No choice. Unless you want to stay in bed. And we really don't want you in bed."

Now pain stabs Thomas in his gut. He gasps.

"Thomas?" Sally looks toward him. "Are you all right?"

He nods, grabs the side of the bed. He tries to catch his

breath. Lexie is staring at him, her eyes wide.

Thomas nods and grunts, pushes himself through the pain.

Sally holds up a finger, says she'll be right back. Both Thomas and his daughter look out the window, watching the squirrels. Thank god, the entertainment has finally arrived.

"How's your mother?" he says, looking at Lexie.

She frowns, as if trying to remember. "Okay. I mean, you know she has dementia, right?"

Thomas nods. "Yes, I did know. I'm so sorry. She's a good woman."

The pipes clank again.

"Then why did you leave her?"

Thomas sucks breath. Well, she's not wasting time. Okay, good to get it out in the open. Good to not keep it inside. Maybe the heaviness in the room can ease up, the air can seem breathable again. Thomas tries to remember what he said the last time she asked him, which was, of course, years ago. Sometimes he thinks Lexie is keeping a file somewhere of answers he gives to this question, checking every so often to make sure, in her lawyerly way, they're consistent.

There's only one answer, he sees now. "I don't know," he says, looking at her. "It was so long ago."

"You don't have a reason?"

Thomas watches the squirrels racing up and down a branch, one with a nut in its cheek. "Sure I do. I fell in love. That's why."

Lexie rolls her eyes. "Just like a man. You FELL in love. Just like Hugh. Like you slipped on a banana peel. Like it's someone else's fault, or just what happened. Like the universe made you do it, not you."

"I didn't say that," Thomas says. "It was my fault, of course."

The pipes rattle again. Now someone is walking into his room, another woman. It's the demented woman from his dining room table. She sits on the edge of his bed, patting the comforter. "Hello!" she says to no one in particular. Thomas is sorry to feel how relieved he is for this weird woman's presence, that there's someone here to break the tension between Lexie and him.

"Hello!" he says back to her.

"Hello," Lexie says, although she's frowning at the woman, then at Thomas.

The woman just sits, staring at the squirrels out the window. They all seem to be watching the squirrel entertainment channel, and the thing about squirrels is, they don't disappoint. "Hello!" the woman says again.

Thomas doesn't respond this time. Lexie is frowning. "Who are you?" Lexie says to the woman. "What are you doing here?"

"Hello!" the woman says again, smiling at Lexie.

"Well," Thomas says. "That's pretty much her repertoire. She's harmless. Is she bothering you?"

"She shouldn't be allowed in here," Lexie says. "Not for what you're paying."

Thomas sighs. Yes, it's expensive to live here. And it is coming out of Lexie's inheritance. Does she resent that? Another difficult topic for the two of them to discuss after they work through everything else. Which never will happen. Thomas feels suddenly tired.

Down the hall, someone shouts, "Hey, throw me that towel." The demented woman stands, leaves the room.

Now Sally returns, pushing a wheelchair. She looks at both

Thomas, then Lexie, before she stops at his bed. She pushes the TV stand back a few inches to make room for the wheelchair. Lexie seems to be watching closely.

"Okay, not a fancy model, but the best I could find. You can do it, Thomas," Sally says. "I'll show you how. First, just scoot over here to the edge."

But "scoot" isn't quite the right word, Thomas sees, for the motion he's making. No, this motion isn't jaunty and quick, it's awkward and labored, his trying to move his weak body toward Sally without causing more pain. It feels as if he's pulling a big bag of potatoes, a bag that's bigger than he is, a bag with huge holes so that potatoes keep spilling out of the bag. Oh, and the bag has tiny knives that poke out and keep stabbing him.

"Ouch. Give me a moment here," he says. Sally nods, holds out an arm.

"Okay," she says. "When you're ready, grab on. I can help."

Thomas gasps as he heaves his legs over the edge. But now the pain seems to be over. He takes some deep breaths. "Okay. I've got it," he says. "Are we done yet?"

Lexie's eyes are wide.

Sally laughs. "Not much more. But a little. Here's what we're going to do. You just wrap your arms around my neck. Hold on tight, and I'll lift you onto the chair."

"Can you do that? Lift me? I'm heavy."

Sally looks down at her legs. "I only use leg muscles. No problem. I've been doing this a long time, never injured my back."

"Not yet," Thomas says.

"Not yet," Sally smiles. "Okay, put your arms up. That's it. Are you ready?"

Sally leans over him and he reaches up, puts his hands around her neck as she begins lifting him. He smells a spicy scent from her hair. It's an intimate gesture and he feels ridiculous, wrapping his arms around a young woman's neck in front of his daughter. But more important, his body feels like dead weight. How long since he got out of bed?

"Heave ho," Sally says, and just as Thomas feels himself lifting up off the bed, his arms burn with pain and suddenly he's letting go, falling back into the sheets.

Damn. Lexie is still watching closely. "Sorry," Thomas says.

"Hey, we're just getting started here," Sally says, smiling. She seems to genuinely not mind, to be infinitely patient. Looking into her eyes, Thomas hopes he won't cry. Kindness has always had this effect on him.

"Okay, one more time," Sally says. Now Sally leans forward, places her arms in his armpits. He places his arms around her neck once again. This is the part where she lifts him, where she maneuvers him into the wheelchair. But as he leans toward her a hot stab of pain cuts him in two. He drops back to the bed once again.

"Damn," he says, holding his side.

"It's okay," Sally says. "Take a breath. Take a deep breath. We'll try again."

Now Lexie is standing. Her face looks flushed.

"It's okay if you want to wait outside the room," Sally says. "We'll be done soon."

As Lexie lifts her chin in the air, the urge to cry washes through Thomas again. His little girl, so grown up. And so miserable.

"No," Lexie says. "I'll stay. I want to stay with my dad."

My dad. Thomas closes his eyes. How quickly and easily

the words fall out of her mouth in spite of the tension between them. My dad. He's her *dad*, the only dad she has, the only one she will ever have. As she says the words, there's an oomph to the "my" and a push on "dad" and Thomas sees he belongs to her, will always belong to her. Of course he belongs to her, he's her father. How could he not realize this?

"I'm sorry," he says again, shaking his head.

"Hey," Sally says, inches away from his face. "No problem. We'll just wait a second, then try again." She bustles around the room for a minute, moving a book here, a washcloth there. She raises the blinds on the window, then comes back to the bed, leans toward him. "Ready?"

Thomas nods.

"Lift!" she calls out, and Thomas lifts, and the pain swoops through him and so does whatever strength he has left in his legs and his arms, pushing up through his body along with the force of Sally's kindness and his own love for his daughter, newly freed from so much confusion. So much love! Here he goes, up, up, up, lifting up and over. He feels himself bolt through the air, plop down on the seat of the chair.

Sally laughs, claps her hands. "You made it," she says.

18.
talking naked

When Sally wakes, Shannon is lying beside her. He is naked. She is naked. Oh god.

What happened? She closes her eyes. She remembers what happened. It was wonderful. And now here he is, in her bed.

Thank god he's still sleeping. She watches him as he sleeps, although just through one eye. Okay, he's got the body. The body is actually pretty amazing. Dark hair swirls on his chest. It looks so soft; Sally wants to reach out and stroke it. She feels herself heating up, just thinking about it. But of course she won't do that. She might wake him. Let's not wake him just yet.

His arms are muscular but not too muscular. He's got muscles where they are supposed to be, no extra fat hanging around in his middle. How do people do this? Sally doesn't have a clue. It seems to her extra fat has always been hanging around, pooching up at her stomach, sometimes less fat if she's been on a diet, but always some, nonetheless. Always there.

Sally looks down at her own body. Okay, she has to remember

to suck in her stomach. Really suck it in now.

He coughs in his sleep. Shannon's breath isn't too bad, sort of beerish is all.

Yes, there was beer last night, lots of beer. At the party. She wasn't even going to go to the party! But then Charlotte reminded her, the retirement party for Norm, head of maintenance. Sally always liked Norm, his quiet competence, his respect for the residents. She wanted to go honor Norm. So after work she walked to his house, a few blocks away. She would just stay for an hour. She's not a party girl, that's for sure.

But an hour turned into two hours, and for some reason Sally just stayed. Because Shannon was there, standing at the edge of the party? Not that. Because she likes Norm and his wife, and they kept bringing out Thai chicken wings, and their grandkids were there, sitting shyly among the adults. Sally had a sweet talk with Norm's granddaughter, what's her name? Finch? Lark? Some bird name.

Still, she was always aware of Shannon, who he was talking to, for how long. She didn't like feeling so aware of him, how her attention stayed with him even as she acted like she was paying attention to others. She hates it when people do this, not really paying attention. And she was doing it.

When she finally got up to leave, Shannon suddenly appeared by her side. He offered to give her a ride home. Okay, she said. Sure, why not?

And the next thing she remembers they were in front of her house, kissing. In his car! His car still had that fresh laundry smell, and the clean, crisp smell made the kissing seem innocent somehow, sort of youthful and silly. Sally was making out in a car! She hasn't done this since high school. Well, except for the vet. What if her neighbors walked by? In between kisses she kept thinking she should open the door and get out, but she just couldn't do it, couldn't get out of the car. And then it grew darker, and she only wanted to keep kissing this man, keep feeling the growing ache in her loins, his soft touch, how his touch on even her wrist, her shoulder, made her skin glow electric.

"Shall we go in?" she heard herself ask, finally, and they did. Oh god.

Shannon coughs again. Now his eyes are open. "Hey," he says, smiling.

"Hey," Sally says back.

What happens now? A strange man in her bed. It's been how long? Really long. Sally should hop up, start making breakfast. But to do that she has to draw attention to her body, have him look at her poochy tummy as she gets out of bed. Damn. She can't even move.

"I like that print. The Monet," Shannon says. He's eyeing the poster on her wall. Water lilies. "Did you ever see it? In the Chicago museum?" he says. "It's there. It takes your breath away. Once I just stood in front of it for, oh, it seemed like hours. Well, I sat actually because there's a bench in the room, which is a really good thing."

"You like art?" Sally says.

Sally hopes this is true. But of course he's probably just full of himself. Sally can't help herself from falling down the rabbit hole of puffing up a man's ego, asking questions. Get him talking! It's what she knows how to do, especially with men. Really, it's so easy. Just ask a few questions and they're off; all she has to do is smile and nod as the man goes on and on. She won't even need to say anything. Seeing herself take this tack, going the route of listening, just listening, Sally feels some relief, but she also feels herself pulling away from Shannon, getting smaller, closing into herself.

"Well, sure, I like art. Doesn't everyone? And anthropology, like I said to Thomas and, oh, there was geography and astronomy and so on. Let's just say I took a lot of classes in my two years of college. And here I am, a maintenance guy."

Okay, now he's talking, telling stories about the classes he took. He does like to talk. And she can listen. She's good at it. She can nod her head every so often, and that seems to suffice. The good thing is, she likes the sound of his voice.

Now Shannon seems to be studying the sheets. His fingers are tracing the flower design on the border. How long since she washed them? She hates washing sheets, the struggle to get them back on the bed. Oh god, Sally can't even remember the last time. Now his finger moves up her arms. Damn. She closes her eyes a moment, then opens them. He is looking at her.

"How about you? How long have you been at the center?"

Sally shakes her head, laughs. She feels giddy and nervous. "Forever!" she says. "For decades! Well, more than two decades, actually. Last year I got an award for being there twenty-five years. A quarter century, dumping bed pans!"

Damn. Now she's done it. Now she's told him she's old, even made it sound like she's older than she actually is. What she didn't say was, she started in high school! She studies his face for a reaction but sees none. He is just smiling, watching her. Damn, his eyelashes are long. Like a girl's.

"Tell me about it," he says. "Tell me about why you stayed."

And so Sally takes a breath and starts talking. She talks about working there as a teenager, feeling frightened at first, all those old people, sometimes seeing them naked. But pretty soon she began loving it, loving the sweetness in the midst of the heartbreak, and while heartbreak was everywhere, she saw so much sweetness. How she worried about herself sometimes, realizing that most people find nursing homes sad, but working in one makes her happy. Happy in a sad sort of way. Does this make sense?

Sally pauses. She's not used to talking so much. Is it okay? She's not really a talker. She waits for Shannon to do what most men do, jump in with his own thoughts, offer the time he did something sort of like what she's talking about, but really not like it at all, the moment when he hijacks her story to bring it back over to him. But he's just lying on his side looking at her, his head resting on his hand. He's not like the other big talkers she knows, who can't seem to listen.

"Tell me more," he says.

Mostly Sally looks down as she speaks, but every so often she glances up into his eyes. They're oddly colored, sometimes green, sometimes brown. The way they sit on his face, so far apart, gives Shannon the look of being always surprised. Pretty soon she's telling him how things at home were so bad, her dad drunk all the time, so more and more she stayed away, stayed at the center.

Here's what happens, Sally sees, when you open yourself to another. When you talk, really talk, when the words are new and fresh, not the prepared script you've said over and over, but new words you hear for the first time as they appear in your mouth, as they roll out into the world. You hear how true those words are, how you are bigger, smarter and more interesting than you ever imagined. Talking like this, Sally feels herself turning into someone she wasn't before, someone she likes very much. She feels beautiful.

Sally sees her arm reach out, sees herself pulling him toward her. She feels her lips seeking his. She feels his body's warmth next to hers, his skin on her skin, the firm weight of it. She feels herself stroking his chest with her whole hand, squeezing his nipples. It's even better than she imagined. She wants to make love so badly.

She pulls Shannon closer, on top of her. She has shown herself, all of her, all she's ever known and more, and now she wants to open as much as she can, as much as she possibly can, open her body as well as her mind.

Ah yes. She closes her eyes. She hears herself moan and doesn't care how loud it is. Now he's inside her. They are moving together. She looks up, into his eyes. He gazes at her, so softly. No matter how long this will last, making love, it's not long enough. Can she open more to this man? Yes, she can. She hears herself calling out.

Afterwards, Sally lies still. She and Shannon lie quietly, holding hands.

Now Panda jumps up on the bed. The cat immediately nestles against Shannon, butting his chest with her head. Shannon laughs, begins stroking the cat. Sally feels briefly jealous. But that's ridiculous. It's just a cat!

"I've been wanting to tell you," Shannon says. "About the day at the vet? The way I kept crying, God, I'm embarrassed, just thinking about it."

"It's okay," Sally says. "Your cat had died. Of course you were sad."

"Well, I was, but it wasn't just that," he says, rubbing Panda's head with his finger. Her purring grows louder. "I mean, of course, I loved my cat. But she was also the cat I shared with my girlfriend."

Sally feels herself stop breathing. She stares down at the bed.

"My ex, that is," Shannon says. "I mean, we broke up about six months ago. You know, we were together for, oh, fifteen years. A crazy long time! We were high school sweethearts. I wanted to get married but she didn't, so we just lived together. Anyway, she left me for some coach. A life coach! And when the cat died, it was like going through that all over again. I just lost it."

Sally remembers Shannon bending over his cat in the back seat, sobbing. Of course. Of course he was grieving for more than the cat. "Oh," Sally says. "Well."

This is good news and bad news. The good news is that Shannon is the kind of guy who sticks with a woman for the long haul. That's remarkable! But the bad news is bad, really bad. The bad news is that he's fresh off this heartbreak, probably not thinking straight. The even worse news is that the old girlfriend is still out there somewhere, hovering around, and when she decides she wants Shannon back, she'll snap her fingers and he'll come running. Fifteen years? Sally can't begin to compete with that. Damn. Sally feels nauseous.

"I'm sorry," she says now to Shannon, although she knows her voice sounds flat. She's trying to be someone else now, someone who cares that he had a hard time when he broke up with his girlfriend. But she's faking it.

"It was hard," Shannon says. Maybe he doesn't notice the insincerity in her voice. Of course he doesn't notice. He is a man, after all. He's no different from any other man. He's no different from any other big talker. What was she thinking? Then he smiles.

"But it's better now." He's smiling at her, reaching out for her arm.

Sally pulls her arm away from him.

"Hey," he says, frowning. "What's going on?"

She could continue the way she began. She could tell him the truth, show who she is. She could say, oh, I can feel myself closing off now because I worry I'm too old and fat for you. Not pretty enough. Also, I'm lonely. And you talk too much. Plus, you have an old girlfriend who will come back. They always do. I just know things will go wrong soon, very wrong, and I'm thinking how you'll break my heart.

This is not what she says. Instead she wraps her arms around herself. "Nothing," she says. "It's nothing."

Shannon is lying on his back, staring at the ceiling. Sally hears Panda purring, nuzzling into the crook of his arm. "Sally?" he says. He's frowning. "What just happened?"

Sally's panties are on the floor. If she makes a deep dive out of the bed, she can put them on before he sees her fat stomach. And anyway, who cares? Who cares if he sees how fat she is? It doesn't matter. What was the thing Thomas said? To not act on your preconceived notions. To let people surprise you. But no. There will be no surprises.

"Nothing," she says. "Nothing just happened. I need to get up now. You have to go."

19.
the room calls

Lillian keeps walking, up one hallway and down the next. She does this most days. She walks because she feels jangly inside, because she can't find her home. The jangly-ness feels like coming undone, like all of her parts might blast into the air and go poof. Just like that, she might vanish. When she's walking this fast, something soothes her, a rhythm of arms and legs working together, propelling her forward. Any moment now, she might find her home, down this hall or around the next corner. So she just has to keep walking.

It helps to look down, at the floor, to watch her feet as they move. Her feet are her friends! Here they are, pushing ahead, hoofing it.

And yet. Are these really her feet, and not someone else's? She likes to wear flats, gold ones, sleek and shiny and slender, she wants to see sparkle when she looks down, her feet moving with a snap and a lilt, a touch of luster. But the feet she sees now are not in gold flats, no, they're stuffed into puffy white shoes, the sort of shoes young people wear when they run. These shoes feel heavy, they're weighing her down, they're bulky and fat. How did these ugly shoes get on her feet? Are these really her feet?

She stops, bends toward the floor. But now something crashes behind her, a loud whack, a deafening a clatter of dishes and metal.

"Lillian! Please! You can't just stop like that when I'm behind you."

It's one of the young men who works here, pushing the tall cart of meal trays. He's shaking his head, scowling.

"Please get out of my way," he says now, his face squinching up. "Just move."

That is rude. Okay, she can move to the side. And she'll move even farther. A door's open and since she's not wanted out here in the hallway, she'll go into this room.

Inside the room Lillian stops short. There's a woman lying in bed. She's fully dressed, maybe taking a nap. Her eyes are closed.

"Hello?" the woman calls out. "Anyone there?"

She's seen this woman. It's the woman with braids, braids that hang down on her shoulders, like a young girl's braids that flap as she walks. But these braids don't flap, no, they just sort of hang there, looking scraggly and grey. The woman's skin looks like chocolate. This woman smiles at Lillian. In bed she looks like a little girl, but an old little girl, a little girl who got old too fast. She'll just sit here for a while next to the woman. She'll keep her company.

"Who are you?" the woman calls out. "Why are you here?" So many photos on the table next to the bed. Lillian picks one up. The woman on the bed is in this picture, surrounded by what must be her family. It's a big one, so many people, squeezed together under a tent. Some of the men are holding up fish. For a moment Lillian wishes she had a family like this, cousins and uncles and whatnot. But it feels wrong to want a family that's not her own. No, she just wants her own little family, she wants Annie and Daniel. She'll find them if she keeps walking.

Where are they? Where is her family?

There are so many photos here, the woman won't notice it's gone. Or maybe she wants it gone, maybe she's been trying to get rid of her photos? You never know.

Something beeps in the bathroom, telling her it's time to leave. Lillian tucks the photo under her sweater and darts out the door.

"Who are you?" she hears the woman calling behind her.

She keeps walking. The jangly feeling is spreading, it's shooting out from her middle to all of her parts. The jangling feels like all of her might explode, and then who will she be after that? Who is she now?

Another door is open, and the room seems to be calling her name.

Inside there's a man on a bed, the same man she sang to before. This man is sleeping, his mouth open wide as if he's yelling something, although nothing comes out but a jagged breath, like his breath might stop any minute.

The man wears blue pajamas with navy blue piping around the collar. Daniel has pajamas like this. In fact, this man reminds her of Daniel. Could he be Daniel? Her heart is thumping just thinking about it.

Lillian sits by the side of his bed. This man only has a few photos next to his bed, so she slips the woman's photo out from her sweater and places it on the table. There, that looks good.

He'll be happy to see it. Lillian studies his face. Daniel wore a hat every day, but of course he didn't wear it to bed. This man has dark hair, like Daniel. He has a square jaw that gets bristly when he goes a day without shaving, just like Daniel.

Could this be Daniel? Daniel has thick, dark hair on his chest. She loves to stroke his chest hair, to feel its softness under her fingers. She pulls down the covers. She unbuttons the man's pajama top. He grunts, rolls to his side. That's okay. She slides her hand into his pajamas. His skin so warm! Yes, he has thick hair on his chest, just like Daniel. Is it him? As she strokes his chest hair, he rolls back toward her, snorts in his sleep.

She's sitting by the side of the bed when footsteps tell her she's no longer alone. She starts. The tall man is standing close by.

"Hello, Lillian," he says. "I have something I want to show Thomas."

He holds a paper in front of him, leans down to show the man in the bed. But the man's eyes are still closed and his head turned away.

"Thomas," the tall man says. "I have good news. I just want to tell you."

The tall man sits down on the side of the bed, right next to Lillian. It feels good to have company.

"Remember those letters I told you about? To men on death row? One of my guys is getting released. He is! He goes free in two weeks. Something about DNA testing."

The tall man is shaking his head. The man in bed, the Daniel-like man, is still snoring, his eyes closed.

"Isn't that something? I'll leave it right here. It's a statement from his attorney. I thought you'd want to see it," the tall man says, putting a paper on the table beside the bed. He gazes at the man in bed, who doesn't wake up. He shakes his head. "I thought you'd want to know."

The tall man reaches out, takes Daniel's hand. He holds it for a minute between his own. He coughs once, then again.

"Goodbye, Lillian," he says as he stands. He turns back to her. "You shouldn't be here, you know. This isn't your room." Then he walks out.

The Daniel man snorts, shifts in his bed. Lillian reaches for the paper. A few of the dark scribbles make sense, but most must be in a different language. Death row. What is death row? It feels like this place, where old people get smushed up together, where someone puts the wrong shoes on your feet so you don't even know who you are. It feels like where she is now.

More footsteps, getting closer. Someone is turning into the room. Lillian's heart thumps in her chest. She shouldn't be here, she's in the wrong place, like the man said. She steps close to the wall, next to the window. She pulls the curtains close, to cover herself. Maybe this is a good place to hide.

Through the curtains she sees someone walk into the room. Now there's a dark outline of a woman standing next to the bed. The woman takes off her coat, sits on the chair. She pulls the chair close to the bed.

"Oh, Daddy," the woman says.

The woman reaches out, takes the man's hand. He is still sleeping. He snorts again, turns away from the woman.

Lillian tries not to breathe or make any sounds. She squishes herself next to the window. The glass is cold on her back.

The woman picks up a photo from the bedside table, the same

one Lillian just deposited there. She turns the photo over, frowning.

"Who are these people?" She puts the photo back on the table.

The Daniel man is snoring, making little yipping sounds.

Now the woman leans forward, her head on the man's chest. Her back begins heaving and Lillian hears sobbing, watery sounds. She pulls her hands close to her side. Even though her feet aren't really her feet, she squeezes them close to the wall. She is squishing herself into as tiny a space as she can.

The woman's cries escalate now, they are ragged and loud as throaty sounds spill out between sobs. The woman keeps shaking her head as she cries, as if her sobs are so big that they're pulling her head this way and that.

It would be the wrong time to step forward so Lillian steps back, trying to smush herself into this space next to the window. But as she grabs hold of the curtain, she loses her balance. She feels herself pitching forward, still holding the cloth. The curtain rod snaps, falls to the floor.

The woman beside the bed suddenly straightens.

"What the…!"

"Yes!" Lillian calls out as she falls into the room in a tangle of curtains, using what she hopes is a friendly voice. "Hello!"

The woman looks up, startled. Her face is twisted, her eyes wide.

"What on earth? What are you doing here?" she's yelling at Lillian. Now her mouth takes the shape of a pretzel. The woman stands and steps back, pointing the way to the door. "Get out of here. Now, right now!"

Lillian's face might burn up. She is hot everywhere. She steps out from the pile of curtains. The man is moving in bed, making noises.

"What? What's going on?"

Now the woman grabs Lillian's shoulder. "Now!"

As she is pushed, Lillian stumbles out of the room. Just a moment ago the room was calling to her and now it's tossing her out. No wonder she gets confused.

Where is her home? The feet that aren't really her feet keep walking.

20.
the parade

When someone steps into Beth's office, she scrambles to take off the headset. She's pretty sure she must look ridiculous. Still, it's amazing what you see in this virtual reality thing. Lillian will love it. Maybe. It's a long shot, but worth trying.

Someone is standing beside Beth, looming over her. That's pretty bold, barging into her office without knocking first. Beth tries to tamp down her annoyance.

"Get her out," the person says, almost yelling. Whoa! Beth jumps out of her chair. It's a woman. "Keep her out of my father's room."

Beth has never seen this woman before. About her age, with bottle blond hair, but she's no one to talk about bottle blond. The woman's face looks twisted with anger. "Keep who out?" Beth is sorry that, as usual, she's looking up at the stranger, who is considerably taller. Everyone is considerably taller. "Out of where?"

The woman steps even close as Beth steps back. The woman won't hit her, will she? It seems possible. But the blond woman folds her arms across her chest, as if she's working hard to keep herself in control. "That crazy woman! She was in my father's room. Again. He's dying!"

Ah yes, Thomas. His daughter. Her words swirl around Beth, so much to respond to: crazy, dying. When angry words come at her, as they sometimes do from residents or residents' families, she tries to imagine the words marching on by, not really aimed at her, just a sort of off-kilter parade out the window. The image helps her stay calm, feel less defensive. Of course her residents' family members are suffering, watching their loved ones age, then slip away. The angry words are just out-of-tune tubas and trumpets blasting their noise; they'll be gone soon.

"Please." Beth stands, motioning toward the chair. "Please sit down. Did you just fly in? You must be exhausted."

"I'm not exhausted," the woman is yelling. "I'm upset, and I have a right to be, finding a crazy woman in my father's room."

Beth takes her coat off the chair, gestures again for the woman to sit. But the blond woman remains standing. She's wearing high heels. Beth stands as tall as she can, but once again it's not tall enough. "I'm sorry," Beth says. "Lillian wanders. We try to keep her out of other people's rooms, but sometimes it happens."

The woman blinks, tosses her hair. "It happens? No, that's not okay. That's not a good reason. It can't just *happen*. You have to stop it. It's your job! My father is paying you I don't know how much, and he can't have a crazy woman in his room all the time. Or ever!"

"She's not crazy," Beth says, although she immediately knows this is the wrong thing to say. "She has dementia."

"I don't care what she has!" Now the woman's voice picks up

even more steam. Outside the door, Beth sees the new aide stop, tilt her head. She's listening, Beth believes, to see if she should intervene. Beth waves her on.

She remembers what this is like, being the advocate for a parent. It was so hard with her mother, trying to make the nursing home staff see her mom as a person, not just a number. So often she felt she was butting her head against a huge wall. She vowed she'd do better at Grace.

But how to do better? She tries to listen, to hear the feelings beneath the sharp words. This woman must be crazy with guilt, having been estranged from her father. Like Beth, with her mother. The emotions so tangled, so raw.

"You know, we could offer some counseling," Beth says. "You've had so much to deal with now, way too much."

"I do not need counseling. No." Now the woman's face blooms red as she spits out the words. "I need you to run this place the way it should be run. I need you to do your job!"

Who knows why things sometimes make Beth angry and sometimes they don't? Who knows why most of the time, almost all of the time, she can stop, take a deep breath, and just let the parade march right on by, tooting its loud and ridiculous horns? And who knows why the parade sometimes stops right beside her and the musicians morph into bad guys with guns? With the guns aimed at her? Now Beth feels herself getting hot. She feels moist under her arms. "Don't talk to me like that," she says in her deepest voice, taking a step toward the woman. "You have no right."

"I have every right," the woman says, tossing her hair again. Huh, she's used to making that hair work for her, that's for sure. "With what we pay you, we have all the rights in the world."

As Thomas's daughter storms out, the new aide stands just outside the door, looking puzzled. What just happened? How can Beth explain, as she surely will have to? Not just to the aide, but to Charlie. Beth shakes her head. Shit.

"It's okay," she says to the aide. But of course, it is not.

• • •

Beth feels sick to her stomach. When she puts on the headset again, she adjusts the goggles to fit snug over her eyes. She presses the button for Ocean. First there's the low rumble of water, a bass line throb of surf hitting shoreline. Now she sees waves, their deep greys and blues melting into white foam. Oh! More sounds: the call of gulls, both lonely and soothing; now the outlines of birds emerge, winging through space, now dipping into the sea. Here's the swish-swishing of waves as they unfurl onto the beach, their rhythm compelling, so soothing. Beth feels her heart slowing down, her breath coming easier. What is it about the ocean?

She closes her eyes. Perhaps it's the constancy, the repetition of waves, the implication that yes, life will go on, it will go on and on just like the ocean. What you love will continue to live through this year and the next, though all of the years, through eternity, and you will live, too. You and your loves will last, you won't end, your loves won't end, nothing you love will leave you, ever.

Except that they do.

The last time Beth went to the ocean, she was with Daisy. It was just the two of them, and she drove from Ohio to the beach in North Carolina. She felt like a pioneer, an explorer, a lone woman in a car with her dog. It felt bold, elemental. Daisy was sitting in the passenger seat, her head so alert, her eyes focused forward, leading the way. Her snout pointed earnestly, as if saying, yes, I'll get you there. No worries! Every so often she looked over at Beth, a doggy smile on her face, then went back to her post as navigator.

Beth had never before made a long trip alone with a dog. She'd always been with Jack, and of course they argued, not bad arguing but pretty much constant, where to eat, where to stop for the night, Beth wanting one thing and Jack another, so much negotiation and bickering that by the time they arrived, they were exhausted.

With Daisy, there was no arguing. None at all.

And even though some hotels allowed dogs, Beth stayed at one that did not, because sneaking Daisy into the room added adventure. Daisy seemed in on the caper; she never barked, never caused trouble, the two of them sharing a secret as they dashed from the car to the room, then huddled together in bed. What's the worst that could happen? They'd be tossed out, and that too added an edge, a risky shine to the trip.

They arrived the next morning, spent the day at the beach. It was grey and chilly and still the best day Beth ever had. The beach was almost deserted but for the gulls and tiny birds skittering close to the water. Daisy dashed after them as Beth unloaded their cooler: a sandwich for Beth, kibble and treats for Daisy. Daisy chased after the birds on the beach, never tiring though she never came close to catching one. Still, she pranced on the sand, looking free and exuberant in a way that left Beth laughing. So Beth joined the game, joined Daisy, the two of them dashing, heading straight into the water, then dashing back out again, chasing birds, never catching them. Beth flailed her arms at the sky as Daisy jumped straight up into the air. The two of them finally collapsed on sand, Beth feeling both exhausted and oddly renewed.

She felt free, a woman alone with her dog at the ocean. And during the afternoon she woke up and realized she'd fallen asleep all alone on the beach. But of course she wasn't alone. There was Daisy sitting beside her, alert and protective, keeping watch until Beth woke up. Why had she never before traveled alone with a dog?

But of course it couldn't be just any old dog. It had to be Daisy.

21.
far away

What was it like, the first time he saw Sarah? Thomas wants to remember.

He is burrowing into his pillow, into his past, into his memories. He feels himself falling but it's not a bad fall, not scary, not his body twisting into a fist. No, it's a soft fall, a gentle slide into a new room in his mind. The door to the room is wide open. He enters. It's a room filled with his life at the college, those thousands, tens of thousands of days, but it all feels like one day, and he's amazed that he can live it again.

He always loved the first day of class.

Now he's standing in front of the blackboard, watching students file in. There really was a blackboard back then. But often no chalk, so Thomas always joked the first day about the financial state of the college. And the college usually was broke, but it was an excellent school and he loved being a part of it.

He was there how many years? His entire career. The college was tiny and there was no chalk, but he had huge windows and high ceilings and the scent of learning, right in that room, the same room every year. The room smelled of sweat and books and the passing of years all mixed up together, and that smell, to Thomas, was heavenly. He felt himself bounce a little walking into class the first day.

Who would have known he liked teaching so much? Thomas knew himself to be shy, an introvert. But put him in front of young people to talk about anthropology and some other Thomas emerged, some show-off, some jokester who came strutting out for his students. He heard himself become funny, surprising. He was good at this! He told stories that made them laugh, widened their eyes. Of course, he had a spectacular topic. Young people never got tired of hearing about the weird things humans can do, and humans do so many weird things.

So as he watched the young people file in the first day, he felt himself shiver with possibility. He saw how frightened they were, how poised to please him, how much they wanted good grades, at least not bad ones. He saw the young men acting tough in their ball caps and sweatshirts, the young women either not speaking or leaning in to assert themselves. The young women changed over the years, that's for sure. So much change. He saw his students through the '70s and the '80s, the hippie days, then the '90s, then the millennium. He saw young people dress in tie-dyed shirts and bandanas, then all black for a while, then tight jeans and T-shirts. He heard so many musicians blast from their radios, then computers, then phones. He heard Bob Dylan to Blondie to Bright Eyes. He had a front-row seat for whatever young people were thinking and doing and hearing, and he loved having that seat.

Now Thomas sucks breath. Sarah? Here she comes, through

the doorway, on the first day of class. Thomas closes his eyes. He wants to remember. Are these the actual details, or is he making them up? It doesn't matter. She's thin, a bit messy looking. In his mind Sarah wears some sort of poncho and jeans, she's always hiding her body. Her dark hair is tussled, not out of design, she just never paid much attention. But he's aware of her from the start, sitting in the front row of class, the intense way she watched him. He felt himself suck in his gut, stand up straighter.

Her questions! Thomas remembers feeling immediately challenged, and the challenge excited him. And he remembers her voice, how softly she spoke, how hesitantly, even while asking tough questions. So many contradictions about her, something odd that seemed to throw sparks out into the room. Who was she? He was curious.

At one point in the class he's aware that he and Sarah are having a conversation, talking to each other only. He sees other students eye each other and snicker. He pulls back. It's the '70s! He's not one of those guys who plays to female students, who ultimately beds them. Oh god, no. Until Sarah. Only Sarah.

Thomas turns toward the blackboard. There's no chalk. He makes his joke about the state of the college. Students laugh. "Moving on," he says to his class, consciously not looking at Sarah. "Let's turn to the syllabus."

"Thomas?" A voice hovers above him.

Where is he? Who is speaking? Is it Sarah? Thomas opens his eyes. He blinks, sees his dresser and chair. Yes, he's in the place with so many old people. He knows this woman, but it's not Sarah. It's the kind woman with the beautiful skin. Her face looms above him.

But he's disappointed. This room, though it's apparently real, feels like a vague memory in his mind and it's distant somehow, not vibrant and pulsing like the classroom he just left. He wants to go back to the classroom, sink back into that day. He feels gravity tugging him back into the past. He closes his eyes. Such heaviness in his body.

The kind woman touches his shoulder. "Hey, don't leave," she says. "Stay with me a while."

He tries to keep his eyes open. What is her name? Sally?

But wait. Who is she really? She's leaning close to him, and Thomas feels himself falling into her smell, her skin. Is this his mother? Thomas thinks she might be his mother, leaning above him, putting him to bed as a child. Is that why he's in bed? Is he a child again? Is he in his old bedroom, the one with posters of Mickey Mantle on the walls, his stuffed walrus?

Thomas blinks. No, this isn't his childhood room. This room is light green, a medicinal shade. Now a clear thought blasts through his mind. His stomach pinches. He's not a small boy in his bedroom, not a college professor on the first day of class. No, he's an old man, getting ready to die. Oh god. How could that be? He was a child just a moment ago.

He feels himself reaching out. She takes his hand. "Thomas," she says, smiling at him. "There you are." Now she moves the pillow beneath his head, plumps it up. "Here," she says. "Let me make you more comfortable."

Now Thomas feels warmth pushing up from his chest, from his center, it feels like heat rushing out of his body. She doesn't know him, not really, and yet here she is, caring for him. He feels like crying.

The woman leans close to him. "I'm here," she says. "I'm here with you."

He closes his eyes and the room swirls again. And now he's back in a dream but it's a new room, a room in which he's lying in bed with Sarah. He doesn't remember how it first happened. But there they are. He knows that it's wrong, that he's making the biggest mistake of his life and he also knows he will do this, will couple with this strange dark young woman. He knows he won't take it lightly, knows he couldn't do that if he tried. He knows he will follow his heart and turn his life upside down.

Thomas sees now what this leads to. It leads to ruining his daughter's life, destroying the happiness of the good woman who married him. These betrayals feel heavy, they are weights on his body, anchors dragging him down.

And yet. And yet.

Now he and Sarah are lying together. The room is dark, only the light from the street in the window. They are naked, holding hands, facing each other. They are taking turns speaking in soft voices. What are they talking about? Maybe their childhoods, their hurts, their wishes, their dreams. They speak of everything, over time. For the first time in his life, the only time, Thomas feels heard and seen by someone who he knows understands him, and he wants, more than anything, to see and hear Sarah as well.

He believes that he did. It wasn't hard. Everything about her was compelling to him.

What was that Beatles song? In my life, I loved you more. The melody plays in his head. I loved you more. More than what? More than was reasonable. More than he loved his wife. More than his love for his daughter? Not more, but this love was so different. It was, for the first time, the only time, feeling known.

Was it worth it? Would he do it again? Was it worth the pain he caused others, to feel that exquisite intimacy, the closeness of body and heart and mind? But it's the wrong question, he sees, because it's a question he only sees now, after decades have passed. At the time he wasn't asking the question, no. Perhaps he should have been asking it. But at the time he was just moving toward love, choosing it.

"Thomas," a voice says, above him, the smooth-skinned woman, Sally. "I'm putting another blanket on you, a comforter. I don't want you to get cold."

Yes, he feels a new layer of warmth, of softness. Such kindness. He can't speak. The softness of his bed feels like waves, like a soft ocean holding him up. He is floating. He drifts for a while, beneath a blue sky.

Now the sky darkens. He sees a huge wave heading his way, a wall of water as high as a cliff breaking above, crashing toward him. He steels himself for the impact. But the wave doesn't crash from above, no, it rises up from below. It is lifting him, rocking him, holding him, a sweet spray of liquid washing his face. This wave feels so soft. It feels amazing. It feels like forgiveness. But who is forgiving him? Surely not Marjorie, not Lexie, no.

Perhaps he's forgiving himself? He's been trying so hard, for so long. He doesn't know what forgiving himself would feel like, can't even imagine after so many years. Maybe what he expected was wrong? Maybe forgiveness is not sudden and singular, not a flash of lightning out of the blue, then over and done. Maybe it feels more like this, a rocking and rolling, an ebbing and flowing, an ongoing motion that tilts toward forgiveness sometimes but recedes shortly after, moving forward and backward through all the days of a life. Maybe it's a wave like this wave, ongoing.

Whatever this is, he feels soothed by it. He relaxes. He'll let this wave rock him, hold him on water. The wave cradles him. Now sleep overwhelms, and he drifts further away from the shore.

22.
on her shoulders

Sometimes when one of her residents dies, Sally feels herself getting bigger. She sees herself hoist the dead person up on her shoulders—but of course, on her shoulders, he's not dead—and carry him. She's like one of those circus acrobats riding a bike while balancing a human standing above her. She feels herself seeing the world through the dead person's eyes. She is living for two! It makes her live better to see life this way. She sees more and hears more. And after a few days the person dims, so she no longer feels their weight on her shoulders. But still, something about that person stays with her.

Do other employees think like this? Sally has thought about asking but hasn't. She's pretty sure the others will say, no, they never think this. Never. Not one single time.

Sometimes Sally's not sure she can get any bigger, what with all those who have died at Grace Woods. But what about Thomas? Will he be on her shoulders? Sally believes that he will be, that she will carry him there, and he will stay longer than most. Except she doesn't want Thomas to stand on her shoulders. She wants him alive, right now, in the world.

She's in his room now and hears him stir in his bed. "Thomas?" she says. "It's time for breakfast. French toast, your favorite." Sally picks up the book off the floor beside his bed. He is still sleeping, though the sounds of residents eating breakfast, the clanking of silverware and murmur of chatter, drift into the room.

What's the book? Sally smiles. It's the book he described just last week, about how differences between cultures are linked to the geographical features of continents. She was mesmerized by his enthusiasm, by his crisp and eloquent sentences, by how he used stories to bring these concepts to life. She imagined herself in his classroom, furiously taking notes. Or rather, probably not taking notes but watching him, seeing these ideas play out across his expressive face. She'd be one of the girls falling in love with him.

Where will all his thoughts go when he dies? What happens to everything that makes a person a person? This is the part that stumps her. Yes, the body runs out of steam, she gets that. But our feelings and thoughts? Thomas is not done! Each time she sees him, he's brimming with things to say, as if trying to say it all while he can. Except for the past couple of days, he hasn't been talking much. Now he seems to be mainly sleeping.

"Thomas? It's French toast this morning."

"Hmmm," he says. She leans over him.

"Hey, want to get up for breakfast?"

He turns, smiles up at her, even though his eyes are still closed. His breath smells musty, an old person's breath. "Lexie?" he says.

"It's Sally," she says.

He frowns as he burrows into the pillow.

"You know me," she says, trying to sound light, although introducing herself makes her feel smaller. "I work here."

But he's off, snoring again.

Sally picks up the blue shirt from the chair, folds it and stashes it in the dresser. The glasses go next to his bed on the table. She sweeps pieces of foil off the table, drops them into the wastebasket. Little pieces of something hard and white—a toenail? fingernail?—lie on the table too. All these little scraps from our bodies. There is so much that we shed, so much to pick up at the end of a day.

Now she's holding these tiny parts of Thomas. What if she keeps them? She could put them in a little jar on top of her dresser. She could stash them in a baggie, carry the baggie around in her pocket.

But no. That's just weird.

Still, she would tell Shannon this, too. She wants to reveal to him her oddest, most embarrassing thoughts. Why? Because she wants him to love her deepest self, the self that secretly harbors these thoughts, and she thought he might, he just might, be the one who can love her like this.

And this is silly, of course, she knows Shannon won't be the one to love her, there's too much to go wrong. There's the old girlfriend ready to pounce, and there's Megan and other pretty young girls and besides, he talks too much. Yet still this part of her, this pitiful part, keeps leaping up in her mind, having imaginary conversations with Shannon like the real one they had in her bed. It felt so amazing, to talk like that. To feel how deeply he listened. She's tingling now, just thinking about it.

She shakes her head, trying to shake off the thought of him.

Now Thomas makes little grunting sounds in his sleep. Sally leans down, pulls the covers up to his shoulders. Someone moves by the door. A woman, just walking in. It's Thomas's daughter.

"Hello," Sally says, but the daughter walks by without speaking. Sally continues to hover around while the daughter sits on the chair close to the bed. In the bathroom Sally sponges the counter, arranges the toothpaste and brush. She hears murmuring from the other room.

It's okay that the daughter isn't greeting Sally or talking to her at all. It's okay that she's not treating her like, well, a human being, like someone she already met. Relatives are like that sometimes, especially the ones that show up out of the blue. The trick is to not let it bother you. It's about them, not about her. She'll try not to take it personally.

The daughter is on her phone. Thomas is still sleeping. Now she sits on Thomas's bed, leaning over him. "Daddy?" she says. "Daddy?"

In high school Sally worried that her father would show up drunk to her conferences. And why not? He got drunk most days after working the early shift. He came home and began pouring Jim Beam, and she stayed at school as long as she could so she didn't have to go home to him. When she came home his head hung on his chest and his words were slurry. Her mother was long gone by then. She took care of her father, cooking dinner each night, but what she felt when he showed up at school was pure shame. Even when he dressed up, he looked like a drunk, a drunk who didn't know how to dress, who still had stains on his clothing.

Now Sally puts clean shirts in Thomas's dresser. What would it be like to have a father who wore a crisp, clean shirt when he came to her school? Whom she could trust to show up and always be proud of?

She turns toward Thomas's daughter. What's her name? Lexie? "He didn't show up for breakfast, so I was worried," Sally says. "It's not like him."

The daughter looks annoyed, then hangs up her phone. "Well, hospice came in last night. They started him on the pain meds. So he's sleeping."

"Oh," Sally says. "Oh."

Shouldn't Sally have known about this? Of course not. Why would hospice talk to her about Thomas, even if she's worked here for twenty-five years? She's only a resident aide. Still, Sally hears the words come out of her mouth before she can stop them. "You know, your dad said he wanted to be drug-free for as long as he can be," Sally says. "He said he didn't want to miss anything. That's so like him."

The daughter looks up at the ceiling. She is frowning.

"I just want to make sure you know," Sally says, trying hard to keep an edge out of her voice. "What he wants."

Now the daughter looks at her, her eyes narrowed. Sally's chest feels tight. She should stop now, but she can't. "I know you're doing what seems the best thing for your dad."

"Yes," the daughter says. "Yes, I am."

She takes a last look at Thomas, who is still sleeping. Now he opens his eyes. Seeing his daughter, he smiles. "Lexie?" he says. "Is that you?"

"It's me, Daddy," she says, taking his hand. Sally's amazed

to see this angry, ungrateful woman turn into a sweet little girl in front of her eyes.

Thomas smiles up at his daughter, a huge smile. His eyes are open. They sit there silently, gazing into each other's eyes.

Sally feels she's been kicked in the gut. Of course she's being ridiculous. Thomas is not her father. He's Lexie's father. But his daughter broke Thomas's heart by moving so far away, not coming home or calling him. She's not the one who cleans up her father when he poops in bed. She doesn't pick up her father's debris, his dead skin, his fingernails, over and over each day. She's not the one who wants to keep his fingernails in a jar. If Lexie picked up his fingernails, she'd toss them right in the trash.

And Thomas forgives her for all that, and more.

"You're here," Thomas says now to his daughter, reaching out for her hand. But pretty soon his eyes close again.

Once Sally heard a deep voice in the back of her mind just as she was falling asleep. It sounded just like her father. Dad? she had said out loud. Daddy? She surprised herself by bursting into tears, not at the sound of his voice but at the sound of her own voice saying, Daddy? She had never once used that name for her father, never felt trusting enough. But in this moment, falling asleep, she felt her own longing just saying it.

"Daddy," the daughter says now to Thomas. She is stroking his hair while he sleeps. She is holding his hand.

Thomas is not her dad. Sally has no right to claim him. He doesn't even know who she is anymore. Still, Sally closes her eyes and imagines. She imagines she's the one bending toward Thomas. Daddy, she imagines herself saying. Daddy.

Now Lexie places her head on her father's chest. Sally hadn't noticed before how thin Lexie is, her backbone jutting out in her sweater. From the back she looks young and frail, like an orphan. Is she crying? When Sally walks to the bed, bends down to touch Lexie's hand, Lexie sits up straight again.

"I'd like some time with him now," Lexie says, her eyes teary. "Some time alone."

"Yes," Sally says. "Yes, of course." Her chest tightens, but she tries to smile as she heads out the door.

• • •

Lillian is walking in the hallway. She seems to walk all the time, up one hallway and down the other. Sometimes she seems happy, and Sally can hear a song as she passes. But other times, like today, her head is thrust forward, her hands stuffed in her pockets. She looks fierce. She looks angry.

Sally falls in behind. Truthfully, it's hard to keep up. This old woman is in pretty good shape.

"Lillian," Sally calls out from behind. "May I walk with you?"

There's a grunt from Lillian, which Sally takes as a yes.

They walk past the living area, where several old women are watching the weather. In the dining room Lorraine and Edward are chatting, lingering after breakfast. The smell of maple syrup wafts from the kitchen, where Sally hears the clanking of metal on metal. Residents are pushing their walkers down the hall, making their slow way back to their rooms.

Lillian keeps walking in circles.

Sally follows. It's a surprise, always, how quickly this feeling can come. This sadness. How quickly it overwhelms her. It feels deep and dark and like the place she's most comfortable, the most comfortable room in a house, the room with a soft chair that envelops her. What house? She doesn't know. But it's a dark place, a sad place, and it feels like where she belongs.

But it's scary too, a sadness that wants to defeat her. Walking helps, even walking with Lillian. "Lillian," Sally calls out. "Where are you going?"

There's a silence, and then Lillian sighs heavily, shakes her head no. She keeps walking. Sally catches up, walks beside her. After a few minutes, Lillian makes a sound. "Hmmmm," she says.

Sally leans toward her. "Can you speak up? I can't hear."

"Hmmmm," Lillian says.

"I see," Sally says. "You're going home."

Lillian suddenly stops, turns toward Sally. She tilts her head, looks Sally up and down. The old woman nods her head yes. "Hmmmm," she says again.

"Okay," Sally says. "I'll walk with you."

Lillian resumes walking. So does Sally. Sometimes the other aides correct Lillian. They try to reason with her, tell her what's true, steer her in the direction of facts. They tell her there's no home to go to, that this is her home. They think facts are good for her. But they're not. Facts only upset her. What Lillian needs, Sally believes, is respect for her own truth, her deeper truth, the truth beyond facts. She's going home. "I'll go with you," Sally says again.

There's a tall figure at the end of the hall. He's just standing there, watching. Just seeing Shannon, Sally feels her heart speeding up. Now he's waving to her, opening his mouth to say something.

Sally puts up her hand as she passes him. "Sorry," she says. "I'm busy. I'm walking with Lillian."

Shannon frowns, shakes his head. What just happened?

Maybe she's just being smart. Now someone stands beside Shannon, gazing up. Such a huge smile. Megan, of course. Shannon looks down at her. Did he just step closer? Did he give her the look? Of course he's talking to Megan, edging close to the pretty young woman. Of course they'll end up together. It's the way the world works. At least, it's the way the world has worked so far for Sally.

Sometimes this sadness feels huge. Sometimes, like now, it wants to engulf her. Why not just let it? She can walk right into its comfortable room, she can pull up the armchair, sink into its softness. She can slide off the chair right down to the floor and let sadness wrap her in its billowy arms. Yes. This is what she wants to do. Just lie down with sadness.

But there's this old woman walking beside her. There's this woman who has lost her home and much of her mind, and this woman is still moving forward. This woman won't stop. Sally reaches out, takes Lillian's arm.

In the dining room, people sit at the tables. The sweet scent of syrup lingers. But she and Lillian are not joining in. They keep walking.

23.
searching for home

"Lillian, I have something for you."

It's the little woman who thinks she's the boss. She's reaching toward Lillian with something that looks like a black mask. Lillian looks up from her puzzle. "I need you to try this on," the boss woman says. "Please."

It's hard to pull away from the puzzle. Lillian has been holding a cardboard piece in her hand, trying to find where it fits. This puzzle box shows a Thanksgiving dinner with a big table laden with turkey and stuffing, lots of happy kids and adults, a mom and dad holding hands, a puppy barking below. Lillian wants to put the pieces together, help this family eat dinner. Without her they'll stay just pieces of cardboard strewn all over a table. But if she can make the pieces fit, the family can be together again.

Where is her family? Where are Daniel and Annie?

Lillian shakes her head no to the boss woman. She focuses on the puzzle. She's been working on this puzzle a long time and has to keep the others away. They just mess it up. Most of the puzzle has come together, but there's a big hole in the center where the turkey should be. Where is the turkey?

"Please, Lillian. Please try this. It's important," the woman says. The boss woman holds out the mask. She's smiling one of those smiles that makes Lillian feel prickly inside, since she can't tell if it's real. "I think you'll really like what you see," she says, thrusting the mask out to Lillian. Now she's putting something on Lillian's head.

Ugh. No. Lillian jerks away.

"Okay, sorry. That was too fast," the boss woman says. She puts the mask over her own head. It has a wide strap that covers the top of the head, with big goggles over the eyes. The truth is, it looks ridiculous, like the boss woman is a huge ant with weird hair sticking out. "See?" the boss woman says from under the mask. "It's okay. It doesn't hurt. And you can see wonderful things when you look inside." The boss woman takes off the mask, places it again on Lillian's head.

Okay, she'll give it a try. Then maybe the boss woman will go away. But it's all black inside. Now the boss woman presses a button and suddenly Lillian hears the roaring of waves. She sits up straight. Now she sees the waves too, sees waves pounding a shoreline. They are moving closer and closer. She starts waving her arms. Help!

"Lillian? Don't you like that?"

No, she does not. The waves are chasing her, almost grabbing her feet! And where is Annie? The only time she and Dan took Annie all the way to the ocean, the little girl zoomed right out into the surf and for a moment they couldn't find her. Lillian dashed into the water and even when waves splashed high on her chest, she kept going. *Annie!* she had called out, but suddenly the surf pulled her down and spun her around so she couldn't breathe. It felt like being inside a washing machine with the lid closed tight, tossing and heaving beneath monster waves. Lillian thought she was drowning.

But she had to save Annie! She clawed water, fought her way to the surface. She gulped air. And when she looked back to the beach, there was Annie! Huddling in her big blue towel, her little girl was alive. But Lillian was so shaken, so upset, that she made Annie and Dan pack up their stuff and head back to the car. Of course they were all mad at each other for the rest of the day and all the way back home. No, she doesn't want to see the ocean again.

Lillian tries to pull off the contraption, but it seems stuck on her head. The ocean keeps pounding. She shakes her head back and forth.

"Oh, Lillian. Don't you like it? Can you watch a bit more?"

No, she cannot. She tries jerking it off again.

"Okay, okay. I can get it." The boss woman presses a button so the ocean disappears, and all Lillian sees is black. The woman lifts the contraption off her head.

She is frowning. "The thing is, we have to do something different," she says. "I thought this might help, give you something to do that you like. You can't keep going outside, Lillian, and we have to keep you out of other residents' rooms."

Going into other people's rooms? She would never do that.

"Let's try something else. Here's a walk in the woods. You like to walk, I know that. Let's try this."

This one's better, not scary. It's a winding path in a friendly woods, all the trees curvy and squat like grandmother trees, the sort that talk to you in Disney movies and give good advice. The leaves are a fresh, bright green, the sky a sweet blue, and even the brown path looks inviting. Lillian hears birds calling out and squirrels scurrying on the ground.

Squirrels! There was a grey squirrel that Daniel used to feed, that lived in their yard. Each night after dinner he took leftovers out to the squirrel. He sat quietly as the squirrel approached, until the animal was almost eating out of his hand. She loved watching him from the living room window, her gentle husband, her Daniel.

She pulls at the mask. She doesn't want to walk in the woods. She pulls at the contraption again. Where is her home? Where is Daniel? "Hmmmm," she says.

"You don't like this one?" the boss woman says. "Okay, we'll find another. I think there's a garden too, an English garden. That would be lovely."

Every woman Lillian ever knew loves gardening. But not her. She's not fond of plants, all those scary green things that jut right out of the ground whether you want them or not. What to leave, what to pull out? She never knew. And the bugs! Don't even talk about bugs. Gardening gave her a headache. No, she doesn't want to walk in a garden.

"Hmmmm," Lillian says. She looks hard at the woman, tries again, louder this time. "Hummmm."

The boss woman tilts her head at her. Her forehead is all wrinkled up. "Oh, Lillian. Do you mean home?"

Lillian nods furiously. Yes! In her mind she sees the white pillars of her red-brick colonial. She sees Daniel out back, feeding the squirrels. Oh, how good it would feel to walk in her front door again!

"We hope that sometime soon you can feel at home here," the boss woman says, smiling. "It can be a new home."

A new home? Doesn't this woman know that's impossible? You can't just get a new home. No. You can't just be plopped in a place with a bed and a chair and call it a home. No. Home is home. It's where you lived your whole life, the place you and your husband were young and in love, with a new baby. It's the place your child grew up, where she climbed the big tree in the backyard, drew on the sidewalk with chalk. It's the place you washed the windows each spring, cleaned out the closets. It's the place you painted the living room the exact shade of salmon you love, then sat in that room each evening, soothed by your favorite color. It's the place where your dead dog Timmy, the Boston terrier, is in the backyard, right next to Tony the poodle. And the cat Butterfly is beside them, and beside Butterfly is Happy Day, the kitten who was attacked by a dog. Happy Day! Just remembering the names brings back that precious time, your daughter a little girl naming her pets.

"Home," Lillian says now, looking into the woman's eyes. She grabs onto the woman's fingers. She grabs the black thing on her head, shakes it.

"You want to see your home in this?"

Lillian shakes her head vigorously. "Yes!"

Now the boss woman looks up at the ceiling. She doesn't say anything. When she looks back at Lillian, her eyes seem all watery, like she might cry. "I wish we had a video of your house. I wish we did, but we don't," the boss woman says. "And we can't make one because other people are living there now."

Other people? Lillian stands. Who's living in her house? Trespassers, that's who. They don't belong there. Why doesn't somebody kick them out? She takes a swipe at the puzzle, sending the Thanksgiving family scattering all over the floor. So what if they don't find their turkey? So what if they never see each other again? Lillian couldn't care less. This isn't her family. These people mean nothing to her. She walks away. When she spies a puzzle piece under a chair, she kicks it further away.

"Oh Lillian," the boss lady calls out, leaning down to pick up the puzzle. "I'm so sorry. We'll find something you like. We will."

Lillian walks as fast as she can down the hall. She won't find her own family until she starts moving. She will find them. She'll find her house, too, and kick the new people out. They don't belong there. She'll call the police. As she walks away, the boss woman is calling behind her.

"Come back, Lillian."

But she keeps walking.

• • •

How long has she walked? It's been a long time. She's still walking even though everyone else has sat down for a meal. When the brown lady tried to get Lillian to sit, she pushed her away. She's still walking.

When she stops walking, Lillian sees strange people living inside her house. How can that be? She sees a strange woman rummaging around in her bathroom, using Lillian's favorite shampoo, spraying her perfume. She sees a strange woman in her bedroom, under the covers, sleeping in her very own bed. The woman might not be clean. Is she staining the sheets?

She sees strange, grimy children in Annie's room, playing with her daughter's favorite Barbies. But where is Annie? Is she hiding in the closet, or under the bed?

These images startle her, bad dreams flashing in front of her eyes. Her stomach is heaving.

But all this walking is making her dizzy. Her legs wobble. She's wearing out. At the door of a room, she pauses. Someone is snoring inside. It's the room that she sometimes hears calling her name, like she's hearing now. Lillian! She steps inside. Someone is sleeping, and there's no one else in the room. A man in bed snores, shifts from one side of the bed to the other. It's the man who reminds her of Daniel, sleeping again. He sleeps a lot.

It would feel good to rest for a moment, before she gets moving again. Lillian gets into bed. It's cold, but when she presses against the man's warm back, she no longer sees the scary dream of strangers inside her house. She takes off her dress, then her slip. She takes off her underwear. Maybe this isn't actually Daniel, but he seems nice enough.

But it's cold being naked in bed. She moves closer to Daniel, scoots to cuddle his back. Now the scary thoughts are all gone. Daniel grunts, shifts, then goes back to snoring again.

A long time ago, when Lillian was cold in bed, she would put her hand in the bottom part of Daniel's pajamas. It was so warm down there, like a small fire. She would stroke Daniel's warm skin. He always liked that, and her hand would get warm, very warm.

Sometimes with Daniel she dove right down under the covers, and now she does this again. Oh my. It's dark and cozy down here, like being inside a tent. She's always liked camping. It's so warm, even though she is naked. It smells pungent, a spicy man smell. It's not a bad smell. It's like Daniel.

Some women don't like the penis part of a man, but Lillian does. It's so funny, so odd, just hanging there and then suddenly sticking straight out. Sometimes she touched it. She did other things, too.

What's that sound?

"Oh my god!" A person is shouting. It's a woman. "Oh my god, I don't believe this. What is going on?"

It doesn't seem a good idea to stick her head out of the covers, so Lillian slides down further in bed, down to the bottom part. Now she feels someone pushing her. Someone is hitting! Now the covers and sheets get ripped right off. She is naked!

It's the woman from before, the scary one.

"My god, what are you doing? Get out of here! We are locking this door!"

She throws Lillian's clothes right at her. Lillian grabs them, ducks as a shoe whizzes past.

The woman is still yelling, throwing things—a book, a hairbrush—as Lillian heads out of the room. It's as if Lillian's not a person at all but an animal, a creature loose from the zoo, a wild thing who doesn't even need clothes. And now she feels like an animal, something furry and free, a raccoon maybe. She scurries as fast as she can. It's faster than she ever imagined.

24.
bring doughnuts

Beth hates staff meetings, even in the best of circumstances. And these aren't the best circumstances. Aides and nurses are straggling into the conference room; just five minutes before the meeting begins. She feels queasy.

It's great being in charge most of the time, one-on-one. Telling people what to do? Yup, she has no problem. But meetings are different. They're unpredictable. Meetings go best when she can go with the flow, go with whomever or whatever hijacks the agenda, and someone always hijacks the agenda. And then Beth feels herself tensing up, hears the crisp edge to her voice that makes others tense, too.

So it helps to bring doughnuts. They blend well with the smell in the room, French toast from breakfast. A big box from Young's Jersey Dairy now sits on the table. Really, it's amazing how effective these balls of fried dough can be. They make her fractious staff seem cohesive, chomping and chewing in unison. And Beth needs all the help she can get.

But now the new aide, Megan, squints at a doughnut, tilting her head this way and that, as if examining the pastries for cooties.

"Are these gluten-free?" she asks.

Shit. Beth forgot about dietary restrictions, which get more complex all the time.

"It's a doughnut. There's no such thing as a gluten-free doughnut." It's Harvey the physical therapist, piping up in his know-it-all way.

"Sure there is. You're calling me dumb?" Megan steps back, her eyes wide. But she's kidding. Isn't she? Okay, it's a rocky start, and the doughnuts seem to be making things worse. Beth just shakes her head, shuffles her papers. It's past time to begin.

Most people are here. Even Harmony has settled into her doggie bed in the corner. Okay, take a deep breath. Lean forward. Now.

The sale went through, as everyone already knows. There are already some changes. Here's one they'll like. New Horizons will now offer employees an emergency loan fund, loans up to $1,000 available with no paperwork and no interest. It's a new perk, something the old management didn't offer.

Some are nodding their heads. But Jen from the kitchen doesn't agree. "Actually," she says. "The best thing would be if they paid us enough that we don't need emergency loans."

Grunts and clapping follow Jen's remarks. "Good point," someone says.

There are other changes as well. Beth announces that beginning next week there will be one less aide on the evening and overnight shifts.

"Next week? When exactly?"

Beth looks more closely at the email from New Horizons. "Actually," she says. "I guess it's tomorrow."

Groans all around.

"Damn!" It's Deborah, of course, looking at Beth over her glasses. "They didn't waste any time." People are mumbling, shaking their heads. "Can't you do something about this?" Deborah says, squinting at her. "Can't you stand up for us? You know this makes things harder for everyone else on the shift."

Heat starts in Beth's stomach, expands upward. She feels her face getting red. "Believe me, I know. I agree," she says. "I hate it too, but I can't stop it."

God, she sounds like a wuss. The truth is, she's feeling her way with Charlie. Before the sale, there was wrangling with the board, needing to be strategic with requests and changes, but no one was looking over her shoulder, telling her what to do. Now they are. At least Charlie is. And she hates it.

Now Sally is nodding in a way that feels supportive. Yes, remember to look at Sally, not Deborah.

"We just have to try it, see how it goes," Beth hears herself saying. "If it's a mistake, we'll push them to change it."

Deborah studies the doughnut in front of her. "Yeah, like after something bad happens. After somebody falls in the bathroom, breaks her neck," she says.

A chain reaction of grumbles floats up from the table.

Okay, try to breathe deeply. Be a leader. Give them some hope, even if you don't have much hope. That's your job. You can do this. "Look." Beth leans forward. "You guys are good. You do good work. We do a good job here, caring for people."

The room becomes quiet. People are looking at her.

"I'm so proud of you all." She speaks slowly, making eye contact with one person after another around the table. "I'm so proud to work here, to work with each one of you."

A ripple of yips bursts from the corner, and everyone turns toward Harmony, sleeping and dreaming. There's laughter all around.

"Excellent timing," Beth says.

People laugh. She still has their attention. "Yes, things will be different. We don't yet know how different. Who knows, it might even get better. There's a window now with the new owners, a window to bring in more resources. Doing new things might get easier, since we don't have to go through a board. We just go through Charlie. So there's opportunity here." Yes, keep speaking slowly, evenly. "But let's stay together. Let's be a family."

Sally is nodding vigorously. If only she'd speak up more in meetings, offer support. But she's careful, probably cowed by Deborah, like everyone. Still, others are joining Sally, nodding along. The new guy in maintenance flashes a smile.

Next Patti from New Horizons marketing appears at the door. She asked to be put on the agenda. Now she talks about social media, how the center needs to rev up its strategies. As if Grace Woods has strategies! Word of mouth, that's the strategy. Until now. Patti says they should put photos of residents having a good time on Pinterest. Testimonials on Facebook. Instagram! Around the table, the younger staff members nod vigorously. It makes Beth feel tired.

Any new agenda items? People shake their heads no, seem ready to leave. Time to close down. Okay, that wasn't awful. As people begin leaving, Beth grabs a doughnut to reward herself for running a not-too-bad meeting.

It happens so fast, Beth feels herself reeling. The door bursts open. A woman hurls herself into the room. It's the bottle-blonde, Thomas's daughter. She plants herself in front of Beth's chair, begins screaming. Staff members look shocked; they freeze, stare at the woman.

"Oh! My! God!" the woman is yelling, leaning over her. Beth can smell her breath, her face is so close. Her breath smells like bananas. "That woman was in my dad's room again. In his bed! My father is dying and I shouldn't have to put up with this shit!"

Beth closes her eyes, as if doing so could make the woman's words vanish. It doesn't work. Some staff members are slinking out of the conference room, others stand still. Her chest feels tight, getting tighter. It's hard to breathe. Couldn't someone stand up for her? But apparently no, they cannot.

"It's bound to happen," a voice says. "Lillian doesn't belong here." It's Deborah, talking to Megan as they walk out the door. Okay. Her staff isn't with her on this.

"Do you have no control? Are you that inept?" the woman is yelling at Beth.

Inept? This is the part where she should yell back. Staff members have stopped in their tracks, wide-eyed. They want to see this. They want to see a fight. But she doesn't yell back. She gulps air, then stands, wishing she were seven feet tall. Or at least, a bit over five feet.

"Let's talk in my office," she says to the woman. She tries to take her arm, but the woman jerks away. Still, she follows Beth out of the room.

• • •

In Beth's office, Thomas's daughter refuses to sit. She stands stiffly, holding on to the back of a chair. She's not a big woman, just tall and slender, but she has a way of twisting her face that looks like she's about to explode. "It won't happen again," the woman says. "If it does, you'll be seeing a lawsuit."

Well, of course. The woman's a lawyer, right? Beth takes a deep breath, tries to slow her heart down. What's this woman's name? Lexie? She needs to remember it.

The woman heads out the door. Then she looks back. "And you don't need to tell me about dementia. I know dementia. My mother has dementia. My mother has dementia and my father is dying."

Beth sighs. "I'm so sorry."

This is the moment in which things could get better between them. Should she reach out her hand? Touch this sad, angry woman on the arm? Tell her own story about having a mom with dementia? But none of it feels right, and the woman's already halfway down the hall. She watches her go.

When Thomas's daughter walks away, Beth closes the door. When was the last time she closed it when she was here, inside? She can't remember. But with the door open, she feels too exposed. Her kitchen staff is scurrying around, getting ready for lunch, but it feels like they're looking at her, angling for gossip to tell the others. They want to know what just happened. She doesn't want them to know. She wants the door closed. She wants it shut tight. She closes it. But with the door closed, the small office seems taller somehow, elongated, like a room in a scary Halloween movie.

Sitting at her desk, Beth feels especially tiny. She looks up at the ceiling, the single light. She feels small, very small, enveloped by towering walls. It's okay to feel small. She is small, in every sense she can think of.

What's that sound? Oh yes, Harmony, breathing heavily on her bed.

Things didn't go as bad as they might have with Thomas's daughter, but they didn't go well. Lexie will file an official complaint. Ouch. But of course she has a right to go up the chain with her complaint, now that there's actually a chain.

A complaint! Has anyone called her inept before? Filed a complaint about her leadership? Not one time. Never. Work is her core, her beating heart when other things fail. Sure, she's screwed up all sorts of things in her life. Her marriage. Too many friendships. But work? Never. She's been the quick study, the one who works twice as hard as everyone else. The one who moves fast, wins awards. That's who she is.

Harmony stands by the door, panting. She makes little whimpering sounds. Beth sighs.

"Not yet," she says. "Not quite yet."

The worst thing is, Lexie is right. The staff is right. Lillian doesn't belong here. It was a mistake to let her stay, and that mistake is harming others. Harming Lillian, as well.

And there's more. Lexie's anger, her impatience, her despair at her mother's dementia and the loss of her father—all of these are very familiar. And yet Beth couldn't connect, couldn't make things better between them.

Harmony is butting Beth's leg with her head. Shit.

"Stop it," Beth hears herself say. "Bad dog."

Outside the door her staff calls out to each other, Jen asking for help with the trays, Megan telling someone the plot to a new show as, judging by clanking sounds, she puts silverware on the tables. Usually Beth loves these sounds, the hum of a staff working well together. It's true what she said at the meeting, that she's proud of being part of this place. Usually. But today she no longer feels part of it; she's off by herself behind a closed door.

Harmony is whining, sniffing under the door.

"Bad dog!" Beth says in her deepest voice. "Bad dog!" she says, louder. She opens the door quickly and shoves the dog out as Harmony looks back with sad eyes, not sure what just happened. Beth makes a face, then slams the door shut. Shit! Now she's smaller than ever. Mean to the dog! She can't remember the last time she was mean to a dog.

She turns off the light. She studies the picture of Daisy on her desk, her father's hat on the wall. She reaches over, takes the hat off the hook. She places it on her head. It's a soft feeling, a melting feeling, rising up in her chest.

"Bethie," she hears a voice say. The hairs rise on her neck. Is it him? Of course not, it's her imagination, it's what she wants to believe. Still, it's his voice, and it's been so long since she heard it. She closes her eyes. Maybe darkness will keep him talking. "Bethie," her father says. "Did I forget to tell you? We all make mistakes. That's how we learn. Then we go on."

It feels like her chest is heaving in on itself, that her bones might be washing away. She's holding her breath, because perhaps if she stops breathing she'll hear him again.

"Bethie," her father's voice says again. "Open the door." She gulps air.

"Bethie," the voice says.

Beth takes off her father's hat, sets it back on the hook. She takes a deep breath, leans forward. She turns the knob. The door opens.

Outside, Sally is crossing the dining room. She waves to Beth as she goes by. Deborah scurries by with a large bowl. Edward and Lorraine are sitting at a table, chatting, already waiting for lunch. Others begin drifting in. The smell of meatloaf wafts into the office. It's the daily life of Grace Woods. It is Beth's place in the world. She's the leader. She'll sit here looking out as others look in. They can think what they want. They can think that she screwed up, that she's old, that she's inept. She won't hide. Life will go on.

25.
on the water

"Thomas?"

Thomas frowns. Someone is shaking him. But he doesn't want to leave. How did he get here with Sarah? Thomas doesn't know how he got here, knows only that he wants to stay.

They're on a ferry, he and Sarah, waves breaking around them, gulls swooping down, the sun shimmering on water. The air smells of salt, perhaps from the ocean and perhaps from the chips that passengers are holding up in the wind. Thomas isn't sure it's a good idea to feed chips to the gulls, but he doesn't protest when Sarah opens a bag. She holds a chip up in the air, as gulls suddenly drop from the sky to snatch it out of her hand.

Sarah is laughing, feeding the birds. He feels himself throbbing with happiness to see her so carefree, his Sarah, her brow always wrinkled, her difficult questions, her intensity. He loves that intensity, but he loves this as well, this new lightheartedness. Did he give this to her? Does their love make her this happy?

"Thomas?"

Something cold now on his lips, very cold. Thomas grimaces, turns his head away. No, he's not leaving Sarah.

Is this a memory? Is he making it up? He's not sure. He just knows it feels real, that he can actually see the shimmer of waves, smell the scent of salt in the air. He feels water splash on his skin, the waves are so high.

What is this?

It's a passage, this ferry ride. They're heading to Martha's Vineyard, their first vacation together. As he sits on the bench beside Sarah, tourists swarming around them, he sees that this ferry ride is something more, it's his passage from one life to the next. There's the life he left behind, the one with Marjorie and their little girl. He left that life back on land, far away. He left his family, just weeks ago. Just thinking about Lexie makes his heart hurt. What if he has a heart attack here on the deck of the ferry? Damn. But he's here now with Sarah. He chose this, his new life, and now he's crossing the water, moving toward it.

Sarah! She turns toward him now, her head thrown back, her dark hair streaming in the wind. You can only love so many people and he has chosen this one, this woman. He made the right choice this time, a woman who shares his curiosity for the world. He will start a new life with her. He's amazed to hold so many feelings at once, the heartache of leaving his old life behind, yet also this buoyancy, this uplift of spirit, beginning a new life, beginning again. He feels like one of gulls hovering above, able to dip and swoop in thin air.

Now there's something stiff again touching his lips. He hears a voice crying out. "No!" Stop!" It is his own voice.

Now it's too late. He shakes his head. He's awake. He's back in the world. Damn. He opens his eyes, then closes them again. He wants to get back to the ferry. Now someone is poking a stick in his mouth, a wet stick. Damn. He turns away.

"Thomas? I'm sorry to wake you. But we have to keep your mouth moist, or else it will dry out. That could hurt you."

Thomas looks up into the looming face of one of the nurses, the short round-faced one. He means to say something but only a grunt comes out of his mouth.

"I know," she says. "I know it's a pain."

She knows? She does not know, does not have a clue. She's holding a stick with a tiny pink sponge on the end, which she stabs in his mouth. Is the ferry moving away from him, taking Sarah along? He will swim if he has to. He'll swim out into the ocean and catch up with the boat, climb aboard from the water. Thomas sucks the pink sponge, if only to get this woman to leave.

When the nurse stops poking the stick in his face, places the sponge on his table, he turns his head again, looks out the window. He closes his eyes. Yes, he's back again, he feels the spray of cold water. The wind has picked up and Sarah's dark hair is flying. She's laughing, her upturned face split in half as she whoops into the air, feeding the gulls.

But wait. Now there's someone sitting in the chair next to the bed. A woman is holding his hand. How can that be when he's on the ferry?

"Daddy?" she says. She seems to be crying. Oh, he hates it when Lexie cries. It makes his heart hurt. She is reaching toward him but she's reaching across a wide expanse, she can't do it, can't quite reach and neither can he. She's not on the ferry. No, she's still on the shore and he's crossing the water. Could he reach out and bring her with him?

He sees her becoming smaller and smaller, still on the shore. Thomas feels himself trying to reach her, he's lifting an arm. He would bring her along if he could. But his arm is so hard to lift. It flops back down on the bed, and he feels himself floating, floating away from her.

But Sarah! Here she is, right beside him, moving across the water.

26.
letting go

Sally tries not to stalk Shannon's car in the parking lot. But it's hard—some days, like today, she has to walk right by it on her way to the door. So sure, she looks through the window. And though outside the car always looks amazingly clean, it's messy inside, with food containers strewn around, envelopes stacked on his dashboard. It's hard to not crane her neck just a tad, trying to glimpse the names on the envelopes. Is one from his old girlfriend?

They haven't talked since that night, when was it? Weeks ago. She wants to stop thinking about it, stop thinking about lying with him in her bed, how close she felt to him then. She wants to stop thinking about making love. When Sally sees him coming her way, she ducks into a room, or scurries after a resident. She's seen him stop, watch her, and then walk away. And why not? She's acting crazy.

Now she's cutting close to his front window. The passenger side door is open, with Shannon's legs sticking out. His big feet. He's talking to someone in the back seat. Damn! Sally walks quickly by. A high voice, then the low tones of Shannon. What if they see her? Perhaps they won't see her. Whatever is happening, no one seems to be looking her way. She leans toward the sounds that drift from the car. What is Shannon saying? Did she hear "love?" Did she hear, "I love you." Or was it "I don't love you?" Or was it another word altogether? Maybe "glove?" Or "dove." Or maybe "above?"

There's a woman's high voice. Is that crying? Is it good crying or bad?

Sally's heart thumps. She walks quickly. Now the back door of Shannon's car opens and other legs stick out. They are small legs, female legs, legs with flip flops on her feet. Small feet. Toenail polish? Of course. A bright shade of red. It's not someone who works here, not in sandals. Sally wants to get back into her car. She wants to gun it and run right over those feet. These feet are tiny and perfect. Sally's feet are big, and she never bothers to paint her toenails. Why should she? That would just draw attention. She doesn't want any attention. She doesn't want people looking her way.

A woman in Shannon's car. The old girlfriend? Maybe. Sally knew she'd turn up, but not quite so soon. Or it's some other woman, a new one. Damn. Of course, she can't run over this strange woman's feet with her car. But she wants to.

Damn. This not thinking about Shannon isn't working out the way she had hoped.

• • •

In Thomas's room, Sally leans over the bed. "Thomas," she says, but there is no response. No fluttering of eyelids, no hint of a smile. No squeeze of a hand. Thomas would usually do all of these things, but now there is nothing.

He is leaving the world. She's seen this so many times. She knows what to do. She dips the Styrofoam-tipped stick on the bed table into the pitcher of water, then places it in Thomas's mouth. It's a surprise, how quickly his mouth comes alive, how fiercely his lips close around the Styrofoam stick. He sucks loudly, his mouth a tiny animal with a mind of its own, hoovering in the life-giving water. Of course. Sally smiles. Thomas wants to stay in the world. He wants it so badly. At the other end of the bed, she reaches under the sheet. His feet are still warm. Death isn't imminent. Not just yet. Relief feels like a sudden swoosh through her body.

She starts, looks up. Did someone just cough? There's someone else in the room, sitting quietly in the corner. The woman introduces herself and points to her name tag—she's from hospice. As Sally keeps tending to Thomas, the hospice nurse sits by the window, shuffling papers around. She's young, with dark hair. Hospice nurses seem to always just sit there, getting paid the big bucks while others do the actual work. Others like Sally.

Sally reaches farther to make sure the sheets are tucked tightly at the end of the mattress. It drives Sally crazy when sheets come undone and her feet stick out of the end of the bed. She doesn't want Thomas's feet getting cold.

Well, he won't be feeling them getting cold, after a while. Damn. Something feels stuck in her throat. It's hard to breathe. She's done this so many times and still it feels new. It's new because this is Thomas.

She's holding Thomas's foot. She should let go but can't quite do it. His foot is so warm, and this comforts her. She leans over, reaches under the covers to take the other foot in her hands. She massages his feet. Can he feel that? She believes that he can, that he feels this small pleasure. She takes each toe and holds it, then massages the toe, the whole foot.

In her mind, Thomas is lifting, lifting out of the bed. He's heading up toward the sky. And in her mind Sally is hanging on, still holding his feet, dangling below. She knows she needs to let go, to drop to the ground while she still can. But she doesn't let go. She tightens her grip. Her hands are so strong. She won't fall. She'll stay with him. Stay here! She wants to call out. Stay with me!

Now the hospice nurse is looking at Sally. "How about giving him a little more water?" the nurse says.

The hospice nurses are so annoying, all so terribly young, like this one, acting like they're in charge. Even worse, once a family has called in hospice, they *are* in charge. What does this young woman know about Thomas? Nothing, that's what.

Still, Sally moves to the other end of the bed. She tucks in the covers, then dips the stick into water, gently rubs Thomas's mouth. He opens it, begins sucking. Sally swabs his mouth again, making sure the water is cool, but not too cold.

There's movement at the door. Now Thomas's daughter comes in the room. She sits on the other side of the bed.

"Do you have to do that? Stick that thing in his mouth?" The daughter narrows her eyes, watching Sally.

"It's to keep his mouth moist," Sally says.

Moist. How long ago was it? She remembers the conversation. For some reason Sally said the word "moist" and Thomas lit up and went into this riff about how "moist" is one of his favorite words, how it rolls right off his tongue, how his mouth feels moist when he says it. Just like Thomas, to get such pleasure from the tiniest thing. Like saying "bamboo." And ever since then Sally's aware of the feel of words in her mouth in a way she wasn't before. The feel of words! Thomas left her with this. He's leaving her with so many things.

She could tell Thomas's daughter this, how much her father means to her. His kindness. His curiosity. His pleasure in the sound of words. But no. She will keep it to herself.

Sally almost trips over the hospice woman's foot. She tries hard not to kick it. Such a tiny shoe, so perfect, with its little black bow. Good lord, another perfect foot! She wants to kick it so much. She wants to drive her car right into the room and run over this foot, too.

"I'm sorry."

Sally looks up. Who said that?

Thomas's daughter's eyes are so puffy they seem barely open. She is looking at Sally. "I've been so short-tempered," the daughter says now. "I know it's come out at you. And you're good to my dad."

Sally blinks. She looks down at Thomas's bedside table, rearranges pill bottles for something to do. What's the daughter's name? Lexie? "Oh," Sally says. "Well."

"You know—well, you don't know, I was a prosecutor. My whole life," the daughter says. "That was my job. You have to be tough, as a woman, to do that. You have to be tough all the time, so the guys take you seriously." She shakes her head. "I don't like what it's done to me."

Sally nods. She hears crying. Lexie is holding her face in her hands. The hospice nurse clears her throat. From Thomas, there's a soft snuffling sound.

Lexie sits up straighter. "I wanted to tell him," she says. "How wrong I was. But I think it's too late."

Sally is surprised to see herself reaching for Lexie, placing her hand on Lexie's shoulders. For such a fierce human being, she has tiny shoulders. "You can still tell him," Sally says. "I think he can hear you."

Thomas's daughter looks at her in a questioning way. Then she reaches out, takes her father's hand. "Daddy," she begins, and then she stops. Her shoulders are shaking.

"Take your time," Sally says. "It's okay."

Lexie scoots the chair close to the bed, leans her head on the edge. She reaches up, touches Thomas's face. "Daddy," she says, and she's sobbing again. Now she quiets, clears her throat. "I love you so much."

Lexie is stroking her father's face. She outlines his lips with her fingers.

"Forgive me," Lexie says, in a soft voice. "Please forgive me."

Now Lexie is draped over her father's chest. As her back heaves up and down and the room seems to vibrate with sobbing, Sally is once again moved by how thin Lexie is, how childlike her shoulders and arms.

In her mind, Sally sees Thomas rising up from the bed again. He seems to be soaring, up, up into the sky. He's moving away from the world. Now she sees that Lexie's holding on too, clinging to Thomas's feet. And she sees herself there as well, holding tight to his feet but cleaving to Lexie as well, both she and Lexie are dangling beneath, not wanting to let Thomas go.

Whoa! The room spins. It shimmies and tilts. But she's rising up in the sky, with Lexie and Thomas. Isn't she? Such a long drop to the ground. Yes, now she's falling, plunging through air. Is she still up in the sky? No, the dizziness is here in this room, right now, nausea in her gut. She is falling, actually falling, tumbling down. She feels her knees buckle, her elbow bangs on the edge of the bed—ouch!—as she drops to the floor. Things go black for a moment, then Sally opens her eyes. She's lying face down on the carpet. Her elbow throbs. Can she move?

"Sally?" a voice says. "Are you okay?" The voice sounds like Lexie. Now someone turns her, puts a warm cloth to her face. "Let me help," Lexie says.

27.
out and about

Lillian is sitting by the front door as the worker ladies busily clean up after dinner. She's mad. She's disgusted. People keep screaming at her, like that awful blond lady. And new people living in her home? Not for long. She'll kick them out. When the Bible man walks in from the parking lot and bends over the guest book, Lillian seizes her chance. As she slips out the door she feels wild, as wild as the screaming woman thought she was, as sly as a raccoon, as sleek as an otter.

Now she's outside.

But truthfully, it's hard to keep feeling wild, what with the asphalt, the hard surface of a parking lot beneath her feet. But she's on her own, out in the world. The breeze on her skin feels like a kiss. The air smells like growing things ready to harvest. The thing is to be brave enough to see what comes next. It helps to start walking, to act as if she knows where she's going. She heads down the street and turns right at the corner.

It seems to be evening. In yards people are doing evening

things, mowing lawns, tending to flowers. These houses don't look familiar, but the town has changed over the years. Even the Spaniards have moved here, although the grown-up Annie says don't call them Spaniards. There's another word that's better, but Lillian doesn't remember that word. She doesn't mean harm by calling them Spaniards, it's a word that says where they came from. And they're not from here, that's for sure.

Downtown now there's a Spaniard grocery store and a Spaniard restaurant. Sometimes Lillian sees the Spaniards walking down the street, and they always have lots of children.

The next house is a big white house with a circle of chairs in the front lawn. Painted in soft blue and yellow and pink pastels, the chairs seem poised for adventure. A party? Lillian hasn't been to a party in ages. Oh, sometimes the worker ladies put out ice cream and call it a party, but the old people don't talk to each other, they sit in their old-person bubble and just swipe at the ice cream. And where is the wine? How about cheese and crackers? These people don't know how to put on a party.

Perhaps if she sits in a chair she'll be invited to stay? Her legs are tired already. This pink chair looks good. She like the big arm rests on the sides where she can put her glass, if someone offers her one. It's been a while since she had a glass of red wine.

Two people on bikes pass her, waving. Lillian waves back. Will they come to the party? No, they keep moving on down the street. Now a tall woman walking a greyhound goes by. She waves too—such friendly people!—but doesn't stop.

Goodness, no one is stopping. No one is coming to the party! It's getting darker and colder outside, and here Lillian sits all alone. She doesn't want to be the only one at the party.

Now a family walks toward her. A short mom and dad, bunches of kids. Are they Spaniards? Lillian leans toward them. She thinks they must be, even though one of the children reminds her of Annie, sort of prancing along with long skinny legs, like a colt.

Wait a minute! Where is Annie? Is she at home, looking for grilled cheese sandwiches? Is she hungry?

The woman who says she's Annie tells her this is not so, says Annie is all grown now and can get her own sandwiches. She says she is Annie! Truthfully, this would be a relief. But Lillian doesn't believe her. She has to find Annie soon. She stands, pulls her sweater tighter. It's getting cold.

She walks up one street, down another. Where is her beautiful home, the red-brick colonial with white pillars? Lights in the house windows are coming on. Lillian used to love looking inside people's houses when she and Dan took evening walks. But sometimes walking at night made her sad. Sometimes when she looked inside houses and saw moms leaning over the dining room table, dads reading the paper, she felt something missing in her own life, her own home. What was it? She wasn't sure. But she wondered if the people inside these houses knew something she didn't, if they weren't living a life just a bit better than hers. Were they happier?

And when she started thinking like this, she couldn't tell Daniel. What could she say? That she was unhappy? How could she say this? Wouldn't it hurt his feelings? And there he was, not glancing into windows himself, just looking straight ahead as he took his purposeful strides.

No, she couldn't tell him.

Lillian hugs herself tight. Oh, she wishes Daniel were with

her now. Lights from a car loom down on her. Where did it come from? Lillian jumps to the side of the road. This car doesn't see her, or if it does it wants to hit her, because it's heading right toward her. Help! Lillian gets out of the way just in time. "Idiot!" someone yells from the car, some man sticking his head out the window. Her heart won't slow down. Goodness! Maybe she needs to stop now that it's dark, walk again when it's light. Her legs do feel funny, like they might buckle soon. In the morning she can keep looking for Annie.

Here's a very big house on a big lot. Lillian likes big houses because she knows the people inside are good people. She can trust them. There's a big deck out back. Oh my, the deck's filled with sofas, beds almost. They have nice looking pillows on top.

It looks like a long climb up the steps, but she begins. Her knees hurt. But she can do it. She can! At the top of the steps she's looking down into the yard and straight into a sliding glass door of a family room. There's a teenager lying on the floor, her head leaning into a computer, a TV in the background. Lillian takes small steps. She doesn't want to scare anyone.

Here's a lounge chair that's almost as wide as a bed. The pillow looks hard, but at least it's a pillow. Lillian sits. Now she lies down. If only there was something to cover her up. She takes off her sweater, tries it out as a blanket. But it's only a sweater, and her feet still stick out at the bottom. What about another cushion on top? Yes, there's one on the other long chair. But as Lillian walks back to her chair, the deck creaks. The girl inside looks up. Lillian stands very still. Now the girl goes back to what she was doing. That was close. Lillian moves slowly, carefully, back to the lounge chair. The new cushion almost covers her. Yes, that's better.

So much stuff on this deck. There's chaise longues and chairs, along with bunches of tables. There's not one but two barbecue grills. A table is all set up with a board and black and white chess pieces. And in the yard there's a pool with chairs just waiting for guests. Goodness! These people must have wonderful parties, high up here on their deck. Lillian imagines the deck on a soft summer night, crowded with guests. Neighbors are here, and friends too. Children scamper up and down stairs, dive into the pool. Clusters of women laugh together; men stand around in their baggy swimsuits like Dan used to wear. Lillian imagines the man who lives here holding court at the grill, swinging his spatula, guys with beers gathered around him. He's the king of the party. And his beautiful wife, the queen, is inside, refilling platters of crackers and cheese. Lillian closes her eyes. She can hear the clinking of glasses, the laughter of children, the splashing of water. Once, long ago, she was queen of the party! And now she's an old woman, trespassing on some rich person's deck. She doesn't know quite how this happened.

But at least she's here, where wonderful parties still take place. She looks straight up at the stars. The sky is the same. The sky was huge and dark and sparkling when Lillian was queen of the party, and it still is now that she's an old person who can't find her home.

She's tired. The stars stop sparkling as she closes her eyes. She'll try again in the morning. Tomorrow, she'll find her house, kick the new people out. Tomorrow, she'll find her little girl.

28.
searching the dark

Shitshitshit. Beth is trying hard to keep her eyes on the road. It's dark out, and she's heading back to the center as fast as she can. But she can't stop scanning bushes and yards, searching for an old woman who doesn't belong out at night by herself. Searching for Lillian.

When the call came, Beth was just walking into her house. It was a long, hard day. Since there's now one less aide on the evening shift, she stays later to help, pushing wheelchairs back from dinner, trying to fill the obvious needs. But she can't keep doing this. Should she try to find volunteers, maybe a college student? Someone retired?

And then Thomas. When Beth stopped by his room before leaving, she heard his daughter's muffled sobs. Outside the room, Sally was leaning against the wall, hugging herself. He's leaving them, fast.

Hearing the phone ring in her bag, she couldn't find it at first, then didn't swipe hard enough. The phone just kept ringing.

"Shitshitshit," she said, before realizing she was cursing at Joan.

Lillian is gone again, according to Joan. Apparently, she just walked out the front door after dinner, just after a visitor came inside. The night nurse and the maintenance guy have searched up and down the street but didn't find her. Should they call the police?

"Yes!" Beth shouted, sorry to hear how frantic she already sounds. "I'm coming in right away. How did this happen?"

Silence on the other end. "I don't know," Joan finally said. "Look, it's not like it's hard. She can walk out any time."

"You need to know," Beth shot back. "You need to know so it never happens again."

Now Beth's stomach churns. Joan is right. Lillian can walk out any time. It's not really Joan's fault. It's her own fault. Peering toward a figure on a front porch, Beth almost runs a stop sign. She slams on the brakes. Shitshitshit. The figure walks into the house.

At the center, several employees are huddled at the front door talking to a police officer. Seeing Beth, they look relieved. There's Shannon, the new guy, and dependable Norm, newly retired, who's come back for the emergency and is passing out flashlights.

"Boss, you don't need to go out. It's cold," Norm says. "Stay here; we'll keep in close touch."

Beth shakes her head. "Of course I'm going. I'll head down Livermore. South? I'll go south."

"Okay, north for me," Norm says.

Ali, the nurse in charge, steps forward. "We think she was wearing a salmon sweater," Ali says. "Sort of peach colored? Pinkish orange?"

"I know what salmon looks like," Beth says, sorry that she's snapping at Ali. She'd apologize, but Ali has already walked away, shaking her head.

It's getting cold, almost dark now. What if Lillian gets a cold? Or pneumonia? Beth feels her heart speeding up as they take off in different directions.

In a big yard a beefy man is walking out to a mailbox. Beth heads toward him. She hesitates before speaking, not wanting to hear the words come out of her mouth. An old woman with dementia just walked out of Grace Woods. Has he seen her?

"Oh, jeez," he says. "I'll get my coat. I can help."

This is bad, the sort of thing that makes total strangers drop what they're doing and join in the search. Still, she's grateful for help.

With the officer, Shannon, Norm, the beefy guy, and herself, five people are searching for Lillian. How long can one old woman with dementia outsmart them all? Well, long enough for something to go very wrong. It's getting colder and darker. Beth checks her watch. Lillian has been gone almost an hour. Beth feels her heart slam in her chest.

She peers into the yards of the houses she's passing. Some people have decorated for Halloween, orange lights strung through trees and front porches, plastic ghosts in the yard. It's a residential area, not much traffic, thank goodness, but no sidewalks. Still, would Lillian have the sense to stay off the road? Whenever a car goes by, Beth holds her breath.

What does Lillian have the sense for? What can she do? Some days Lillian seems completely befuddled, yet other days she surprises Beth, surprises everyone with her moments of clarity. People know so little about dementia, so little about what people can do.

Now she's passing a large white house with a big yard. There's a grouping of chairs in the front, arranged in a circle. Beth aims her flashlight. In her mind's eye Lillian is sitting in the circle expectantly, waiting for others to join her. Beth smiles. While Lillian doesn't exactly love other people, she loves getting attention. But the chairs are all empty. No Lillian.

A dog barks, a big dog. Is it tied up? Beth's heart skips a beat. Now a car passes going too fast, and she practically jumps out of the street.

"Lillian?" Beth calls out once, then again.

What is it like to be Lillian, alone in the dark in a strange neighborhood? It must be terrifying. Beth's stomach tightens as she imagines the old woman falling as she tries to find her way home, or being charged by a dog, or hit by a car. And it's all because Beth made a bad decision. An awful decision. Was it hubris? Sure, it was. It was Beth thinking she knew better than everyone else, taking a chance with a human life. Lillian's life.

What if this had happened to her mom? What if her mom had walked out of the facility and into a strange neighborhood in the dark? Beth would have been frantic, of course. But this never happened because her mom was behind a locked door.

But maybe, for Lillian, being out in the world isn't terrifying? Maybe she's having a good time? She might be excited, traipsing through the night by herself. With Lillian, you never know. Above Beth now there's the hooting of owls; below, the crackling of leaves. In yards squirrels are screeching and scampering. It's chilly, yes, but not freezing. The air smells of dried leaves and earth, an autumnal smell. Beth takes a deep breath. It smells wonderful.

But it doesn't matter if Lillian's having a good time or not. Of course she's vulnerable. Of course she's in danger. And while Beth is sorry to feel the thought slip into her mind when she should only be thinking about Lillian's safety, it's already there, a jagged edge lodged behind everything else. She'll lose her job now, for sure.

Beth is passing a sprawling dark house when a bush by the door seems to move. Wait a minute. Is that a person? Can Beth just waltz into someone's property? Yes, she can. She darts up the front walk. But when she reaches out to the bush, she feels only leaves. She'll never find Lillian by staying out in the road. These days, do people get shot for trespassing? Or is that only in Florida? She'll find out.

Now she cuts through a side yard, keeping her flashlight aimed low. Shit, the light's getting dimmer. She shoves it into her purse, pulls out her phone. Okay, the phone flashlight works. Inside the house she sees the backs of heads in chairs, the bright square of TV. It's getting colder. She digs in her bag for her hat. What's Lillian doing to stay warm?

"Lillian," she calls out, but not so loud that the people inside will hear. "Lillian!"

Where would she be if she were Lillian? She would go home, of course, but Lillian's home is in another town, another state. Of course, Lillian probably doesn't know this. Beth tries to imagine herself inside Lillian's brain. Hmmm, this is interesting. She sees in her mind an imaginary plate of food at a pretend table, feels herself lifting the plate, higher, higher, now dumping it, potatoes and eggs flying every which way. She sees the others scooting away, watching her in alarm. Beth imagines herself with just a hint of a smile as people scramble around her, swiping washcloths to clean up the mess that she made.

Hmmm. Here's the surprise. Thinking like Lillian, Beth feels her mind getting not smaller but bigger. Or not getting bigger, exactly, but it's definitely different. She can't think about options, she can't weigh this fact over that, she can't plan a course of rational action. No, imagining herself thinking like Lillian, she can't do these things anymore. But she can do something else. What she can do is see that thinking she knows what's up and what's down, what's true and what's false—well, none of that makes sense anymore. And thinking like this feels freeing, almost expansive. This thing in front of her, a dark metal hood with four legs beneath, Beth sees it now not as a grill, not as something with a particular function, cooking hamburgers, no, not anymore. No, it's just a dark metal thing that feels cool to touch, comforting when she strokes it. And these metal spatulas hanging here on the side? These aren't spatulas, no, they're shiny things that could become weapons, or maybe something to put in her pocket to rattle around. In her new way of thinking, Beth sees that these things don't have names, or uses, or any of the other ways we diminish them. They are just what they seem, interesting objects, full of wonder, of new possibilities. The world according to Lillian.

Beth shakes her head. It is surprising, thinking this way, although of course she actually has no clue how Lillian thinks. What would Lillian do alone in the dark? Beth sees she has no idea, no idea at all.

From inside the house, a dog barks. There's the dog, at the window. Here's a new yard, and Beth sprints into it. The house windows are dark. In the backyard sits one of those miniature barns. Yes, Lillian might go inside. Beth runs toward it, low to the ground. The door is unlocked. She aims the light. Not much to see, just a lawnmower in the corner, rakes hanging on walls. A big bag of mulch pumps out a cedar aroma. But no Lillian.

Whoa. Something presses against Beth's shin, something slinky and warm. An animal, rubbing against her. She lets out a shriek. Shit! It's just a cat, sprinting away. She made too much noise. But inside the big house no one seems to have heard.

"Lillian!" Beth calls out, she hopes loudly enough but not too. "Lillian?" Beth bends toward the ground, takes off toward the next yard. How long since she's raced around strangers' backyards? Maybe never? It feels oddly exciting.

And yes, she did do this before, ages ago. As a kid. It's been so long since she remembered. Each night after dinner and just before bed, Beth and her friends ran wild, careening from one backyard to the next in the neighborhood, running loose, like a pack of small ponies. Beth felt like an animal then, wild, dirt-covered, smelling like air and moist earth. She was the fastest! She outran the rest, she even outran Dickie Hanshew, who lived down the alley. Everyone, even Dickie, knew she was the fastest.

What was that game? Yes, they were horses, wild horses, and she was the leader. She was Blaze Star, the head mustang. She ran first, ahead of the others, galloping, leading her herd. She felt fearless then, leaping bushes and gardens, running faster as light bled from the sky, stampeding, trying to outrun the night as the darkness, the unknown, loomed both scary and thrilling.

They ran until their moms appeared at back doors, calling them in. Then she and her friends slowed down and trotted back home, suddenly tame and exhausted. Still, that sense of freedom, of wildness, lingered just like the smell of damp earth, which her mom never could wash off in the bath.

It was ages ago. What happened to that little girl? Where did that courage, that wildness go? She grew up. She no longer ran so fast that she felt like the wind, was no longer queen of the mustangs. She got a job, then another job. She got married. Who knows what happened?

"Lillian!" Beth calls out. "Lillian!"

She hears herself call out again. She hears how frantic she sounds. Now a sound pierces the night, a jazzy tune that floats up from her hand. Oh, it's the phone. Beth sees that it's Charlie. Shit. She asked Ali to call him because, well, they had to. Of course.

She holds the phone to her ear. This is bad, Beth hears Charlie say. She believes she can see his white teeth flash in the darkness.

"We need to talk. Tomorrow. This is bad," he repeats.

"Yes," Beth says, hearing the words tumble out before she can stop them. "Think of the lawsuits."

A silence. A long silence. She hears Charlie take a breath on the other end of the line. "Actually," he says. "I wasn't thinking of lawsuits. I was thinking of the resident. As I'm sure you are, too."

"Yes," Beth says, closing her eyes. "I'm sorry." She heads back to the street and walks slowly now, aiming her phone light into yards. When the phone rings again, it's the police.

Maybe Lillian's been found? But no, the officer says they'll go another half hour, then they'll call off the search for the night.

"We can't stop," Beth says, using her deepest voice. "We have to keep going."

The police will keep looking, the officer says, but citizens have to go home. That means her, too. They can't risk injuries, having people just wandering around in the dark. They'll start again first thing in the morning.

"I'm not stopping," Beth says, banging her phone shut. Inside houses, lights in living rooms are being turned off as second floor lights come on, then go off again. The darker it gets, the more things look blurry. The edges of houses and garages seem to bleed into the night, porch lights morph into streaks of yellow. Beth shakes her head. She needs new glasses.

Most houses are dark now. She'll keep walking. Lillian is out here, somewhere, alone in the dark. It feels like Beth's mother is lost here as well, maybe everyone with dementia who the world doesn't yet know how to care for. And then there's that little girl, that wild child leading her herd through neighborhood backyards at night. Where is she?

Beth will keep walking.

29.
one more day

Sarah!

She's here. Thomas can't quite believe it. His eyes are closing, but he so wants to open them again, to see her. Yet it's hard. His eyelids so heavy, like tiny pillows have been placed on each one. His body so tired he can't move. But his Sarah is here, and it's not a dream. No, she has come to him. He'd know her anywhere, all that dark hair.

He opens his eyes just a bit. So much light! He doesn't remember this, doesn't remember light as a shock every morning, so much light from the day slashing its way into his awakening brain. But here it comes, a flash and a burst, like the fireworks he and Lexie saw every year, the night sky exploding in color.

Is Sarah smiling? He thinks that she is. There she is, sitting in a chair at the end of his bed. She's writing something. Just like always. What's that? It looks like a name tag, on her chest. But he knows who she is!

Yes, he's in his bedroom. Now something seeps through his

lips. It's cold! Thomas feels himself sucking, feels his lips move. Someone is squeezing water into his mouth; his lips are lapping it up.

It feels good. He hadn't realized how dry his mouth was, how parched, until he tastes this water. And water has such a taste! How did he never know that? It tastes like silver, crisp and metallic and with a citrusy edge and right now it feels like the best thing he's ever had. A sip of water! Still, even his lips feel tired, just from sipping.

He can't quite tell who is giving him water. It doesn't seem to be Sarah. She's still sitting, still writing something. Things look so blurry; is it the darkness? He knows he's in bed, yet he feels himself somewhere else too, although he doesn't know where. Yes, he's floating, floating on waves, on a ferry crossing the ocean. A woman hovers above him, the one with the water. He wants to look into her eyes, to let her know how grateful he is. Yet his eyes feel so heavy. So he closes them.

"Thomas?"

Who is speaking?

A soft voice makes its way to his ear. He knows this voice, though he doesn't know who it is. "I'm having a baby," the voice says. It seems to be close to his ear. A baby? "I don't know what kind it will be. I mean, girl or boy. But I want you to know."

Thomas blinks, tries to open his eyes. The shape above him so fuzzy, he can't make it out.

"If it's a boy, his name will be Thomas." Is it Sarah? Is she having a baby? "Thomas," the voice says. "After you."

Thomas. Yes, that's him. That's his name.

"And if it's a girl? Well, I'm not sure exactly. Thomasina?

We'll figure out something." Someone, the person above him, is holding his hand. Such warm skin! It feels so good to hold someone's hand, to feel the warmth of this person's body, even if he doesn't know who she is.

Thomas. It's a good name, an honest name, a rock-solid name. It has served him well. He likes the sound of the name; he would like this name even if it weren't his, but of course it is his. He likes the feel of his own name in his mouth.

Are he and Sarah having a baby?

While this baby will grow into his own person, his own self, still he will carry something of Thomas into the world. Thomas will still be here, in the sound of his name. He feels his mouth widen. Is he smiling? It hurts a bit, to move his muscles this much.

Sarah is still here. In his real life. Thomas looks now at her, her dark hair falling around her face. She's sitting next to the bed, absorbed in her thought, still writing. Of course. That's his Sarah, always thinking. How lovely she is, lost in thought.

Still, he wants her to look up, to see him. Why isn't she looking his way? Why doesn't she speak? Still, she's here. Her presence soothes him. He wants to call out. Thomas opens his mouth but this is hard too, his jaw heavy, so much effort required. Pushing even the smallest sound from his mouth feels beyond him. But he wants to tell her what it's like, dying. She was the one who listened, always listened. She'd want to know, he's sure of it.

He would say he's still frightened. He would say he still can't imagine no longer being a part of this world. He would say that thinking about it still sends a wave of cold fear pulsing through him.

And yet. He'd also tell Sarah that dying is different than he imagined. When he's not drifting off somewhere, off into space, he feels so intensely alive. All of these memories, cascading through him, lighting him up. Sometimes his memories get bigger and brighter until he seems to be living them all over again. The memories tumble on top of each other so that each is held in another, and when they open out, he sees they're not separate at all, no, they're all part of each other.

And time goes so slowly! These moments when he's awake—hearing the song of a bird, feeling the softness of sheets—crawl by as if they won't end. Finally, time has slowed down. It's like he's living a whole extra life, packed into these moments.

Yes. He wants to tell this to Sarah.

Thomas opens his mouth, but again, nothing comes out. How did she get here? She came from so far away. He wants to say how thankful he is that she came.

But he's not ready! He's not ready to leave the world. He doesn't want to leave Sarah. He doesn't want to leave the sound of the birds. He'd like more of it. He'd like one more day.

But what is that sound? It's a weeping sound, low and mournful. Someone is crying. Is it Sarah? No, Sarah's head is still bent over her papers. Someone else is making the sound, someone at the end of the bed. Someone who is holding his hand.

Oh Lexie! Please don't cry. He always hated to see her cry, see how her whole face collapsed in when she was a child, how her little features squished up and he worried his little girl's sorrow would swallow her whole. Lexie always seemed to be crying, she wanted this or that, she was mad at her mother or someone at school was mean to her. He remembers coming home from work at the end of the day and thinking, please, Lexie, stop crying!

Just give me a few minutes here to get settled. And deep down he blamed himself. What sort of father had such a child, what had he done to make her unhappy?

Now she is holding his hand. She is squeezing it. "Daddy," she is saying. "Oh, Daddy. I will miss you so much."

He is making her cry. This time his dying is making her cry.

"Please," she is saying. "Please forgive me."

Forgive her? If he could, Thomas would say this to his daughter: You were just being human; you were a mash of feelings and fears just as I was, and our fears got all out of whack, they tangled until we had to be apart for a while. Oh, if only he understood this at the time, if only he didn't take it so personally. Of course I forgive you, Thomas would say if he could. Also: there is nothing for me to forgive.

But Thomas can't speak. Yet he feels his daughter's pain, how his dying is making her weep. What can he do? He can do something. His love for Lexie, like his love for Sarah, feels huge. He feels his love as a surge lifting the ferry, higher, lifting it on the water. Even though his body can't move and his mouth can no longer speak, he feels this love buoying him up, like waves on a shining sea.

For Lexie, he can be brave. He can offer her only one thing and that thing is a good death, a gentle death, a death that doesn't make her suffer more than she has to. He can do this. He is so frightened. But this wave of love makes him strong. Did he ever know before how strong love can be? He's not sure. But he knows it now. He will stop crying. He will die in peace, not in anguish. He will try to do this.

He can give Lexie this. And Sarah, too.

Up, up, one wave, now another.

Outside, the birds are beginning to sing. He can hear them! He is grateful to them. They are helping him, in their way. They are carrying him. Now the birds have turned into sea gulls, squawking their calls. What? The gulls are dipping and diving, coming close to him.

What is this?

He's on top of the water, on the ferry again. He feels the spray of cold water. He hears the gulls. He seems to be moving from this place to the next, lifting out of this world. Sarah is no longer with him; she is waving to him from the shore. Ah, but how can he be making a crossing if there's nothing there, on the other side? Where is he going? He doesn't believe in a place after death. He never has.

And perhaps there is no spot where he's heading. Perhaps he's just moving in place. Perhaps he's just feeling the swell of the waves, the spray of cold water, hearing the call of gulls overhead. Perhaps he's not going anywhere. And perhaps that is enough. Just this.

He can do this.

Still, he wishes he had one more day.

30.
fly away

When Sally comes on her shift, she goes straight to his room.

The hospice nurse is standing, looking out the window, talking into a phone. Lexie is holding her head in her hands. She is crying. Great deep sobs pour out of her.

The hospice nurse turns. "It just happened. About twenty minutes ago?"

Sally places her hand on Lexie's shoulder. Her small shoulders are quaking. "I'm so sorry," Sally says.

When Sally fell to the floor a few days ago, Lexie took care of her. She washed Sally's face gently with a warm cloth, then helped her up. She sat with Sally until the room stopped spinning, then walked Sally out to her car. Humans! That's what Thomas always said, smiling and shaking his head. They're full of surprises.

Now Lexie's sounds are muffled, watery. She reaches up, takes Sally's hand. "Oh god," she says. "Oh Daddy!"

Thomas's hand is still warm. Sally sits next to Lexie, on the side of his bed. Thomas lies on his back, his eyes still open. But he is gone. He doesn't look to be in pain or distressed. He just looks like Thomas, thinking something interesting, being amused by the world. Sally reaches up, closes his eyes.

"I'll wash him," she says, and the hospice nurse nods.

Does it really matter if the water is warm when she wipes a dead person down? Still, she wants to get the temperature right. In the bathroom, she sticks her finger into the water streaming out of the faucet. Her hands are shaking. She doesn't want him to get cold. She pauses, holding the washcloth in her hand. Sally grabs the porcelain, holds on. She can do this. She can take care of Thomas. She can care for his body.

In the bedroom. Sally starts with his arm. She lifts it. She washes first the outside of his arm, then the tender skin inside, then his armpits. All the while, she hears the sobbing noises of Lexie, the rustling of pen on paper from the hospice nurse. She can do this. She knows what she's doing.

His skin is starting to cool. How does this happen? How can a person be living one minute and dead the next? This is the part she doesn't get. A dying person may be sick, very sick, barely breathing, his body destroyed inside and out and yet his skin is still warm; he's alive. He still feels her touch. He can make sounds. Then everything changes.

Most people here at the center would say his spirit has flown away, off to heaven or some other kingdom or new consciousness. Thomas didn't believe that, Sally knows. He believed that what she sees here, his dead body, is all that is left of him. Sally doesn't know what she believes. All she knows is that this moment, caring for Thomas's body right after he's died? It's the most stunning moment she knows, the moment that turns her world upside down. She wants to lean down and kiss him. The hospice nurse is looking away and so Sally does, she kisses him on the forehead.

Now she washes his hands, taking care to wipe clean each finger, the space between fingers. She cleans his fingernails. Now she unbuttons his top and washes his chest. His nipples are pink, still alert to cold air.

Sally drapes the sheet on the side of Thomas's bed close to Lexie so she doesn't see. Now she pulls off his pants, washes his genitals. She pulls the washcloth softly between his legs before washing his knees, his calves. Now she is washing his feet. She lifts each foot, holds it carefully, washes between his toes. She washes the bottom of his feet. A tiny piece of blue paper is stuck to one foot. When did that happen?

Sally takes a deep breath. Thomas won't be walking the earth anymore. It doesn't matter if he has something stuck to his foot. Still, she picks the paper off his skin. Gently, very gently. She washes his foot once again. Tears are welling up in her eyes.

"The crematory people will be here soon. Within an hour or so," the hospice nurse says.

Lexie is still by the foot of the bed, sobbing.

"Goodbye, Thomas," Sally says softly, so no one can hear. Her chest seems to cave in on itself. She stands still for a moment, tries to breathe. She touches his cheek. It's getting colder.

Now her hands relax. Sally lets go. Thomas wouldn't like this, yet she can't help but imagine his spirit moving up and out, he's flying away now, up, higher and higher, into the blue horizon. She looks out the window, to the maple he loved, the squirrels chasing each other, providing him so much pleasure. Is that him? That speck in the distance? It might be Thomas. She watches him go.

Now he's just a dark dot, alone in the sky. But she's still here. She's not flying. She's rooted here, in this place. She's still on the ground.

• • •

Sally barely remembers how to get to the cemetery. It's been a while. Two lanes snake through the grounds, and she should either take the first lane or the second. She turns at the first. This looks familiar. She pulls off the lane, parks on the side.

It's a warm day for November. Leaves crackle underfoot. Yes, these are the headstones she remembers: there's the Bentleys, the Hoovers. Have more Boyles died? There seem to be more Boyle headstones than before, when her father's sat on the edge of that sprawling family. Now his is not so much on the edge as in the middle, since the Boyles are slowly surrounding him. And their headstones so big! Lots of pink marble, borders of roses etched into stone. They look elegant. And also expensive.

And then there's her father. A tiny headstone, provided by the government. The stone was described as "upright granite," and at the time she was amazed and grateful that his veteran status got him a headstone for free. Of course, when he died there was no money for anything. So she ordered it.

The Boyles are taking good care of their headstones, which all look freshly swept. Leaves have piled up at her father's. Sally bends to push debris out of the way. The ground so cold! There's a newspaper in the car. She heads back to the car to get it. Okay, now she can sit.

While the headstone is small, it is dignified, like the simple white stones at Arlington. Her father a veteran! It continues to catch her off guard. He was in Vietnam. Why doesn't she know more about this part of his life? She knows nothing. He never talked about it, and she didn't ask. She wishes now she had asked.

"Hello," she says to the headstone. "It's been a while."

She seems to be the only one at the cemetery. Overhead, some sort of bird is making a racket. A nut drops to the ground. Sally looks up. A squirrel overhead, chattering away. She smiles. Thomas would love this.

Now an SUV pulls up a few headstones over. A woman gets out. Kids tumble out of the back seat. The woman sets out a planter of crimson mums as the kids scurry around, chasing each other. Is this how families behave in a cemetery? Well, Sally has no clue how families behave. There was no family when her father was dying, only her. A quick, deadly cancer, in the liver. Sally worked up to his last week of life—of course she didn't know it would be his last week—and then cared for him. Was he frightened? His eyes looked frightened as she scurried around his room, but she never asked. She didn't want to slow down, didn't want a deathbed scene where she would feel pushed to forgive him for his years of neglect, his preference for Jim Beam over her.

Did her father neglect her? Yes, he was drunk all the time. And yet. He was there. Her mother had left, years before. Still, her father got up each morning, stayed sober long enough to do his job at the warehouse. He earned a living for both of them. He never left her.

Now the woman and kids pile back into the SUV, head out of the cemetery. Overhead, birds are singing. She closes her eyes, listens. Thomas would love this. Did her father love listening to birds? Watching them? She doesn't know. There's so much about him that she doesn't know. Really, she never asked.

Let people surprise you, Thomas would say. Don't let your preconceived notions of who people are get in the way of seeing who they actually are. Well, her father won't be surprising her, not anymore. He is dead. He is under the ground.

But maybe Thomas meant this, as well. Maybe he meant that just as you can let others surprise you, you can surprise yourself, too.

"You tried, I think," Sally says now, reaching out to touch the cold headstone. "I think you were trying."

You can be someone you weren't before, Thomas would say. You can be someone new. You can start over, right now. You can start anytime.

31.
the raccoon family

"Hey," a voice says. "Who are you?"

Lillian opens her eyes. She sees the outlines of trees. The sun is coming up. Where is she? There's porch furniture all around, chairs and tables. Did she sleep here? And there's a creature standing in front of her.

"Hello!" Lillian says, staring at thin legs in jeans. Now she looks up, into the face of a tall animal with spiky green hair. Lillian blinks. Green? The creature has something dark on its eyes, like a raccoon. If this is a raccoon, then Lillian might be one, too. That would explain things. Maybe the mean woman was right, maybe she's crazy or wild. Or could this be a dream? She's not sure. But whatever this creature in front of her is, the creature seems friendly.

"Hey," the creature says now. "I think you should leave. Sorry, but you don't want to meet my parents. They'll be downstairs soon. I hear them upstairs."

Parents? Downstairs? Upstairs? The creature can talk. Where

is she? As Lillian looks around, she remembers last evening. Yes, she walked out of the place that she hates. She just up and walked out. And then she found this big deck and lay down. She must have fallen asleep. Now Lillian sits up. She's a little damp, this lounge chair is damp.

"Are you hungry?" the creature says. "I can bring you something before you go."

"Yes!" Lillian nods. There's a rumbling in her stomach. As the creature goes inside, Lillian surveys her surroundings. How far away did she get? It feels like a long ways away. The last time she slept outside was with Annie. Sometimes they put up a tent in the backyard and slept there the whole night. Daniel wouldn't join them; it was just her and Annie, but Lillian remembers how sweet and snug she felt, cuddled up in that tiny tent with her little girl. Oh! She hasn't thought about this for so long. Where is Annie?

Now the creature appears again. Lillian's pretty sure it's not an animal but a girl, since she seems to live in this house. She has a half sandwich in her hand, another wrapped in a baggie. She hands it to Lillian. "It's just peanut butter," the girl says. "I hope you like peanut butter. I do. I live on peanut butter."

"Hello!" Lillian says, and when the girl frowns, she wonders if she said the right thing. But now the girl is smiling again, so Lillian smiles back. You can never go wrong with a smile, even if the wrong words sometimes follow.

"I can help you down the steps," the girl says. "If you don't mind. You seem a little wobbly. And I brought a jacket. You might need it."

My, this girl is so kind! Yes, Lillian's grateful for the jacket because at least it's dry, although it's long and dark and baggy and not the sort of thing Lillian would ever pick out on her own. When she turns it over, she examines the words on the back: Arctic Monkeys.

The girl shakes her head. "Yeah, I know. Sort of ridiculous. It's a band. I used to listen to their stuff all the time but now, well, I'm sort of over them. You can have it."

Oh my. If Lillian didn't need to find Annie she could rest here a while, get to know this strange girl. But the girl is scanning the house, looking restless.

"You have to go now," the girl says, when they get to the bottom of the stairs. "I hear them inside. They're always yelling."

Lillian nods, takes the girl's hands in her own. These are definitely hands, not paws.

Lillian takes her sandwich and waves goodbye. She starts walking, crossing the big backyard of this house. At the street she turns right. She still doesn't recognize these houses. Thelma and Marion had big houses out in the new part of town, and Lillian often came to their houses for bridge club, but this doesn't look like that neighborhood. Could a whole new section of town have been built while Lillian's been gone? Well, they had to make a place to put all the Spaniards. Not that Spaniards could afford these houses. No, not at all. The Spaniards would live somewhere else. How long has she been gone, anyway? Has her town changed this much without her?

Lillian takes the half sandwich out of the baggie, chomps down as she walks. It tastes wonderful. But wait. What about Annie? Lillian can't eat the whole thing, though she is starving. She wraps up the rest of the sandwich, puts it in the pocket of the girl's jacket.

Maybe she could keep going like this. She'll keep walking and at night stop on porches and decks until she finds her own house. She could do this. People could give her sandwiches to take on her way. Long, long ago when Lillian was a little girl, scruffy men used to show up to the back door of her home and her mother would feed them. Her mother gave them a bag of sandwiches and sent them on their way. What were they called? Hobos. Lillian could be a hobo. For a while, anyway. She has to find Annie soon. The thought of Annie roaming an empty house with nothing to eat makes Lillian stop in her tracks, bend over to hug herself. Her stomach balls up with the thought. She picks up her pace. She must walk quickly.

There's something stuffed in the pocket of the jacket. It's a hat, a black knit hat with daisies stitched into the border. Lillian puts it on. It's good to cover her ears. More important, Lillian hates hats, she refuses to wear them. Now that she's wearing this hat, along with the new jacket, she's pretty sure she's turned into a different person. Or perhaps not a person at all. She's a monkey! An Arctic monkey.

She passes a woman getting into a red car. Maybe this woman has seen Annie? "Yes!" Lillian calls out. My, that was loud. The old Lillian wouldn't have raised her voice, but the new Lillian likes to be forceful. But she needs to get the woman's attention. Still, the woman frowns, gets into her car and drives off.

There's a thunk-thunk sound off to the right. It's a tennis court, two young men playing tennis. Now one of them hits the ball and they both look up as it sails right over the fence. It drops in front of Lillian. "Ma'am?" one of the men calls out. To her? She picks up the ball. It's a bright yellow, like the sun at midday.

She likes the fuzzy feel of it. She could use something soft in her pocket, just to touch now and then. She stuffs the ball into her jacket. "Ma'am?" the young man says again. "Over here. Please?"

But Lillian doesn't give back the ball. The person she used to be would give back the ball, apologize even, for the crime of having it land at her feet. But this new Lillian, this Arctic monkey, does not. No, the ball is hers now. The universe offered it, plopped it right down in front of her. It's a sign that she's on the right track. She'll keep the ball. She could give it to Annie. She waves to the tennis players, then walks off.

"Ma'am?" she hears the man calling after her.

Now big brick buildings appear, lots of young people moving about. It must be the new college she saw before, the one that suddenly sprouted up in her town.

Someone is huffing and puffing behind her. Lillian turns just as a young woman trots up.

"Whoa, your jacket! It's amazing! Where did you get it?" A young woman with red hair and a blinding smile is tilting her head at Lillian. "I mean, Arctic Monkeys is my favorite band. They're the GOAT, don't you think? I've never seen a jacket like that before."

"Yes!" Lillian says, although she's not sure what goats have to do with it. "Hello!"

The young woman squints at her.

"Well," the young woman says, frowning before she erupts into a smile again. "Nice to meet you!" She jogs away.

Did they actually meet? Was that a meeting? Lillian's not sure. But whatever just happened, the morning is going nicely, what with her new jacket and hat, a half sandwich and a tennis ball stuffed in her pocket. And now a new friend. Whoever this new creature is that she's turned into, she's happy to be her.

Wait a minute. A car has pulled up in front of her. What's that noise? A siren is blaring, lights are flashing. It's a police car. Now someone is opening the door. A tall man steps out. It's the same man as before, the man who started out handsome and then turned ugly. No! She won't let this happen again. The old Lillian would just stand here, let him lead her away as if she's a lamb, a delicate lamb who can't put up a fight. But the new Lillian won't have it. She's no lamb, she's a monkey. She takes off, through a yard. The policeman is following. He's moving faster. Well, Lillian can play that game. She can run, too. How long since she's tried to run? Her legs feel like she's running through pudding. It's been quite a while.

When her foot trips over something, Lillian pitches forward. It's the hard ground, smashing into her face. Eew. Her mouth stuffed with grass. She's eating dirt. It's cold and gritty and bitter. She spits it out. She rolls over. The policeman is standing there, looking down. He looks far, far away.

"Okay, I guess we have to do this again. You have to come with me," he says, leaning toward her. How did she ever think he was handsome? He extends his arm. There's still dirt in her mouth, crackling like sandpaper. She spits it out, up, up, up into the face of the policeman. He looks stunned, wipes his cheek.

"You little bitch," he says.

Is she a bitch? That sounds hopeful. Perhaps she's a bitch and a monkey as well, a bitch monkey, and whatever she is, Lillian sits up, tries to sprint away from the policeman. But his long arm shoots out. He grabs her. Do monkeys bite? Lillian's pretty sure that they do. She aims toward the pale skin on his arm.

"Damn!" he says, jumping away. But he's pulled something shiny out of his jacket. "Can't believe I'm cuffing a little old lady."

Lillian knows she is fierce, not a little old lady at all. She's wild, that's for sure. Her hands may be cuffed—ow!—but she still has her mouth. But now he stuffs something into her mouth that's mushy and tastes like aluminum foil, though she's never actually tasted aluminum foil.

"That should do it," he says, shaking his head. "Damn!"

Does he have to shove her quite so hard into the back of the car? He's muttering, still shaking his head. Okay, then. So what if he treats her like dirt. She is dirt, or at least, she tasted dirt in her mouth. She's a wild thing and he knows it. He has no clue what she'll do next. That's good. Neither does she.

32.
leaving

Beth kneels by Lorraine's chair. The old woman nibbles a bite of cake. It's Beth's favorite, carrot with chunks of pineapple, and Jeff the cook made it today in her honor. Now Lorraine dabs her mouth with a napkin. Beth smiles. It's just like Lorraine, always so feminine.

Harmony is beneath the table, hoovering up crumbs. Next to Lorraine sits Edward, who has maneuvered two slices of cake onto his plate, one hidden, unconvincingly, under a napkin. Everyone knows about Edward's sweet tooth.

Now Lillian walks by, scowling. She tilts her head and widens her eyes at the dining room, as if affronted by seeing them there, sitting together.

"Lillian," Beth calls out. "Have some cake with us?"

But Lillian just shakes her head. She keeps walking.

A demented woman walking in circles, a dog under the table scarfing up crumbs, old people dressed in their best to eat cake and, well, to honor her. People who think she's a rock star, a hero.

Beth smiles. Ah, yes. This is her world. "Lorraine," she says.

Now Lorraine looks down at Beth, reaches out to her face. Beth's knees hurt, but she doesn't move. This is important. She tilts her face up, lets it be touched. She closes her eyes. Opening them, she holds Lorraine's gaze. Lorraine's eyes are blue, and she does not look away. Neither does Beth. She hears the clanking of plates, the human calls from the kitchen. Time slows to a crawl. Now it stops. Such a simple thing, looking into somebody's eyes. Is there a feeling more intimate? I see you! And yes, I am seen.

"You're so beautiful," Lorraine says.

And now Beth feels beautiful.

She will miss this so much.

Beth kisses Lorraine's hand.

"Lorraine," Beth says. "I have to say goodbye."

Lorraine tilts her head, as if trying to see Beth's words from a different, more reasonable, perspective.

"Not goodbye forever," Beth says. "But I won't be working here anymore. I won't see you each day. I have to leave this job. Today's my last day."

Of course, leaving is not her idea. Charlie canned her. He didn't even wait until Lillian turned up. The morning after Lillian escaped, Charlie showed up to say this wasn't working out. "This" meaning "Beth." She had defied his instructions, and there was that business with Thomas's daughter. But given Beth's four decades in the business, he'd allow her to save face, to announce her retirement.

Her retirement? Hell, no. She chose not to save face, especially not Charlie's face. So no, she didn't retire. She got fired. It's okay with her if everyone knows. Jeff whipped up this low-key party at the last minute, under the radar. Low-key is good. For one thing, Thomas just died. For another, well, she got fired.

Beth stands, moves next to Edward. "Edward," she says, as she touches his arm. "I have to leave."

He looks down at the table. "I know. Someone told me. I don't like it. I don't like it a bit." Now his hand disappears into his shirt pocket. He pulls out a tiny box. Now he extracts a ring from the box, a gaudy green ring with rhinestones, but a ring nonetheless. "It's my mother's," he says. "I want you to have it."

Beth takes a breath, then another. "Oh, Edward," she says. "You're so kind. But I can't take it. How about giving it to one of your granddaughters?"

He frowns, looks at the ring. "I'm not sure which one," he says.

She puts the ring on her finger. "How about I wear it today, then give it back when I leave? I would be honored."

Edward shrugs. "Well, okay. If that's what you want."

Now Elsie Bull reaches toward her. Elsie usually seems grumpy, and Beth never thought the old woman liked her that much. She rarely speaks. Even now she's looking the other direction, not saying anything, yet her hand has grasped Beth's hand, and she's holding on. How tiny and wrinkled her hand is, and yet how fierce her grip. Beth squeezes her hand.

Edward leans toward Lorraine. Beth has seen them together more often recently. Are they a couple? Beth hopes so. She reaches for the little vase on the table. The flowers look old, but at least they're real daisies. She'll change their water after everyone's done.

What will happen to meals here at the center? It's important they continue to be restaurant-style; the residents like it so much. Joan needs to stand up to Charlie. Beth sighs. She can't make this happen. She has to let go. Has she ever let go of anything, even once in her life?

Edward turns toward her. "Are you talking to me?"

"Sorry," she says. "Just a sigh. A loud one, I guess."

He nods slowly. "I know what that's like."

Now Sally walks up. She looks different somehow. She seems taller. Sort of glowing.

She leans down, gives Beth a big hug.

"You're the best," Beth says as Sally blushes, turning even more radiant. If only Beth had realized, before now, that Sally indeed is the best. It took too long, way too long, for her to see this.

Edward leans close, whispers into Beth's ear. "I'll miss you," he says.

The sadness begins in Beth's middle, oozes up to her chest. She doesn't clench her body against it or stiffen. Rather, she lets it flow. You can't outrun sadness here at Grace Woods; it's everywhere, every day. Beth has learned this. So you just have to feel it. She's feeling it now, the softness of sadness, its deep squishiness. It's not so bad, feeling it. And after the sadness flows through, something opens inside her. Beth doesn't know what this something is, but it's opening now, and it's stretching her, making her bigger, and she feels big enough to hold all of life, each bit of it, its sweetness and heartbreak as well. Look at me! life seems to be saying. See me in my glory! And Beth looks.

She takes a deep breath, twirls the ring on her ringer. She squeezes Edward's hand. "Yes," she says. "I'll miss you too."

• • •

It's the last box, and it's heavy. This one is filled with slippers and shoes. Beth is surprised how much stuff there was in her office, personal stuff she left over the years, stashed into drawers and beneath her desk. Sweaters and jackets, slippers and socks. Bottles of lotion. Vases that once held flowers, little gifts people gave her that she forgot to take home. It's like she was moving in slowly, so slowly that no one would notice.

And now she's moving out. She's walking across the parking lot, carrying boxes. Her legs feel wobbly. Can she really do this? Can she leave this place? Of course she'll be back, maybe she'll volunteer, help one way or another. But she won't be the queen.

Her legs are shaking. Maybe she can't do it, after all. Maybe her legs will buckle, right here and now. Maybe someone will find her collapsed in the parking lot, the center director who just couldn't leave. Beth stops for a second, takes a breath. The walk to her car appears endless. She puts the box down on the pavement. It's evening, and the air smells of autumn, the season of leaving, of leaves spiraling down to the ground. But then, at the Grace Woods Care Center, it's always the season of leaving. It's just that now it's her turn. Beth closes her eyes, takes in the scent. She can do this. She can go forward. She picks up the box and walks on.

In the car, she checks her rearview mirror. There's her building, glowing tonight, glowing and throbbing. And yes, it's humming, too, humming with life. She can hear it. She rolls down her window to listen. Is the building really humming, and trembling too? Is it quivering and quaking with the pulse of lives being lived? Yes, it is. Of course it is. Absolutely.

33.
new beginning

Sally's been trying to get the center leaders to perk up the staff room, so maybe she should be happy with this. It's not a new coat of paint, no. Rather, it's an art show of sorts, small paintings hanging around the room as if it's a gallery. Most of them are ink drawings of eyes, eyes in bizarre places. An eye perched on top of a cactus, an eyeball sitting alone on a porch swing.

Goodness. A note says the paintings are the work of one of the nurses, a male nurse who's been here almost as long as Sally. She didn't know he was an artist. She's not sure he is. Well, maybe this art show is a step in the right direction. Maybe not.

Sally intended to stop eating junk food today. But maybe tomorrow. She grabs a package of Doritos from the machine, sits back down.

The door opens. Sally's stomach jumps each time it does, then settles back down. It's just one of the kids who works in the kitchen, getting a soda. He waves, goes back out.

It's been how long since she spoke to Shannon? She begins

counting back days. It's been more than a month since they spent the night together, and they haven't talked since. Way too long. How did this happen?

At work he kept trying to talk to her, she could see that. But she avoided him, dashing out of rooms when he entered. She didn't know what to say. When she spoke to him in her mind, which was almost all the time, she heard her voice tinged with anger. Anger so soon! She didn't want Shannon to hear that ridiculous anger, so she just didn't speak to him. She was scared, is all. She just couldn't imagine him loving her. Anyway, he talks too much. So why even start? She is hopeless.

And then he vanished. She hasn't seen him in, oh, maybe a week? She doesn't know why. She doesn't want to ask the others about him, get them talking. Damn. Maybe he quit? Maybe he's gone for good. And she did it again, she pushed him away. Sally grabs another handful of Doritos, although her stomach already feels queasy. She pours more sugar into her tea. She knew the coffee is bad here, but the tea is much worse. Maybe more sugar. Who cares how much sugar she puts in her tea? She's alone in the break room for once.

Now the door opens. Shannon walks in. Her stomach falls to the floor.

His eyebrows raise when he sees her, then he looks down. He shifts his weight from one foot to the other as he waits for his coffee from the machine. He sits down across from her. He's frowning. Uh-oh.

"Well," he says, looking at her.

Sally nods. Damn, those eyelashes! Like a Kardashian.

He sips coffee, then looks around. "Whoa," he says, pointing to the wall. "What's this?"

Sally looks too. "I think it's art," she says. "It's Rusty's work, you know the nurse who's been here so long? Who knew he did this?"

"Huh," Shannon says, taking it in. "Who knew."

"It makes me feel weird, though," Sally says. "All those eyeballs. It makes me feel sort of, I don't know, itchy."

Shannon looks at her, then at the wall again. He smiles. "Yeah," he says. "I get that."

Does he? Sally thinks that he does. What is it with some people, that even mundane moments between you feel weighted somehow, heavy with some sort of meaning. It feels that way, being with Shannon. It makes time slow down. Sally had forgotten this part, but now she remembers.

"We need to talk," he says, squinting.

Sally feels herself tighten, yet she can't help but smile. He's such a girl! We need to talk. This is her line, not his. It's the line Sally said over and over to her past boyfriends, trying to get them to talk about feelings. She doesn't know why she kept saying this; it never worked anyway. She was the only one who ever talked about feelings. And here Shannon goes, stealing her lines in this movie.

Now his eyes widen, he leans back in his chair. "But first thing is this," he says. "Thomas. I'm sorry."

Sally looks up, holds his gaze. Oh my. His dark eyes look steadily at her and she feels herself held by his eyes, soothed by them. He seems to be seeing her, in all of her grief. Is she making this up? But of course it won't last. He'll jump in now, begin talking as if he's the one who was close to Thomas, not Sally. That's what a big talker would do.

But no. Shannon is silent, watching her. Sally looks at her coffee.

"He was such a good guy," she says.

Shannon leans in closer. He puts his hand over hers. "I know," he says. "You loved him."

His hand is so warm. Sally feels tears welling up. She closes her eyes. Now the door opens again and someone else comes in, she hears the rumble of a bottle in the soda machine. Whoever just walked in takes the soda and leaves.

Sally opens her eyes. Shannon's dark gaze is still holding her. She wants to lean into him, put her head on his chest. But of course she cannot. Still, she could do this more. She could do it a lot more.

Now something about the silence, its quiet power, pushes words from her mouth that Sally didn't expect to say. She didn't expect to be brave. Still, the words have appeared, and she follows them. "I'm sorry," she says now, her heart pounding in her throat. "I was avoiding you. I made it so hard."

Shannon nods, frowning. "You did," he says.

"I was scared." Sally looks into his eyes. "I just thought, you know, your old girlfriend would snap her fingers and you'd go running back. So I just didn't want to see you." She shakes her head. "It was stupid."

The coffee vending machine rattles and burps. On the other side of the door someone calls out, "Hey, turn down the TV," but no one comes in the room.

"Well," Shannon says. "She did come back."

Sally's stomach does a flip. Of course she came back. The woman with the perfect feet, sticking out of the car. Sally was right. This time she hates being right. So it's already over with Shannon. Before it began. Well, it began, that's for sure.

"She wanted to get back together," Shannon looks at the table.

Another flip in her stomach, plus one further up in her throat. She can't breathe. Sally closes her eyes. How much more does she have to hear? Outside a truck makes the beeping sound it makes backing up.

"But we're not getting back together. I tried. I tried for a couple of weeks. We went away for a week, to give it a shot." He looks up at Sally, tilts his head. "It didn't work out. It won't be working out. Not with her."

The beep-beeping of the truck gets louder outside. Sally realizes she is holding her breath.

"She and I, we were together a long time, like I told you," Shannon continues. "Too long, really. About fifteen years. But what I realized is, it wasn't because of her that we were together that long. It was me. I just loved the life. I loved living with someone, having someone there every morning and night." He shakes his head, looks at the table. "I just love that," he says.

He looks up at Sally. She nods. "But for so many of those years, she was unhappy. She didn't tell me. Well, I should have known and maybe I knew a little, but she wasn't talking about it. She just wasn't honest, with herself or with me. I don't think she can be. And I can't do that again." He tilts his head. "She said it would be different now. But I don't think so. And so I said no."

Now he puts both hands around Sally's hand. His hands are so big. For a moment she's sorry her hand is so close to the bag of Doritos, that he might judge her for this. But wait a minute. That's just silly.

"What about Megan?" Sally says, feeling her breath leave her as the words come out of her mouth.

"Megan? Megan who?"

"The young woman who works here."

"Oh, that Megan," Shannon says, nodding. "She's a flirt, a big flirt, is all. There's nothing between us."

He looks out the window, smiles, then looks back at Sally.

"There's something between you and me, though," he says. "Something in just that one night. I don't know what it was. But something. Did you feel it? I did. I kept trying to find it with Marianne." He looks down at the table. "That's her name, Marianne. I kept trying. But I couldn't find it with her." Now Shannon is looking into her eyes. "It's with you," he says.

Sally hears the ticking of the clock overhead. Should she be back on the floor? Yes, she should be. But she's glued to her chair. "Oh," she says, feeling foolish. "Well." Sally takes a deep breath. She takes several deep breaths. The clock overhead keeps ticking. The truck outside is beep-beeping. Now she feels her throat heating up. Oh no, here it comes.

"I'm pregnant," she says. "I'm having a baby."

Shannon's eyes widen. He pushes his chair back from the table so fast he almost falls over. "Whoa!" But now his face clouds over. "Is it..."

"Yes! It's you. It's yours! There's no other contenders, not even close!" Sally is laughing.

"Whoa!" he says again. Now his smile is huge.

He's shaking his head, looking at her.

"A baby," he says. "A baby? For real?"

"For real," Sally laughs. "Believe me, very real."

The door opens and the physical therapy guy grabs a bottle of water. He waves to them and walks out.

Shannon has pushed his chair out. He stares at the floor. He almost whispers, so Sally leans in to hear. "I've wanted a baby so long," he says softly.

Now they are sitting together in silence. The clock ticks loudly. Sally couldn't get up if she tried.

Shannon looks up. "So should we get married?"

"No!" Sally is surprised that the word comes out with such force, and she sees that it shakes him. Such a girl! This must be how guys feel when the female claims all the commitment in a relationship and runs with it, when the guy is still trying to figure out where he stands. It must be annoying. She leans toward him, smiling. "I mean, no, we can't do that yet. We don't even know each other."

Shannon nods vigorously. "Right. You're right. Okay. Well then, what should we do?"

"Look, I'm forty-two years old. I'm having this baby," Sally says. "That's what I'm doing. And it sounds like you want to, well, be a part of it."

"Yes!" he says.

Are these tears rushing up through her throat? Yes, they are. She lets them come; she can't stop the tears even though the staff room door opens again. She pulls away from Shannon for a moment. Whoever just came in, the person walks back out again. Shannon takes her hand again, and they sit in silence. Outside the truck keeps beeping, and Sally realizes it's like a bird song, only louder and brassier. She thinks of Thomas, how much he liked birds. What would Thomas say now, what would he tell her to do?

Should she risk it, loving Shannon?

Yes, Thomas would say. Yes, you should.

"I'm so glad," Sally says, although she seems to be whispering. They are silent again. The tick of the clock sounds like life, like life announcing itself. Tick-tock! Time is passing! Keep moving ahead! And yes, that's just what she's doing. She is moving ahead. She doesn't know why she feels so sure about this, why she never thought of not having this baby. But she never even considered it. She wants to do this. And she wants to do it with Shannon.

"So," Sally says. "We'll just, you know, have a baby. We'll get to know each other. We'll give it a shot."

Shannon's forehead is wrinkling. She likes this about him, how transparent he is. She doesn't have to try hard to read him.

"We'll give it our best shot," Sally says. "We'll do our best. We'll make it work."

Shannon is smiling again, nodding.

"And then, maybe, we'll get married," she says.

"Sounds good," Shannon replies. "Actually, that sounds amazing."

34.
monkey do

Lillian does not like this woman. She doesn't like her at all. The woman has too-black hair and a big butt, and she's trying to make Lillian get into bed. Her jeans are tight and worn low, so that squished-up fat overflows the top of her pants. Lillian wants to grab the fat roll, give it a pinch.

"Lillian!" The woman is yelling now as if Lillian can't hear. As if she's an old woman.

"Lillian, you have to take off the jacket. Right now."

No, she does not have to take off the jacket! She does not have to do anything. Lillian hugs herself tighter, clamps her arms across her chest so the woman can't pull at the sleeves.

"Damn it, Lillian! Just take it off!"

Lillian turns so she's facing the corner of the room, away from the woman's big ugly hands.

"Do you know what it says on the back? Do you know what it even means? Arctic Monkeys! It looks ridiculous!"

Lillian doesn't feel ridiculous, not at all. This jacket knows her. It's her friend. It knows just how she feels. The Arctic! This jacket knows that for Lillian, each day is a blizzard. The jacket knows Lillian feels cold and alone in this world. The jacket soothes her, tells her why she feels lost. It's because she IS lost, she's trudging alone in a faraway land, in deep snow and ice. She's lost in the Arctic. Of course! That explains everything. And the jacket also knows she's a monkey, a creature full of surprises.

Now the woman appears in front of Lillian. She's grabbing the jacket, spinning her. Before she can stop herself, Lillian reaches out, pinches that big roll of fat.

The woman widens her eyes. "Damn! That fucking hurt!"

For a second Lillian thinks the woman might hit her. She doesn't mind. She's ready to fight. And she's a monkey. She can bite.

The woman sucks breath. Her face is red, getting redder. "You're on your own now. Fuck it. Just do it yourself. You think it's bad here, Lillian, wait to see where you're going. Any day now. A place with locked doors! You'll never get out." The woman bolts from the room.

Fine! As if Lillian can't get ready for bed by herself. She'll take off the jacket, then put it back on over her nightgown. Sleep in it? Yes, she'll sleep in it, if she wants. But the sleeves do something funny, they drop to her elbows. They squeeze her, hold her arms tight. They're not letting go. What is this? Now the jacket seems not her friend at all, but her enemy. What happened? Why can't she take off her clothes? This shouldn't be hard. She sits on the bed, pulls on one sleeve. There's another sleeve underneath, and if she tugs on this sleeve everything will work out. But it's not working out. She feels stuck, her clothing has captured her, won't let her go. Heat flashes through her legs, her chest. She hates it here!

She didn't want to come back and they made her. Now everything here is against her, the worker ladies and even her clothing.

But a place with locked doors? What does that mean? Lillian imagines trying to get out of her bedroom, then finding the door is locked. What would she do? She sees herself banging on her bedroom door, desperate to leave. She sees herself rattling the doorknob, but the door remains locked. Would people come help her? Not if she pinches them. Not if she bites.

She's dizzy; her head might explode. At least she can get out of this bedroom right now, even if the jacket is holding her captive. She'll just keep it on, keep her clothes on. She can walk right into the hallway, though her arms are stiff at her sides. The hall is deserted, only a man pushing a cart full of trays.

The lights are low. At the other end of the hall, a woman walks slowly in circles. From here the woman looks like a zombie, already dead yet endlessly circling. Now a man with a walker comes out of a room, moving stiffly toward the circling woman. He steps back away from her, then toward her again. It's a zombie do-si-do, the sad dance of this place. But Lillian is not a zombie. She's not doing this dance. Why is she even here? She needs to go home. She needs to find Annie, make her a sandwich.

Where is everyone? Maybe that nice man who seems like Daniel might help her, might pull off her jacket. But when she turns into his room, he's not there. There's no one there, no covers or sheets on the bed, just a bare mattress. The whole room looks empty. Is this the wrong room? Where did he go? A queasy feeling slinks through her stomach.

Lillian stands at the back door, hikes the jacket back onto her shoulders. At least now she can move again. Walking would help calm her down. It's almost dark. Is that someone walking outside? She leans closer. Yes, it's the nice lady she likes, the blond worker lady, walking with the tall young man. She likes him, too. When he sees her he always laughs, then he winks, as if they're sharing a joke. Lillian's not sure what the joke is, but she likes thinking they have one.

The back door opens into a courtyard. The blond lady and young man are heading past the pond, toward the walking path in the woods. She'll stay back a ways so they don't see her.

Lillian opens the door. Oh my. Cold air blasts her face. If she walks fast, she can stay warm. Is this where they took the path into the woods? She'll follow them. Such tall pine trees. Everything smells different in here, a deep, earthy smell, like the dirt that stuck in her teeth when she fell into the grass. Wind rustles the trees. A squirrel scampers in front of her, climbs up a tree. Another squirrel dashes up after.

Why hasn't she walked in this woods before? It feels good to be here. When Lillian was little, she'd walk in the woods with her dad. The sounds! She remembers the crackle of her dad's feet walking before her, the leaves rustling, the calling of birds. But sometimes Lillian lost sight of him. Was she all alone? What if she had to stay all night in the woods with no one to care for her? Maybe she'd be kidnapped by bad guys or eaten by bears. She tried to call out—Daddy!—but fear gripped her throat, no sound came out until her dad suddenly scooped her up in his arms.

Lillian stands still. She's surrounded by trees. There's no sound of people walking, no crunching of leaves beneath feet. It's dark now. The nice man and woman must have gone back inside. But so what if she's alone in the woods? What's scary is not the woods, no, it's the building she just left, the old people inside with their zombie dance, their stiff do-si-dos. What's scary is being among them.

The sidewalk winds around in a circle, all smooth concrete, smooth enough for a wheelchair. But no wheelchair for her. She can still walk on her own legs, thank you. Where does this sidewalk go? She can stay on the concrete and find out where it goes, or she could veer right off into the trees.

Yes, she can veer off. She's pretty sure that's what a monkey would do.

And here she is, standing next to a tree. It's short and squat with comforting limbs that reach toward her like arms, a grandmother tree. Lillian leans closer. She embraces the tree, breathing deeply. The tree smells like growing things. She can feel the tree breathe beside her.

Now the grandmother tree says something. Lillian leans closer, puts her ear to the bark. It's a bit damp but smells strangely sweet.

"Keep going," the tree says. "Don't stop now. Get out of here."

Get out of here! Yes, this tree's on her side. Lillian keeps walking. Now that she's off the sidewalk, she walks gingerly, dodging roots. As a child she loved making piles of leaves, then sitting down smack dab in the midst of them. Now she kicks leaves into a pile. She feels tired. She could sit here, take a rest. She could roll her sweater into a pillow. She can go to sleep here in the woods, smelling the deep earthy smell and hearing the calling of birds. Oh, how lovely it will be to fall asleep to this sound. She could start again in the morning.

But no. She has to keep going. Now! Get out of here. That's what the tree said.

But wait. What is this? There's a fence on the edge of the woods, a tall fence made of metal. Made of chains? The kind you can see through. When Lillian presses her face against it, she sees the outline of houses beyond. Her house might be close, with Annie inside, looking for sandwiches.

Is there a gate in this fence, some place to get out? Lillian tries following the fence one way, then the other. No gate, anywhere. This fence is making her mad. She's in prison!

She stands still, looking out into the dark, her face pressed to the fence. Annie is out there, somewhere. Daniel, too. When she pulls the fence toward her, it snaps back. The snap makes the fence rattle and clank. Now she shakes it.

"Hello!" she hears herself calling. "Yes!"

She pulls the jacket tight around her. It's getting cold, Arctic cold. It could start snowing. Ice could form underfoot; she could slip and fall. At the least, she would have to go slow. But she would rather, much rather, trudge along in the snow, in the Arctic cold, rather than stay here with these old people. Or be at the place where she's going, the place with locked doors.

Can she climb over? Of course, she's a monkey! She steps up, puts a foot into one of the fence holes. But she can't lift herself. She tries again and again. Pain shoots through her arms as she tries to lift up. She may be a monkey, an Arctic Monkey, but she's an old monkey, a weak monkey, not strong enough to climb up a fence.

But she can make noise.

"Yes!" Lillian calls again, shaking the fence. "Hello!"

The sound thrills her. It's a blast in the night, a shout in the silence, her own voice piercing the dark.

She shakes the fence again. It's a good sound, the shaking, but it could be louder.

There's a stick on the ground, a big stick. But she can lift it. She can swing it hard, bang it against the fence. Ouch! But it's worth the pain in her shoulders to make a big noise. Now this fence turns into a drum. She is smacking it. Metal rattles and shakes. So much clanging and banging!

The fizzy feeling is exploding inside, energy zapping her arms and legs.

"Let me out!"

Wait a minute. Who said that?

"Let me out!" Lillian yells again, as loud as she can.

Yes, these words came out of her mouth. These words knew just what to do. They lined up as they should, in a sentence, bang, bang, bang, all in a row. Words that make sense! There are no flying birds, no scratchy feathers stuck in her throat. This is her own voice, her own words, and she has something to say.

"Let me out!"

The night turns into dark curtains opening onto a stage and her words step out, beneath spotlights. They are taking a bow. Her own words! The audience claps for them. Now the audience rises up from its seats. People are standing, women in gowns, men in tuxedos. A standing ovation. Bravo! Bravo!

But there are footsteps coming toward her. Someone is running. Whoever it is, they're getting closer.

Who is coming? She can't tell for sure, but it looks like the big-butt woman, heaving herself forward.

But Lillian has the big stick to swing. She can throw the tennis ball at the butt-woman's face. She can bite. She'll put up a fight, just like any monkey.

"Hello!" Lillian yells at the top of her lungs, as she takes another swing with the stick. "Yes!"

35.
which road?

It's oddly quiet as Beth opens the door to the animal shelter. Inside, a dark-haired young man in a uniform sits at the front desk. He looks up expectantly. "Can I help you?"

Beth says she's looking for a dog. He squints as he asks: did she lose a dog that she's now seeking, or is she looking for a new dog, a stray?

"A new dog," she says, although of course the truth is more complicated.

She needs to sign the guest book, the young man says. Above the book are posters of adorable puppies, sweet kittens. Buttering us up, Beth thinks, but she's okay with that. She's the third person today to sign in.

She needs to turn right, then turn right again at the dog area. As soon as Beth opens the door, the din begins. What a racket! About a dozen large cages are filled with dogs, leaping into the air, as if some blast of air beneath them is lifting them several feet off the ground. And of course they're all barking. It's astonishing how high they jump, all four feet in the air, like cartoon animals. Me! Me!

It's as if the dogs have been training for this, competing to see which can wiggle its butt with the most vigor, thump its tail with the most force. As they leap, each dog's rear end squeezes up to its shoulders so they look like barking doggie accordions, squeezing out their canine songs, their raucous tunes. And the names reflect the dogs' goofy, exuberant spirits. Murphy! Boomer! Spike! Most are pit bulls, with a few hound mixes too.

Only one dog refrains from the commotion. Willow, the name tag says, a hound mix. She's smaller than the rest, a soft copper color. As the others leap into the air, Willow sits patiently at the front of her cage. Beth holds out her hand, lets Willow lick her fingers. The dog has spectacular eyes, big and light brown. But don't all dogs have beautiful eyes?

Beth bends toward Willow, which sends the dog in the next cage into spasms of leaping. But the cage says that dog just got neutered, that it shouldn't make vigorous movements. Vigorous? This dog is heaving itself right off the ground. Beth doesn't want the dog to be hurt, so she turns to leave. As soon as she walks out the dog area door, the barking ends.

"Did you find something you like?" the young man in the office says, looking up.

Not today.

"Come back Thursday," he says, looking oddly hurt, as if he really, really wants her to find the right dog. The vet releases new dogs on Thursday, he says, dogs that have passed all the tests. Passed the tests? For a second Beth considers asking what tests, exactly, the dogs passed, but she doesn't want this sweet young man to think she's mocking him. Having expected a no-nonsense bureaucrat, she's charmed by his caring.

It's a sparkling November day, the leaves spiraling down to the ground, the sky a cornflower blue. Beth turns out of the lot. Which way to turn to get home? At the first corner, she decides to turn left. And why not? It's a country road, weaving through old barns and farmland. It might take her in the direction of home, or it might not. But she doesn't have to go home. She could keep driving. She goes slowly, no one behind her, slowing further to watch baby goats in a field. She could turn right, then left, and just drive wherever the road takes her. She could just stop and watch baby goats. Or she could hop on the interstate and keep driving, end up in Kentucky by dark. Kentucky! A whole different state. What's it like in Kentucky? No one expects her at home, or anywhere else. No one. She could go anywhere. She could travel the world. Where is it that she's always wanted to go? Someplace, surely. The Yukon. She's always wanted to go to the Yukon.

Or she could stay home. She could get another job in the profession she loves, caring for old people. There's so much to learn, to understand. Like how to more humanely care for those with dementia, like Lillian, how to balance their need for safety with a life that's worth living. She's researched an explosion of new ideas, ideas so bold few have been willing to try them. Perhaps Beth could try them. That is, if she can still get a job.

It's a queasiness she's feeling, deep in her middle, a feeling of not being settled. Her stomach's a mess. On top of that, her life's all in flux. But it's a good feeling, little sparks of excitement spiraling through her. But wait! It's a bad feeling, the queasiness deepening. Beth takes a deep breath. She's not sure if this feeling is good or it's bad. But she'll stop at a 7-Eleven, pick up a box of Saltines. The crackers can settle her stomach.

She pulls the car to the side of the road, takes her phone out of her pocket and clicks in the familiar numbers. Pammie picks up on the second ring.

"So that trip to Seattle? I think it may be pretty soon," Beth says.

"Woo hoo! You got the time off?"

"I quit." Beth watches a herd of cows that are walking toward her in a pasture. The cows are next to the fence now, watching her with mournful eyes. "Actually, I got fired."

"Oh," Pammie says. "Well, that's good. Or bad. Which is it?"

"Not sure yet," Beth says. "But anyway, I have the time now. I definitely have the time." One cow has thrust its head over the fence, and Beth longs to pet the furry face. "Can I bring my dog?"

"You have a dog?"

"Well, I don't actually have a dog now. Maybe soon, though. Maybe I'll make this a road trip."

After she hangs up, Beth pulls back on the road.

As she drives, she keeps eying the passenger seat. It looks empty. She can imagine Willow there serving as navigator, her graceful head pointing forward, leading the way. Willow would look over at Beth every so often and smile in her doggie way, letting Beth know that wherever Beth wants to go, she's got it covered, no problem. Beth would rest her hand on Willow's soft fur as she drives, sometimes rubbing her velvety ears.

Off they would go, she and Willow, into the hopeful blue afternoon.

epilogue

Thomas is born in the summer. He is, in fact, a boy.

The center does its best to schedule Sally and Shannon on different shifts, so one of them can be home with the baby. Things have changed, not for the better, with the new owners, though so far Sally's hung on. She's sorry that Beth is gone. The new director, Wayne, is way too corporate.

But Sally's preoccupied with her baby. When she and Shannon are both working, Linda, Shannon's mother, takes care of him. Sally likes Linda. She's a longtime cashier at a supermarket in a town about ten miles away. She says she loves her job because she gets to meet so many people. Every day she gets to see what they eat! Knowing this feels like intimacy, Linda says. But she's been thinking about retiring, after all these years, because standing so long is hard on her feet. And she wants to spend more time with baby Thomas. Sally thinks she sees where Shannon's kindness comes from.

Not surprisingly, Shannon is a wonderful father. He loves nothing more than lying on his back on the floor and putting

Thomas on his chest so that the two of them are staring into each other's eyes. The baby coos and smiles when his father's face is so close. Sometimes he sticks his chubby fingers into Shannon's nose or mouth, which makes his little body shake all over with laughter.

Truthfully, sometimes Shannon is a bit annoying. Sally worries about this. She's not used to having so much power in a relationship. Sometimes that power feels thrilling, but other times she wants Shannon to take control. Sometimes he seems like a dog, a big, handsome Labrador puppy trotting along at her heels, and she has the urge to, well, kick him. But when things with Shannon get hard, she forces herself to talk about it. This is the deal they made, that they would talk about whatever bothers them.

Sally feels astonished, again and again, amazed at the power of something so simple. When she begins to talk, her stomach churns with anxiety. Is it really okay to be feeling this? To be talking about it? Yet as she speaks, as Shannon listens, Sally feels herself soften and bend, she feels her hurt and defensiveness melt away. He doesn't interrupt her, doesn't try to make her feel differently. He just listens. And when he talks too much, she gives him the thumbs-down sign. It's what they agreed on, a hand sign, since asking him to stop talking feels stressful. And he stops talking. And soon she's able to move over and around the walls she built between them, able to take a step toward Shannon, to hear him as well. So far, it's working. He surprises her, every day.

She didn't expect how much she loves being a mother. Did Sally's mother feel this pleasure when Sally was little? Sally can't remember ever seeing joy on her mother's face, and it saddens her to think how her mother missed out.

Ever since baby Thomas began smiling, Sally and Shannon have laughed about how the baby has trained them. As soon as the baby begins to pull up the sides of his mouth, lo and behold, they're smiling too. And when she sees it with Shannon, sees him and their child engaged in a duel of smiling, both of their bodies twitching with joy, Sally closes her eyes. It is too much. It's just too much happiness.

Are there differences across cultures in how babies are cared for? Of course there are. Thomas, the first Thomas, would have so much to say. And what about raising a child? Childcare practices must be all over the map. Sally could Google them, but she wishes she could hear them from Thomas, hear his tone of wonder at the amazing variety of human behavior. Sally thinks about these things now, when she didn't before. Knowing Thomas has changed her.

Now Sally looks down at her baby awakening from his nap. She's leaning over his crib so that her face must look huge to him, like the moon. He blinks, opens his eyes. His eyes widen. His whole face lights up. And his smile spreads even further, his feet pumping air, his fingers clasping and unclasping some invisible hand. And here it comes, her return volley. Could she stop smiling if she tried? She doesn't think so. She's smiling so wide her face hurts.

Now her baby seems to be looking up, just over Sally's shoulder, smiling at something above her.

"Thomas?" she says out loud then, though she doesn't know for sure if she's speaking to the first Thomas or to the tiny new version in front of her. Then she feels him, the first Thomas, standing on top of her shoulders. He's still with her, just like she knew he would be.

The tiny Thomas locks eyes with her, squeals in delight. How can she resist? And on her shoulders, the other Thomas leans forward, ready to guide her into the world.

Perhaps it doesn't matter which Thomas she's speaking to.

"Thomas," she says again. She loves the feel of the word in her mouth. She says the name over and over.

acknowledgments

Big thanks to Emily Hitchcock of Boyle & Dalton for her belief in *One More Day*, along with her savvy guidance through the process of publication. Thanks also to Heather Shaw of Boyle & Dalton for magnificent editorial help. A round of applause to my writing group—Ed Davis, Joe Downing and Susan Carpenter—for their kind support and helpful feedback during early drafts of the book. And thanks, too, to first readers Kay Kendall, Jim Klein, Alisa Isaac, Lee Huntington, and Katherine Merrill. A tip of the hat to Lauren Shows for her generosity and formatting skills. And thanks to Matt Minde for never-ending (it must seem) tech support, and for random laughter.

about the author

Diane Chiddister is a journalist and former editor of the *Yellow Springs News* in Yellow Springs, Ohio. She's also a short story writer and 1981 MFA graduate of the University of Iowa Writer's Workshop, where she was a Teaching-Writing Fellow. This is her first novel. She lives in Yellow Springs, Ohio.

Made in the USA
Monee, IL
29 October 2021

81027683R10177